A Wiser Girl

Moya Roddy

WORDSONTHESTREET

First published 2020 by

Wordsonthestreet

Six San Antonio Park, Salthill, Galway, Ireland
www.wordsonthestreet.com
publisher@wordsonthestreet.com

© Copyright Moya Roddy

The moral right of the author has been asserted.

A catalogue record for this book is available from the British Library.

ISBN 978-1-907017-59-9

Cover design, layout and typesetting: Wordsonthestreet

A Wiser Girl

Praise for Moya Roddy's other work

Out of the Ordinary

Each poem finds its careful focus, allowing us to ...enter into dialogue with a poetic voice that is authentic and truth-filled.
Mary O'Donnell

Stunning and memorable poems
Rita Ann Higgins

... a book of minute observations, of stolen glimpses and sudden seismic epiphanies.
Jessica Traynor, *the North*

Other People

... the writing is so good ... the stories vivid, multi-layered, subtle ... with the sensitivity to language of a poet. Beautifully written.
Eilís Ní Dhuibhne

... very much a literary writer, her breezy style borrows something from the best popular fiction writers; Wordsonthestreet have done short story fans a big service by publishing Moya Roddy ...
Kevin Higgins, *Galway Advertiser*

... entertaining and thought-provoking ... often haunting
Eamonn Kelly, *Books Ireland*

little time-bombs
Lelia Doolan

to all who struggle for change — young and old

Roma 1975

1

Italy ... Italy ... Italy ... Italy ... the insistent rhythm of the train inveigles its way in and Jo wakes feeling cramped and cold. As she gropes in the dark for her jacket, a Donegal tweed her mammy insisted she bring, an avalanche of misery guts her. *Why did she leave! Why!* Pulling the coat over her head, Jo tries to lull herself back to oblivion. Across the aisle, an elderly couple sharing the compartment shift and re-arrange themselves beneath a cocoon of rugs and shawls, the man muttering, the woman emitting little put-putting sounds like a candle guttering. Jo listens enviously: if she hadn't turned up her nose at the blanket they'd offered, she wouldn't be shivering as well as miserable. How was she to know the train went that close to the Alps! One minute the carriage was baking, the next freezing, a weird light illuminating everything. Then she saw them: vast, majestic, gleaming – peak after peak receding into the distance, moonwhite, ghostly. If only she could go back and see them again ... But there's no going back. No going back to Dublin either. Jo burrows into the corner of the narrow seat, the threadbare fabric rough against her face. Dublin. *Dubh Linn.* Black Pool. Black hole. A hole she almost drowned in-

The train swerves, lumbering like a huge animal as it changes track and Jo's eyes jerk open. She didn't drown, she escaped, is on her way to the sun. The land of *spaghetti bollock-naked* a lad in the office had joked the day she'd handed in her notice. Goodbye Tax Office, goodbye old self, Josephine Nowd, clerk-typist. Goodbye Eamonn- Pain knifes Jo's heart. What is she doing on this train? What possessed her to leave! *She loves him!* At least if she'd stayed, there was a chance they'd get back together.

As the train settles into a steady rhythm Jo's heart stops

thumping. Who is she trying to fool! She had to leave. She'd no choice. Living in Dublin with a broken heart was like crossing a minefield every day. She'd never realised how small the city was, how incestuous. Eamonn was everywhere. If she didn't come across one of his photos in a newspaper, she heard him holding forth on a chat show: talking with a passion she hungered for — for herself. Bastard! To think she'd been eejit enough to imagine she could lure him back with her own words. She'd done her best the night she'd bumped into him in McGraths: rabbiting on about a project at art college, hoping to impress him, hoping a pretence of indifference would do the trick. Too carried away to notice *he* was the one weaving the spell. Forgetting the way his voice could arouse her as surely as physical contact. Words! He could twist them into any shape he liked: make her laugh, make her cry, make her want him. If he'd touched her up or tried to kiss her, she might have copped on, might have objected when he'd slipped his arm around her, led her tipsily from the pub. She might have had the savvy not to ignore the sly wink he'd given one of his cronies; might even have realised as they tottered back to her flat that the only thing lying in front of them was their past.

It had all been over in a matter of moments, his desire sated. When he'd walked out the door, she'd felt cheated — realising she'd given away something without really knowing what it was. An idea of herself. He hadn't asked to see her again. There'd been no mention of love, no words at all.

Now she's going where words will echo meaninglessly and for a while she won't understand any of them.

'*Matina, matina*, morning, morning,' the old woman chants softly.

Jo breathes in the smell of food, hears a rustle of paper. She groans inwardly: it's way too early to be trying to make conversations in broken English.

'*Matina, matina*, morning, morning!' This time the chant's harder to ignore.

Making a yawney sound as if she's just woken, Jo half-turns, is met by a pair of button-black eyes.

'*Carina*,' the woman says, drawing out the "a". Her husband, happily demolishing a doorstep of a sandwich, gives Jo a grin, the inside of his mouth shiny with gold.

'*Mange, mange*, eat, eat,' the Italian coaxes, proffering a roll. 'Brickfast.'

Pearls of fat glisten on a piece of protruding meat and Jo's stomach heaves.

'Have to go … toileten.' She tacks on "en", hoping to make it understandable. Grabbing her handbag, she rushes out.

The train shakes and buckles and Jo has to stretch out her arms to stop herself falling. Opening the door of the jacks, she flicks a switch and a light blinks on. Yuck! The place is manky! Avoiding a puddle – the floor's swimming – Jo hovers above the toilet. When she's finished, she washes her hands in a trickle of water, dries them on the back of her dress. The pocked mirror above the sink reveals a puffy face, mascara streaked, her mane of red hair matted and curly from sleep. Thank goodness, Eamonn can't- No!! Jo slams her mind shut. She will not allow herself think about him. In defiance, she purses her lips, slicks on lipstick, pulls a comb through her hair. She'll come back later; do herself up before they get to Rome. With a bit of luck, someone might have cleaned the place by then.

The old woman's lying in wait when Jo gets back, a bulging roll in her hand.

'Eat, eat, *buono*, good,' she encourages, tipping her fingers to her lips, making a kissing sound.

Jo takes it, hoping she can get it from her mouth to her stomach without tasting it. Outside, night is waning, an invisible hand painting the horizon a shimmering rose pink. A new day is beginning. Jo sinks her teeth into what turns out to be lumps of white cheese, something red and spongy. Flavour explodes on her tongue, salty, tangy. Delicious! She gives herself a metaphorical clap on the back. It's a new day for her too – a new life – and this is just the start. From now on she's going to taste everything that comes her way.

'*Brava, brava.* Good!' The woman gives Jo's knee a hearty slap and lifting her skirt flaunts a patchwork of pockets on her rough underskirt, all filled with neat little parcels. '*Troppo, troppo*! More!' Jo gags. The woman nudges her husband, points to the girl's face.

'No, no, enough, not hungry,' Jo shakes her head as the old lady extracts one of the packages, begins to unwrap it.

'*Magri, magri*!' the woman cries, leaning across and squeezing Jo's thigh.

Jo's eyes fill and she fiddles in her handbag, pretending to be looking for something until the danger passes.

'*Perche*- Why you go Roma? Holiday eh?' the man enquires, spreading his arms wide, his head and shoulders doing a little dance.

'No, no holiday.' Without thinking, Jo imitates him. 'I have job with family, look after children-' she stops. 'Au pair,' she explains, tapping her chest.

The man frowns, repeats the words, his eyebrows knotting.

'Ah, cheeldren! *Bambini, Si! Si! Brava*, good!'

Jo nods, feeling a bit of a hypocrite. She's not even sure she likes children, always crying and wanting to be played with. She took the job to have somewhere to lick her wounds, somewhere far away from Dublin. In Italy, she'll re-invent herself: turn herself into an artist. A great one! She'll become a woman of the world too, teach herself to love the way men like Eamonn love: with their bodies. And from now on, she'll keep her soul for her work: she isn't going to make the same mistake twice.

As the train lurches drunkenly past fields of umber soil, past medieval villages with crumbling ochre walls and terraces of dusty green vines, Jo soaks up the colours. These shades and more are in her suitcase, stashed away beneath her new underwear. As soon as she's settled in, she'll start painting. Paint all the way to forgetfulness. Tears that have been threatening prick her eyelids and Jo leans her forehead against the glass. How is she going to forget? The biggest item in her luggage is pain. A fat tear escapes and she wipes it away surreptitiously, contemptuously. It was her own fault for believing a man like Eamonn could love her. Or someone the likes of her could make a leap into the privileged world he lived in. Slag. Hole. That's what girls who "did it" are called where she comes from. "*I love you.*" She'd hoarded those words for the right moment, the right man. Only to find out that like all the stupid girls in all the stupid songs she'd been a fool! Not in saying the words. Only in meaning them.

Without warning the muted tones of the landscape burst into technicolour – field after field of giant yellow flowers. Sunflowers! Thousands of them! Jo gawks; she's only ever seen them in paintings by Van Gogh.

'*Girasoli,*' the old man tells her, pointing.

'*Girasoli*', she repeats, the word wrenching her heart open, the golden brightness spelling new promise. Hearing the door slide across, Jo drags her eyes away. It's the young fella who's been looking after the old couple, seeing they're comfortable, getting things down from their luggage, taking the old man to the toilet.

He hangs out in a different carriage and Jo wonders if it's because theirs is non-smoking: there's always a whiff of fags off him. In daylight, she can see he's the spitting image, a grandson or nephew most likely. She's nicknamed him "Romeo" on account of his long black hair and sultry good looks. Today, he's all spruced up in a snazzy pin-stripe, flares you could sail a boat with.

'*Buon Giorno! Buon Giorno!*'

He includes Jo in his greeting and she gives him a self-conscious nod. He can't be more than a year or two older than she is – twenty-three max – but he acts older. Jo listens in as they begin to chat, talking over each other, hands embroidering whatever it is they're saying. She loves the lilt in their voices, as if each word is having a ball.

'You don't have to eat if you don't want to,' Romeo breaks into her reverie.

She hasn't heard him speaking English – hadn't realised he did; his flat accent disappointing, all the lovely sing-song gone.

'They're my grandparents,' he informs her. '*Nonna* – grandmother – thinks all English girls are too thin, don't you *Nonna?*'

'No understand, no understand,' the old lady protests.

The young man pats her affectionately, kisses the top of her head.

Jesus! Imagine an Irish boy doing that in public! Jo can only remember kissing her mother on special occasions, pecking her really; has no memory of ever kissing her father. When she was growing up, anything to do with bodies, anything physical was *verboten*.

'You don't approve of English girls, do you *Nonna?*'

'*Boh,*' she grunts, looking at her husband to rescue her but he seems to have nodded off, his chin knocking on his chest.

'I'm Irish,' Jo corrects the boy, annoyed at herself for saying it so bluntly. Still, it pisses her off anyone could mistake her for English.

With a shrug he makes for the door. Agitated, his grandmother raises her voice, a volley of words ricocheting round the compartment. When he attempts to pacify her, she brushes him off, raises her arms to Heaven.

'*Vergogna!*' The sound explodes like a sausage bursting in hot oil. Having uttered it, she settles back, hisses it a second time. Her husband opens one eye, shuts it quickly.

Jo stares at the woman, amazed at her vehemence. Then, like the sun emerging from clouds, she produces a round of cheese and cutting off a chunk, offers it to her grandson.

'Thank your lucky stars you're not Italian.' The flat English accent's back.

'She seems angry. What does that word mean?'

'Shame! Big shame. She's dead set on me marrying some Italian girl. Won't stop going on about it.' He nods towards his grandparents. 'You'd never guess they've been living in Birmingham for years. All they do is mix with Italians, re-live their youth. I'm sick telling her the past's the past, Italy's changed. Everywhere has. People don't go in for that sort of thing anymore. It's the 1970's for crying out loud, not the 1870's!'

A brooding expression clouds his handsome face, as if he's staring into a future he doesn't like. He's right, Jo thinks, the words finding their mark, the past's the past for her too.

'*Siamo arrivata, siamo arrivata,*' the old man croons, 'we arrive!'

Getting to his feet, he blows his nose noisily before rummaging through a worn leather bag. As the train shunts into a garishly lit station, he pulls out a bottle of colourless liquid, brandishes it.

'*Roma*,' he sighs, kissing the bottle, '*Roma*'. Crying and laughing, the woman blesses herself over and over. After taking a slug, her husband wipes the neck of the bottle and with a little bow presents it to Jo. Aware of the honour, she puts it to her lips, shutting out the image of his old man's mouth.

"*Roma*", she toasts, repeating the magic word.

'*O Solo Mio*,' he croons, his eyes misting as he serenades his wife, a thin crackly voice filling the compartment. Jo's heart contracts: why are some people lucky in love when others are not? Don't begrudge them, she warns herself, reaching for her bag. The case is crammed to the gills which means she's going to have to wear the stupid tweed jacket; die of heat. Shuffling it on, she shoves her train ticket into one of the pockets, snags on something small and hard. Turning out the lining, she sees a tiny miraculous medal, the bluest of blue. So that's why her mammy made such a fuss about bringing it! She might have known. Jo can imagine her – murmuring prayers as she sews the medal in, a raft of good intentions woven into every stitch. The woman will never give up!

All the same, venturing out of *Stagione Termini*, Jo finds herself running her fingers over the shiny surface of the medal, sending a plea to the shimmering ball burning up the sky. She needs a miracle. Badly. She needs the sun to scorch Eamonn from her memory, blast her into the future as someone else.

2

Dumping Jo at the side of a dual carriageway, the autobus disappears in a cloud of diesel. Ugly tower-blocks elbow each other for room. So much for the luxurious *palazzos* she'd passed on the way! With a screech of tyres, a low-slung E-type hurtles past, horn blaring. Madman! Jo swears, watching the car overtake a snarl of traffic, a second lunatic on its bumper, the sun sparking off the gleaming metal.

Picking up her suitcase, she looks up and down the street, not sure which way to go; is relieved to see a guy in singlet and shorts with a row of corks swinging from the brim of his cowboy hat ambling towards her. Beggars can't be choosers, Jo thinks, plonking herself in his path, her lack of Italian sticking in her throat like a gobstopper.

'Excuse me, do you know where this is?' She enunciates each word, holding out a piece of crumpled paper with the address of the hostel in block capitals.

'Relax, I can speak English. It's round the next corner, far end of the block. Follow me.' His accent sounds as if someone's squashed it.

'Are you staying there?' Jo asks, hurrying to keep up, the case banging off her leg; her attention side-tracked by a waterfall of creamy-white flowers cascading all the way to the ground from a third story balcony.

'You should get yourself a haversack if you're travelling. It's less hassle.'

'I'm not. I've got a job as an au-pair.'

'Cool. The name's Kevin, from Oz if you haven't guessed.'

'Australia, you mean? I'm Jo, Irish.'

'Kinda thought you might be. Well, here we are.'

Jo grimaces. The pale stone building looks more like a posh office block. 'Wow! It doesn't look like any of the youth hostels in Ireland.'

'Sounds quaint. I'd love to go there someday.'

Jo's blood boils. Who does he think he is with his "quaint"! 'We do have buildings like that too, ye know. It's not all cottages and thatched roofs.'

Kevin grins. 'I see you've got one of those Irish tempers. Matches your hair.'

Before Jo has time to reply, a moped roars up, sputters to a halt.

The Australian groans. 'Shoot, you might as well meet Gino. Everyone does sooner or later.'

'Watch your valuables, he's a pickpocket,' he warns, raising a hand to the stocky figure swaggering in their direction.

'*Ciao* Gino.'

Ignoring the Australian, Gino makes straight for Jo, one hand rubbing his crotch.

'Americana, Americana?' he questions, '*Bella, bellisimma.*'

'*Basta* Gino.'

Jo gives Kevin a look.

'"*Basta*" means "enough" not "bastard" in case that's what you're thinking,' he laughs. 'Good word to know if you're planning on spending any time around here.'

'You like fucka with me?' Gino tugs her sleeve.

Jo's mouth falls open. 'Are you mad! Fuck off.' Jesus Christ, she thought fellas at home were bad with their "How's your gee?" but they'd never come right out and say that. Even if they're thinking it. Besides, she'd left that sort of crap behind once she'd started a relationship with Eamonn. Not that his middle-class

19

friends were all that different, they just had different ways of being vulgar. Amounts to the same thing if you're female.

The Italian's eyes pop. 'Hey, no lady talk,' he complains, wagging a finger.

'I'll say what I like, none of your business.'

'No American?' Gino frowns at Kevin.

'*Irlanda, Irlandaisa*,' Kevin tells him.

Jo rolls the words round her tongue, relishing them.

'*Irlanda?*' Gino scratches his head. '*Irlanda! Mama mia!*' Before Jo can dodge out of the way, wet lips are planted on her cheeks. '*Irlanda*: boom, boom!' he laughs, taking aim with an imaginary gun. Jo gives him a stare. Ireland isn't only the North, she'd like to tell him, not everybody goes round taking pot-shots at one another.

'I think he likes you,' Kevin teases. 'Maybe it's time to go in and register.'

'We have to go,' he says loudly to the Italian.

To the sound of kisses, Jo traipses up the steps after the Australian, jostling behind him through revolving doors. The reception's crowded with frazzled-looking back-packers, a few of them conked out on the ground, fast asleep. Jo gapes: she's never seen so many people with long blond hair or long tanned legs! Not to mention so many half-naked girls. Eyes on stalks, she tags on the end of a straggly queue, pleased when Kevin joins her.

'They hold onto your passport,' he fills her in as they inch along. 'Once you hand over the dosh, you'll get a number. That's for your bed. Don't forget to keep the receipt. Part of it's a deposit so you'll get it back when you leave.'

'If you're looking for haute cuisine, the canteen's in the basement. Follow your nose, you can't miss it. The food's not bad, and the portions are big. It's cheap too.'

Jo sighs with relief, she's starving, hasn't had a bite to eat since the train. Not that there weren't fantastic looking cafes near the station but without the hang of the money, she was scared they'd overcharge her.

'The only lousy thing is the bogs.' Holding his nose, Kevin pulls an imaginary chain. 'Maybe the Sheilas' ones ain't so bad.'

Jo shrugs. She's used to awful toilets. When she was young, they couldn't always afford toilet paper, so sometimes all they had was pieces of old newspaper. And her granny didn't even have a toilet: you went in the field or the shed, depending.

'Does he speak much English? Gino,' she asks, worried Kevin's getting restless.

'Mainly the few choice words you heard. You seem kinda familiar with them yourself.'

The remark hurts.

'Don't look so serious, it spoils your charms.'

'Fuck off,' is on the tip of Jo's tongue but she bites it back. Why is she surprised? It's probably the same no matter where you go: guys get to say what they like, girls are supposed to zip it.

Since dinner, something unbelievably scrumptious called "lasagne" – mince in a creamy sauce between layers of pasta – Jo's been holed up in the common-room, poring over a dictionary. "*Abbastanza*" she's discovered is a different kind of "enough" to "*basta*". Well, the chef certainly gave her "*abbastanza*"; if all Italian food tastes as good, she'll be needing new clothes in no time.

She's positioned herself near the door and hearing a squeak glances up but it's only the two Asian-looking guys who were sitting at the next table in the canteen. They'd spent the entire meal arguing over something; at least it sounded like arguing. She gives them a little wave, not too friendly, she doesn't want them joining her, cramping her style. Jo stifles a yawn. If the Australian doesn't show up soon, she's going to have to call it a night, give the bunk bed a test run. Luckily, she got a top one so it shouldn't be too bad. This could be the United Nations, she thinks, glancing around – every nationality under the sun seems present, all talking at the same time. Disregarding the babble, she makes a stab at pronouncing her new word: *abba...stanza*, *abb...a...stanza*; gives up. Language is funny: how did *abbastanza* get to mean "enough" or "enough" get to mean "enough" for that matter?

The answer, my friend, is blowing in the wind, a stoned-looking guy strumming a guitar moans like he's tuning into her thoughts. Dylan on a bad night, Jo grins, singing along under her breath. Skipping through the dictionary, she stops at the 'M's'. The old woman on the train had said something like "*magra*" or "magri". "*Magri*": thin! No wonder she was trying to feed her up. People are always saying she's too thin and since she broke up with Eamonn, her weight's-

'Hi there,' Kevin's twang intrudes.

'Oh hi!' Jo takes her time looking up, intending to look surprised. She doesn't have to: without the silly hat she hardly recognises him; realises he's actually good-looking. And the denim shirt he's wearing make his eyes look startlingly blue, like Terence Stamp's in The Collector.

'Gonna grab a coffee, get you one?'

'Thanks. But that machine's dicey, only works some of the time.'

'There's a knack. You have to kick it. That's the only language it understands.'

Kevin aims a right foot at the drinks dispenser and Jo giggles as liquid spurts out.

'Mustn't speak Australian!'

'Very funny! Got yourself sorted?' he enquires, handing her a dripping plastic cup, pulling up one of the hard orange chairs.

'Yeah. Thanks. You were right about the jacks. The women's is yuck!' She does a bad imitation of flushing a toilet and he laughs.

'What are you reading?' Kevin turns the book round. 'A dictionary? Fuck me pink! Found any dirty bits?'

Jo purses her lips.

'Pulling your leg. Okay, okay, let's change the subject. You staying long?'

'I have to catch a train *Domenica*, Sunday, I mean,' Jo blushes, afraid she sounds pretentious. 'I'm starting work in Pavia on Monday. It's near Milan. What about you?'

'Been here a week. I'm off to Greece in a couple of days. Can't wait. Thelessa! That's Greek for water – although I'm more of a retsina man myself.'

He nudges her. 'What's the plan? Eat, drink and get laid by some hunky Italian with smouldering eyes?'

'Yeah. Gino. I suppose that's what you're doing?' she fishes.

'Eating and drinking. Gino, who knows? I'd prefer a *signorina* if I can find one without her mama.'

'You're as bad as Gino!' Jo snorts. 'At least he's honest.'

Kevin raises his hands. 'There goes that Irish temper. How have I offended you this time?'

Jo shrugs, sips her coffee. Most likely he is going to eat, drink and get laid. If anyone's being dishonest it's her.

'If you really want to know, I'm going to visit as many churches as I can.'

'You're in Rome for a weekend and you're gonna spend the time look at buildings! I don't believe it, a culture freak.'

'I'm not a culture freak. I like art. You can eat and drink anywhere.'

'True. But then you haven't tasted *Zuppe Inglese*.' He smacks his lips. 'It means "English soup": ice cream with lots of rum and sponge cake. Now that's what I call a religious experience! C'mon man, churches are full of dust and dead things. You can do that kinda stuff when you're old.'

'Not everyone's a philistine, ye know.'

'Your choice. Me, I'm gonna hang out, sample a few more Italian restaurants, eat as much *vongele* as I can – clam's to you. Of course, there's the Spanish Steps if you're into something a little more stimulating-'

'I get the picture,' she interrupts.

'Scared I'll corrupt you? You're more than welcome.' He winks. 'In case I don't get lucky, I definitely wouldn't say no to an Irish colleen.'

'You'd be lucky.'

Jo makes a little tower out of sugar sachets, tries to make them balance. It would be great to "hang out" but this isn't a holiday for her, it's her life.

'Are you a painter?'

'Kind of. Well, I went to Art College. For a while.'

'How'd you get started on something like that?'

'Dunno. I was always into drawing. Not that I ever thought of becoming an artist. There's not too many painters where I come from. House painters alright. There was a shop near my work, had tons of art books. One day I picked up one ... ' she stops, reminds herself to speak normally. 'It was about Siennese Art. I didn't even know where Sienna was! I'd never heard of it.'

'What happened?'

Jo searches for words to convey how the book had changed her life: within a year of chancing on it she'd applied to go to Art College. The problem is she's no idea why those particular paintings affected her: what gave them the power to invade her heart. All she knows is they set off a tumult in her body, set it on fire. There was something about them, something intangible ... mystical.

Jo doesn't believe in God anymore but religious words are the only ones that come anywhere close to describing what she'd felt – what she feels. Although sometimes, when she and Eamonn made love, she'd experience something similar: awash in him her body would melt... fall away, leave her spiralling towards another world. A world she never encounters in real life.

'I suppose they blew my mind,' she says lamely, looking at him, trying to write on her face all the things she's too embarrassed to say.

Kevin cracks his fingers. 'Hey man, I know exactly what you mean. I'm into surfing. Big time. You wait for the right wave to come along, when it does ... wow! You stare that fucker in the eye and you ride it. Nothing else matters, just you and the wave. It's better than sex – lasts longer too.'

Mentally, Jo re-opens the book, is overawed once more by the beauty, the colours: a blue so pure it hurts, red to stop your heart. Even though most of the paintings are about ordinary things – interiors or street scenes, women going about their daily tasks, episodes from the life of Jesus – within them Jo catches a glimpse of her own Being. She lets out a long breath. Only a gink would compare it to surfing! What she's talking about is ... sacred!

'Welcome back to the land of the living.' Kevin jumps to his feet, his tanned belly exposed as he stretches. Alarmed by a sudden lurch in the pit of her stomach, Jo busies herself putting the sachets back in the bowl.

'Guess I'll hit the sack. By the by, if you don't have a guidebook, I can lend you mine. At least it'll get some use. I'll bring it down in the morning. Course you might not want to have breakfast with a philistine.' With a lazy wave, Kevin strolls away.

The door swings shut behind him and the warmth inside Jo ebbs. It was idiotic thinking a guy like Kevin would understand. Surfing! What would Eamonn say? Jo's heart free-falls. Who does she think she's fooling? If Eamonn as much as crooked his little finger, she'd be back in Dublin in a shot. To hell with Italy, to hell with painting! To hell with everything.

3

Halfway across the bridge, Jo pinches herself: she's in Rome and the dirty-looking water beneath her feet is the Tiber! Instead of the usual rainy grey streets, a panorama of spires, domes, bell-towers and *palazzos* vie for her attention. Even the ruins are imposing. What's weird is that although everything's new and strange, it's also familiar, stockpiled in her brain from paintings, books, films like La Dolce Vita, Bicycle Thieves, cards from girls in the office in Rome on their honeymoons.

Still, whoever built the Eternal City wasn't thinking of tourists, Jo grouses, glancing enviously at a pair of statuesque angels gracing a parapet. She could do with a pair of wings; her legs are falling off and she's going to keel over any minute from sunstroke. Further up the street, a knot of tourists – cameras like third eyes – are taking photographs of the facade of a building and Jo says a prayer it's the ninth century chapel she's been trying to track down. As the group trundle inside, a Japanese couple hang back, the man holding open the door, grinning and bowing as he ushers Jo in.

'*Tesserae!*' the word for the tiny sequins in mosaics pops into Jo's head as she examines the glowing Redeemer in the lunette above the altar, one hand raised in benediction. On either side of His golden throne, angels flash jewel-crusted swords while in ever-widening circles saucer-eyed saints gaze adoringly in His direction. Out at the edge, ordinary mortals – rich patrons by the look of their opulent clothes – cower on bended knees. These figures are miniscule in comparison, their faces overflowing with humility, fear. Nothing's changed, Jo thinks, scoffing at the intended meaning, delighting instead in the glitter, the splendour; her own body starting to feel more and more insubstantial. As shafts of light pour through rows of narrow windows, the gold background of the enormous mosaic splinters, blazes, transforming the chapel into a burnished cave.

Reluctantly, Jo drags herself away and finding an out-of-the-way bench, kicks off her sandals. Despite all the cream she's lashed on, her feet have still managed to get burnt. Worse is a worrying redness at her heel. Gingerly, she presses her hot sweaty feet to the flagstones. Shivering pleasurably at the utter coldness, she leans back, allows the quiet of the ancient building wrap itself around her. Her eyelids droop. Sounds filter through and she hears them in a desultory way as if coming from a long way off – footsteps, a cough, the click-click of a camera...

"Don't pose! I want you to look as natural as possible."

Jo shifts on the hard stool, trying not to feel intimidated by the well-known faces lording it over her from the walls of Eamonn's studio. As the camera clicks, her face changes expression: becoming thoughtful, enigmatic, girlish-

A door slams and Jo's jerks forward. With a little shake, she shudders away the daydream, conscious of an ache where her heart should be. Time to face the cauldron again, she distracts herself, fishing for her shoes.

"Captured for life!" Eamonn's words surface as she buckles a strap. He'd said it that same afternoon, stepping from behind the camera, gathering her in his arms. Jo had held onto the remark, repeated it like a mantra, taking it literally, trying to convince herself he'd meant it.

One of the tiny squiggles on the map turns out to be a tree-lined street and Jo dawdles, taking advantage of the shade.

'*Signorina, signorina*' a voice calls, a car cruising to a halt.

Jo's smile disappears as she encounters a pair of leering eyes. Shit, not another one!

'*Aspetta!* Wait! *Aspetta!* Lika lift, *signorina?*' the man cajoles.

With a toss of her head, she marches on.

The man drives alongside at a snail's pace, spouting what sounds like a string of obscene suggestions.

At the last second, Jo veers down a side street, not stopping until she finds herself in a piazza dotted with umbrellas. Out of the sun's reach, holiday-makers talk and laugh and cram their faces, silver forks spinning, sunlight glinting on lush red sauces, twinkling off sparkling glasses. Kevin would be in his element: eat, eat, *mange*, *mange*! Enjoying food as much as this has to be a sin, Jo thinks as she keeps on the move, evading eager waiters who try and catch her eye, shove menus into her hand. There's no way she could afford to eat here; she'll have a coffee somewhere cheap; eat at the hostel later.

Spotting it, Jo sprints across the narrow street, leaping out of the way of a speeding Vespa that beeps her angrily. Breath held, she touches one of the yellow globes, half-expecting the fruit to be made of plastic but it's real. A lemon tree! If only she had a camera. She lingers – captivated – then turning to go, looks back longingly at a table placed tantalisingly beneath the tree, a large white umbrella offering extra shade. Crazy! Absolutely crazy! Kevin had warned her that prices were different depending on where you sat: outside was the most expensive. Outside, under an umbrella beneath a lemon tree was most likely off the Richter scale!

Just once, a voice in her head wheedles.

'*Signorina!*' A waiter in a smart maroon jacket and fancy bow-tie pulls out a chair, gestures expansively.

Too embarrassed to refuse, Jo sits, blushing when he hands her a menu. '*Cappuccino per favour.*' The smile fades from the man's face. With a sneer, he shouts something unintelligible to one of the waitresses – making fun of her no doubt – then removing a white cloth from his shoulder swipes uselessly at the spotless table. An imaginary till ring up extra lira.

'American?'

'Irish, *Irlanda*.'

The waiter's shoulders hunch to meet his ears, his mouth curving downwards at the same time.

'*Dublino?*' Jo suggests.

'English no?'

Jo smiles, shrugs.

'*Bella no?* Bea-u-ti-ful?' he asks, plucking one of the lemons from above her head. A quick movement and it's cut and peeled. With a bow, he offers her a piece. Grimacing, she shakes her head. Grinning, he bites into it, spits it out, his face contorted.

'Bitter?' she winces; startled to see him put the remainder in his mouth, chew eagerly.

With a flourish of his towel he ends the performance. Jo claps.

'Lika woman,' he tells her, pointing at another lemon.

Jo shakes her head.

'*Si, si,*' he insists. With his hands, he carves a woman's body in the air. 'Bitter,' he nods, clenching the word with his teeth.

'No, no,' Jo disagrees, quickly adding '*Si, si,*' as a stunning young woman arrives with a tray.

'*Si, assolutamente si,*' he emphasises, trying to catch the waitress' attention.

As she hustles away, her manicured hand strays to the waiter's bum. With a mischievous wink, he blunders after her, calling as if in pain. As soon as they're out of sight, Jo checks her heel, disappointed to see the patch of red has blossomed into a blister.

She'll have to ignore it, hope it doesn't get worse. Raising the steaming coffee to her lips, the smell fills her nostrils and from an ocean of well-being a wave of happiness bubbles up.

Roma you are *magnifico*, she toasts, imagining herself – pale, foreign, alone beneath a sun-kissed lemon tree. Mysterious. Beautiful.

A camera clicks.

'Pardon me Ma'am. You look quite a picture sitting there. I hope you don't mind.' A lanky American sporting a necklace of cameras, gives her a goofy grin.

Jo smiles. With a salute, he lopes off, his attention hooked by something else.

Jo picks up her cappuccino but the moment has passed. She isn't alone, she's lonely. She stares after the receding figure, wishing he'd sat down instead of taking a photo.

A feeling bitter as coffee fills her. Bitter as lemons. Nothing lasts. Sooner or later, lemons are plucked and eaten. Just like oranges, she scoffs, recalling what one of the nuns at school used to say. Intent on putting the fear of God into them about sex, she'd warned them girls were like oranges: men would suck dry them dry then throw away the peel. If only she'd paid attention, Jo thinks, finishing her coffee.

Piazza di San Pietro! Even without a guidebook nobody could mistake St Peter's Square. Least of all Jo: the phantom of her past is buried here. Years of fear, of obeying or failing to obey commandments trace their origin to this spot. Once upon a time – not that long ago – Jo believed Heaven and earth converged right where she's standing; that the man who preached from the balcony wasn't just Pope but Christ's Vicar on earth, privy to God's wishes.

She wills herself to see beyond the soaring dome and circle of columns, past the famous window. But the too well-known image gets in the way; only the saints circling the rooftop carry an air of unfamiliarity. One hundred and forty of them, according to Kevin's guidebook. Although she can't see them properly, it isn't difficult to envisage their stern faces; and she is suddenly beset by the idea they're aware of her presence, are standing in judgment over her, chastising her for abandoning her faith. If she'd taken her religion seriously, Eamonn would never have happened and she wouldn't be here.

The doors of a touring bus glide open, disgorging a sea of the faithful. Cameras on overtime, they surge past and Jo lets herself be swept along. Now she's here, she might as well do the touristy thing and visit the Sistine. Spotting a couple of sure-footed priests, she follows their swishing skirts. At least she'll be out of the heat, she thinks, as ginormous doors open, swallow the newest arrivals.

Inside, the chapel's sardine-packed, people jammed up against one another, pointing, exclaiming. A woman in a large-brimmed sunhat sways as if in a trance. Jo skims the entry in her guidebook: "The Sistine chapel was painted between 1508 and 1512. The dimensions of the church meant the artist Michelangelo had to lie on his back and paint looking upwards for almost four years." Craning her neck, she attempts to take in the entire ceiling. She allows herself time, waits to be awed but all she experiences is a chill of disappointment.

Of course, only an ignoramus could deny the ceiling's incredible; most people regard it as the crowning glory of Western Art. But for Jo, the depiction's too real, too carnal; her soul cries out for something ethereal, something less voluptuous. Her thoughts drift to the Russian Icons in the National Gallery –

she's taken to visiting them during her lunch-breaks at college – to the shimmering transcendence of those small offerings, most no bigger than postcards.

She re-opens the guidebook: "More than 300 figures take part in this grand drama of the human race. To the artist the body was beautiful not only because of its natural form but also because of its spiritual and philosophical significance. He saw it as a manifestation of the soul."

Nothing could be further from what Jo had been taught. All her life, it had been drilled into her to regard the body and soul as separate, antagonistic; the soul superior to the body, something to rise above, conquer. Not something to perfect, as Michelangelo had wanted to do. Scrutinising the powerfully-sculpted bodies colonising the heavens, Jo can't help thinking that in the quest to perfect the physical, something immeasurable, indefinable, had got lost.

A throbbing in her own flesh brings Jo back to reality and pressing her way through the incoming crowds, she searches for an exit. She could kick herself for coming, wasting money paying in; it's not as if she didn't know this would happen.

Looking at the metal shutters barring the door of the Farmacia, Jo feels like crying. She'd totally forgotten about siesta and the whole of Rome seems to be on lock-down.

Walking away, she keeps to the shade, but the sun, drawn like a magnet to her pale skin, stalks her. Spotting a bench in the shadow of a wall, she hobbles over and peeling off her sandal, groans. The blister's ballooned up, looks as if it's about to burst. Jo sits, cradling her foot. She gives up. She's had … "*abba*" "*abbis*" – whatever the stupid word is – enough! Rome's defeated her. She'll have to take a bus to the terminus, another to the hostel;

spend all the money she saved today by walking and not eating.

Indifferent to her plight, Rome consumes itself in a haze of yellow fury. Gritting her teeth, Jo eases on the shoe, shaping the serviette she nicked from the café into a pad. Half-walking, half-hopping, she makes her way slowly, doggedly, oblivious to her surroundings; is startled when a figure swathed in black appears from nowhere, blocks her path. Punctuated with a streel of Italian, she gestures towards her own dark robes, at Jo's foot, at the sun.

Jo backs away.

Keeping up a diatribe, the woman scuttles off in the opposite direction. A few yards down the road, she turns and delivers a parting tirade before making the sign of the cross and disappearing in through a doorway as if spirited away.

That's right, Jo rants inwardly, be horrible the way the nuns at school were horrible, then act the hypocrite and pray. Cautiously, she tests her foot. *Chiesa*, church, *chiesa*, church, the rawness at her heel seems to hum. Where's God when you want Him? *Chiesa*, her heel sings. *Chiesa*! Shit! Siesta must be over! Jo raises her eyes in thanksgiving: to have somewhere to rest, somewhere away from the inflamed eye of the sun: Heaven.

With a little sucking sound, the padded doors fit snugly, blanketing out heat and noise. From years of habit, Jo genuflects before slipping into a pew. Apart from a few old women shrouded in shawls – one slapping a heavy crucifix to her forehead as she kneels and rises in quick succession – the church appears to be empty. Intrigued by the woman's supplications, Jo wonders what on earth she could be praying for, what could have her in such a state.

The silence is suddenly shattered by raised, excited voices and the woman with the rosary jumps to her feet, fiery eyes raking the church. The voices sound German; seem to be coming from one of the smaller chapels. Feeling guilty, Jo catches the Italian's eye, tries to communicate an apology on behalf of obtrusive tourists everywhere but as soon as the woman turns away, Jo sneaks from her seat, curious to find out what's causing the commotion. As she nears a side chapel, she almost collides with a man backing out: his head bent over a cine camera, another man close behind.

'Sorry, *scus-*' the words die on Jo's lips: above the altar, amid a halo of dazzling rays, a woman in a nun's habit floats on a bed of clouds; a smiling angel with a golden arrow leaning over her, about to pierce her breast. Jo stares open-mouthed: she's never seen anything so... so extraordinary in her whole life. Half in awe, she tiptoes closer, squint-reads a plaque in front of the altar: *Extasis de Santa Teresa per Gian Lorenzo Bernini*. Fumbling through the guidebook, she finds a blurred reproduction: "In The Ecstasy of St. Teresa, a masterpiece of Baroque art, Bernini unites architecture, sculpture and painting. The saint, a mystic and writer, is portrayed in visionary bliss, penetrated by Divine Love. The work's based on the Saint's own description of a Heavenly visitation."

Jo lifts her eyes. The expression on the woman's face – a look of agonizing pleasure – sets her heart trembling. How could the sculptor, how could anyone, create something so sensuous out of marble! In a church of all places! If Sister Rosario was here, she'd have a seizure. When Jo thinks of the sexless plaster-cast saints she grew up with; the unbridgeable chasm preached between sexual and spiritual. A sculpture like this would be banned in Ireland. Even the idea of connecting bodily pleasure and closeness to God would be considered a sacrilege! Jo studies the glazed eyes, thrown-back head, the body arched suggestively beneath the flowing robes: Teresa's inner passion paraded in front of the whole world. I could be looking in a mirror, Jo thinks. She has the woman in black to thank; if it hadn't been for her, she might have left Rome without seeing it.

4

'Don't forget to keep your receipt,' Jo reminds a Dutch couple as they pick up their bulging rucksacks. It's later the same day and she's lounging outside the hostel, a plaster courtesy of Kevin adorning her heel.

The Australian glances up from the magazine he's thumbing through: 'Roll on sun and sea. Naked German girls doing yoga on the beach. Yippee.'

'I suppose you need a rest after all your strenuous activities!'

'Too damned right. Old buildings sure are tiring.' Without a thought, he dismisses the treasures of Rome with a snap of his fingers. 'Can't wait to get away from all these culture vultures.'

'Meaning me, I suppose?'

'Hell no, you're the real thing!'

As Jo settles herself into an alcove to avoid the sun, Saint Teresa blazes for a moment like an after-image. She'd love to tell someone about her discovery: share it. Definitely not the right person, she decides, watching Kevin tip a piece of gum into his mouth. He'd be good to draw though; good for other things too, a voice in her head hints. At the thought of Kevin's lips touching hers, a tingle runs up Jo's spine. What's stopping her? Loads of things! For starters, she's only met him and she doesn't want to spoil things. Knowing someone can spoil things, love can spoil things, the voice reminds her.

'Kevin?'

'Huh?'

'Wanna go for a beer?'

'Sorry. No can do. Got a date with a Sheila, last night and all.'

'Oh!' Jo flushes. 'Thanks for telling me!' The words are out before she can stop them.

'Hey, didn't know you felt that way.'

'I don't, for your information. It's your problem if you want to hang out with women who haven't a brain in their head!' She forces a laugh.

'Aw Jo, Jo, little Jo,' he pleads, touching her arm. The dipping in her stomach is unmistakable. She brushes him away.

'Think I'll go for a stroll. Enjoy yourself,' she calls over her shoulder.

'See you later for *cioccolata*.'

'You'll be lucky!'

Jo walks away quickly. Overhead, an enormous sun seems determined to set the city on fire. This is stupid. She couldn't seriously fancy a guy who's into surfing; never mind contemplate getting off with him. The idea she's even considering it shocks her; she hasn't felt the slightest attraction to anyone since Eamonn.

Hearing an engine growl, Jo spins round-

'*Bella, bella!*'

Switching off the bike, Gino grins cheekily.

'You - I …' Jo throws her hands in the air. What's the point of even trying, he won't understand.

'*Ciao Irlandaisa.*'

Even so, her heart does a little jig when he calls her that. It makes her feel special—as if Italy's reaching out a hand, welcoming her.

'You like ride with me?'

Jo giggles, wishing she could explain the meaning the words have in Dublin. Their eyes spar across the moped and something inexplicably touching in Gino's expression makes her warm to him. He's so Italian with his dark hair, his neat little body squeezed into too tight clothes. Beautiful enough to be a cherub.

A cherub who can't stop scratching!

So what! 'Let's go! *Andiamo!*' she cries, hopping on the back of the moped, her bravado deserting her as the bike almost topples.

'Not too far!' she yells, her cry lost as the engine belches into life. She clings on as he recklessly takes a sudden right, scootering down a crowded street. Oncoming cars honk, drivers rolling down windows, shouting and making obscene gestures. Gino bats them away, giving as good as he gets.

'*Basta, basta*, stop!' Jo pulls at his shirt. Then all of a sudden she couldn't care less; experiences a rush of adrenaline as they rocket past a queue of backed-up cars without dropping speed. It's obvious he's showing off, proud to have her on his bike, proud of her long foreign hair blowing in the breeze.

Expertly, he manoeuvres the moped down a long winding street presided over by gloomy palazzos. The bike bumps along the cobbles, scattering pedestrians before skidding to a halt. Dismounting, he grabs her hand and before she has time to protest, leads her under an archway.

Coming out the other side, they have to duck beneath lines of billowing clothes. The washing, strung across the alleyway from window to window, reminds Jo of an old tenement she used to pass on her way home from town as a little girl. From the top of a double-decker she was able to see into the rooms; would find herself yearning to live in a flat surrounded by people instead of out in the suburbs. As her and Gino pass the dingy entrance to one of the buildings, a man and woman batter one another with words as sharp as weapons. Unconcerned, the air vibrates with music – opera, smaltzy pop, jazz – blaring from wide-open windows and doors, from tinny transistors turned to full. Above the din, Jo can make out the high-pitched wail of a child but when she glances at Gino, he appears oblivious. Passing a row of stinking bins Jo holds her breath; tells herself it's only a kitten as something sleek and furry scurries out of sight. It feels scary and exciting, and she wonders where they're going, why he's brought her to such a place.

They round a corner and a still life of bored young men –
propping up the wall of a derelict house – breaks into life.

'*Ciao Gino. Ciao, ciao.*'

'*Buona sera, signorina. Buona sera, Gino!*'

This must be where he lives, Jo realises.

'*Ciao amore!*' One of them sniggers.

'*Come bella!*' A hand reaches out. Tongues flick. Gripping her
shoulder, Gino pushes Jo through a tatty beaded curtain into a
dingy bar; the walls pasted with faded pin-ups, plump foreign-
looking women in old-fashioned swimsuits. Near the counter, a
group of workmen in dirty overalls thump coloured pieces onto a
board, their bushy eyebrows meeting, blood vessels in their necks
pumping. Motioning Jo to one of the greasy-looking tables, Gino
shouts an order, nods to the men. Without missing a turn, they
grunt. Gino grunts back, swaggers over to Jo, a challenging
expression on his face.

The game ends abruptly in a barrage of recriminations, the
men swearing and threatening each other. Almost as quickly, they
fall silent. While the next game's being set up, they tilt their
chairs, suck on cigarette butts as they eye Jo lewdly, lingering on
her breasts, her pale legs.

The silence makes her nervous. '*Cappuccino,*' she says for
something to say as a tattooed arm dumps two steaming cups on
the oilcloth.

'*Capputch,*' Gino corrects her. 'Where I come, my home,
"*capputch*", no "*cappuccino*". *A Roma se dice* "*cappuccino*." '*Io,*' he
points at his chest, 'I', "*capputch*," *capito?*' Scornfully, he clips his
chin.

'*Capputch,*' Jo repeats, wondering what the gesture means.
He's made it a few times; something like contempt, she guesses.

'*Brava.* Good.'

'*Aspetta*, wait.' Gino goes back to the counter, returns with two enormous chocolates.

There's a picture of an elephant on the wrapper and opening hers, Jo sees it's shaped like one inside. Noticing her about to break off the trunk, Gino shakes his head, pulls at his lower eyelid for her to watch. With a flourish, he dunks the whole sweet into his coffee, scooping it out almost immediately and sucking noisily.

'*Buono*, good. *Prova, prova.* Try.' He pronounces it "dry".

Jo does what she's told: it's scrummy.

'*Andiamo*, we go!' he announces, tossing back the rest of his coffee.

This isn't in the guidebook, Jo thinks, sloshing back the remainder of hers, pushing her way through the flapping curtain after him.

Gino parks close to the Spanish Steps. Walking purposefully, he steers Jo along a dimly-lit street. They come to a door studded with nails, haloed with tiny coloured light bulbs and he nods her in.

It's a cut above the last dump, Jo thinks, luxuriating on one of the velvet banquettes, surrounded by art deco lamps. Running her hand over the silky pile, she notices several not-so-angelic cherubs getting up to all sorts of antics on the opposite wall. Eyebrows rising, she sneaks a look at the customers. They'll all men, young and good-looking, dressed to the eyeballs. Even so, there's something not quite right about them, something uneasy, like actors waiting in the wings for a play to begin. Now she thinks of it the whole joint has the look of a 20's gangster film. Gino, making his way back from the bar, looks totally out of place with his short chunky body, innocent big grin. Seeing her watching him, he allows his legs buckle, pretends to sag under the weight of the bowls he's carrying. Jo's glad it's not Dublin: she'd be mortified. Suddenly, her thoughts flip. Could this be some sort of meeting place for pick-pockets? Drug dealers!

'*Divino Tartufo*' Gino announces, setting down pyramids of dark ice-cream with spikes of even darker chocolate. '*Specialita!*'

'*Divino Tartufo*,' Jo echoes. 'Thank you. *Grazie.*'

'Welcome, *prego. Sei simpatico, capito?* You understand? You *simpatico.*'

Jo nods. She sort of understands. Then again, it could mean something completely different, she thinks, as Gino shimmies closer. Kevin flashes into her mind and she wonders how he's getting on with his "Sheila"?

The Italian grabs her arm. '*Guarda*, look!'

Following his finger, Jo sees two women, who must have just come in. They are leaning provocatively against the counter and catching sight of Gino, they wave theatrically, blow kisses from the ends of silky gloves. After a quick confab with one of the barmen, they pick up their drinks and flounce over, tottering perilously on high stilettos. Eyes follow them. Both are tall as models with legs that go on forever. Up-close, their faces are plastered with pan-stick.

'*Ciao amore*,' the blonde purrs as she bends to strike a match on the table, her breasts jiggling into Jo's face. They light up; clouds of smoke mingling with the reek of perfume.

Demurely, the dark one lowers her eyelashes.

They are so false, Jo thinks, and her hair looks like a wig.

'*Come stai Gino?*' The blond tweaks his chin. 'How are you Gino?' Her accent is straight out of a B movie.

Gino whispers something in her ear and she laughs, throwing back her head.

'*Innocente*,' she smirks at Jo, guffawing as she turns on her heels. Wiggling their bums, the women sashay back across the room. They're prostitutes, Jo thinks; laughing because they think she's too innocent to suspect. Jesus! Maybe Gino's a pimp, although she has only an inkling what a pimp is.

'You like? *Bella no?*' Gino asks.

Jo shrugs: if they're prostitutes she doesn't approve so "like" doesn't come into it.

'*Angel e Maria.*' He explains. '*Miei Amici*, my friends, *Angelo e Mario.*'

She squints at him.

'*Travestiti*, men,' he sticks out his chest, pouts his lips.

Jo's ice-cream is suddenly fascinating. As she stirs the mixture, something connects at the back of her mind: an article in one of the Sundays about men dressing as women. Transvestites! *Travestiti*! She doesn't believe him. They couldn't be men!

Gino leans his face into hers: she can feel the cold on his breath. Playfully, he plops ice-cream on his tongue, sticks it out.

He doesn't expect her to lick it off, does he? Disgusted, Jo eyes the clot of brown cream, rivulets running down his chin.

'Look at the time!' she exclaims, pointing at an imaginary watch on her wrist. 'Hostel, hostel,' she adds, trying to make it sound urgent.

Gino seems perplexed then with a disdainful sneer pushes his bowl across the table. 'Don't worry baby, we go.'

Nearing the Coliseum, Gino cuts across a line of cars, shears off the roundabout. 'Shiiiit!' Jo screams, her voice joining a cacophony of horns. What's he up to? He can't be thinking of sight-seeing at this hour! In the fading light, the famous ruins are skeletal: a monument to death. As the rumble of traffic crescendos Jo hears the roar of a mob, shivers.

'*Freddo?* Cold?' Gino asks, helping her off the moped. She shakes her head, wonders if she should make a run for it, find her own way back. The problem is if she wasn't already lost, she'd get lost. Jo looks around: it was stupid ending up in a deserted place like this with someone she barely knows. A pick-pocket, Kevin had warned. Maybe worse. She wishes she was back at the hostel, drinking *cioccolata* with Kevin. Safe.

The ground's strewn with rubble, heaps of it, and Gino guides her towards a gap in the perimeter wall. Moving stealthily ahead, he drops her hand and Jo takes the opportunity to pick up a piece of masonry, conceal it in her fist. If he tries anything, he won't know what hit him.

Stopping beneath a crumbling archway, Gino puts a finger to his lips, beckons. Once she's beside him, he picks up a handful of small stones, holds them out to her, an inscrutable expression on his face. Jo's mystified. Taking a step back, he heaves himself up on a narrow ledge and with a bloodcurdling yell pitches the stones into the night.

There's a ping ping as stones land, followed by shrieks as hordes of mangy cats, bodies elongated, hurl themselves through the air, spitting and yowling, yellow eyes flaring. In the almost-dark, mutilated faces appear and vanish; the night hacked with growls, snarls, sounds that are almost human.

'*Selvaggio*!' Making claws of his hands, Gino pretend-scrabs at her face.

Savage is right, Jo thinks; sickened at the sight of the scabby animals attacking each other.

Roaring with laughter, Gino chases her back the way they came. 'Catz,' he yells running after her, 'catz!'

5

A little way off from the hostel, close to a clump of bushes, Gino cuts the engine; is waiting when Jo hops down, his face shiny, expectant.

'Oh Gino.'

She knew he'd try something, had spent the journey back wondering how she'd handle it. To him she's just another foreign girl – a bit of free fun – just as the German girls are for Kevin. Still, if she intends to try and learn to love the way men love, here's her first opportunity.

Quelling her reservations, Jo allows him edge her into the shadows.

'*Amore, amore*,' he whispers, pressing against her. His body feels different to Eamonn's, hard and muscular, his hands rough as they find their way under her top, fiddle with the snap of her bra. Instinctively, she pulls away but he clutches at her.

Clenching her eyes, Jo tries to make herself feel something. Gino's kisses are rapid, impatient. A knee pushes between her legs. Against her will, Jo melts. Tears flood down her cheeks.

'*Stronzo*! *Che cosa*? What?' Gino demands, throwing up his hands.

Jo crumples. Even if he had perfect English, it would be hard to explain to a guy like him that this is as far as she's gone with anyone except Eamonn. Or that he's the first person to touch her since they broke up.

'*Abstanza*,' she shouts to cover her embarrassment.

'*Abbastanza, abbastanza*,' he corrects, glaring at her before doubling over with laughter. '*Madre di Dio*! *Catholica*!'

'*Si, si*,' Jo latches onto the excuse. 'Hostel *per favore*,' she begs, feeling suddenly wrecked.

Stooping, he makes an exaggerated Sign of the Cross on her skirt.

'*Irlandaisa!*' he shakes his head.

As she races up the steps, the moped whizzes past, hooting loudly before vanishing.

Jo peers into the foyer. The last person she wants to bump into is Kevin. Keeping an eye out, she tiptoes up the stairs, creeps into her room. Not bothering with lights, she slips out of her clothes, climbs the little ladder. Relief, she thinks as she collapses into bed.

A moment later, she's sitting up; a familiar cramp twisting her gut. Shit! Shit! Her period must be coming: no wonder she felt so bushed. Straightening out her legs, she winces: it's as if someone's sticking arrows in her. Not arrows of Divine Love either! Mario and Angelo should be careful what they wish for.

The pain intensifies and she massages her abdomen, circling round and round. Beneath the thin sheets her breasts harden. Guilt rears its head. Why? It's her body! If Eamonn was here, he could- Oh Eamonn ... how can it be over when her body is crying out? Craving his touch.

Feeling a dribble, Jo reaches down and bringing her fingers to her nose, inhales the dark blood.

Out of nowhere, comes a smell of lemons. The waiter's wrong, it's not women who are bitter, it's life.

Jo scrapes the last honeycombs of froth from her cup. Although Rome's been on the move for ages – kicking up a row on the far side of the window –the canteen's almost empty.

Excitement wells inside her. She's only been out of Ireland a few days but already she feels different: as if the world's revealing some of its secrets. Her evening with Gino was an eye-opener. She doubts if half her friends have ever heard of transvestites; never mind meeting them in the flesh! And she's glad she allowed Gino kiss her, even if her body mutinied.

'*Tanti auguri!*' she laughs to herself. It means "good wishes", is probably where "augur" comes from. What does her future augur? She'll have to wait and see. She hasn't the faintest idea what the Robertsons will be like. Or their children.

What does it matter: she's going there to paint. Eamonn may have plucked her from obscurity, catapulted her into a different world, but now it's up to her. When she's an artist, when she's made it, Eamonn will regret going back to … Deirdre. Jo acknowledges her rival's name, makes the woman real for the first time. Yes, Eamonn will be sorry, she'll make sure of that. *Tanti auguri*, she repeats, *tanti-*

'The big day, huh'

Kevin slides his tray along the table, pushes in beside her.

Jo nods, envying the huge breakfast he's planning on scoffing.

A smile plays on his lips as he tears open a tub of yoghurt. 'Thought you might have changed your mind, got hitched up with Romeo aka our very own Gino.'

'I don't see myself as the Juliet type,' Jo replies, furious he found out.

'A little birdie saw the two of you canoodling. Got the impression you didn't go in for that sort of thing.' Carefully, he spreads jam on his roll, raises it to his mouth.

Jo scowls. Kevin's no right to make her feel cheap. She isn't one of his interchangeable little "Sheilas".

'I suppose you go in for that crap – women should be virgins!'

'No way, man. I'm all for women's lib. Just wish you'd let me know.'

Jo leaps up. What is she doing wrong?

'Hey, what's up?'

'The curse, what else!' she covers.

'You women sure get a raw deal!' Kevin sympathises.

'You can say that again.'

'You women sure-'

'Shut-up!' Jo punches him playfully and he grabs her hand. As their fingers entwine, her heart leaps.

They look at one another.

'It's been a real pleasure meeting you Ireland.'

'You too Australia.' Kissing him quickly, Jo speeds from the room.

'Have a good trip,' he calls after her. 'And hey, hang on to the guidebook, you'll probably need it.'

Pavia

6

It isn't hard to spot Tim Robertson at the train station. He looks exactly the way Jo imagined a professor would look: all elbows and tweeds, hair greying at the sides, a distracted expression on his melancholy face.

'Josephine Nowd?' he inquires, holding out a hand. 'Tim Robertson. How do you do?'

Jo drops the book she's been reading. He bends to pick it up and she hopes he'll notice it's about art, but he hands it back without a glance.

'Our last girl was from Dublin,' he tells her as they squeeze into a tiny car. 'She was with us almost two years. Fiona Sweeney, you don't happen to know her?'

Jo shakes her head; strange the way everyone thinks people in Ireland all know each other.

'We find Irish girls make the best au-pairs. They're …' He searches for a word, settles on '*simpatico*'. 'Speak any Italian?'

'A bit.' Jo takes a quick peek out the window. She's been looking forward to seeing Pavia but the area they're driving through is modern, boring-looking, not a patch on Rome-

'You'll pick it up. *The Scuola Inglese* – the English School – runs classes. We encourage our girls to attend.'

As Mr Robertson chatters on about times of classes and what looking after the "brats" entails, Jo sees her free time slipping down the drain. As far as she knows, au pairs are only obliged to do certain things: attending Italian classes isn't one of them. Maybe she should say something – make sure he knows she has her plans of her own.

'I loved Rome,' Jo announces as soon as he finishes talking.

'Had a good time?' The question's throwaway; her new employer's attention focussed on a right turn he's making.

'Yeah. Thanks. I was only there a few days but I managed to see quite a lot – churches mainly. Some were really old – one was actually fifth century – the mosaics anyway. And I saw this amazing sculpture by Bernini!' It's on the tip of Jo's tongue to say 'The Ecstasy of St. Teresa' but remembering the expression on the saint's face, she changes her mind. 'I don't usually like art after the fifteenth century,' she informs him before remembering Bernini is 16th century so maybe it's not quite true anymore.

That shook him, she thinks, seeing one of Tim's eyebrows shoot up.

'You're interested in that sort of thing?'

'I studied at the College of Art, the national college' Jo explains, leaving out the fact she'd only gone three nights a week; had jacked it in a year later, soon after she'd met Eamonn. Taking a deep breath, she continues, 'I want to become an artist.' There, she's said it.

As soon as the words are out, Clive Mullins, one of her tutors, puts in an appearance. He was forever tearing strips off students for imagining they could 'become' artists. He believed you were born one or you were wasting your time. He wasn't a fan of Siennese painters either, Jo remembers, disparaging them in favour of Giotto; never missing an opportunity to remind the class how the Florentine had single-handedly changed the course of Western Art. The first time he'd mentioned Giotto, Jo – who'd never heard of him – had gone straight to the college library, excited at the prospect of discovering someone whose work might surpass her favourites. But his frescos had left her cold; they hadn't even seemed that well painted. How could such primitive looking stuff change anything! Santa Croce in Florence has a whole chapel of his frescos and she's hoping to visit them as soon as she gets a chance; maybe after seeing them, what Mullins said will make sense.

The car slows at traffic lights and Mr Robertson looks at her more attentively. 'I'm glad to hear it. Most girls have their heads filled with nonsense. I presume you visited the Vatican?'

'I didn't like St. Peters. The proportions seemed wrong. It was ...' Jo clams up, wishing she'd left well enough alone. She can talk about films or books until the cows come home but when she opens her mouth about art usually she ends up tongue-tied or making a fool of herself. Words that describe art don't come naturally to her; using them makes her feel like she's showing off. Architecture's worse, even though she adores Gothic and Baroque, Rococo most of all; she's give anything to see the Wieskirche in Germany.

'You might have a point.' Mr Robertson's freckled hands grip the wheel. 'I think it was Ruskin said it was only fit to be a ballroom!' He laughs and Jo joins in, relieved he's easy to talk to; not as pompous as he looks. 'I'm sure Michelangelo would appreciate your opinion – he was the architect.'

There were several architects but Jo lets it pass; her stomach getting the jitters as they turn into a courtyard and Tim backs the car into a tight parking space.

'We're here!' he declares, getting out and coming round to open her door.

"Here" turns out to be an old-fashioned mustardy-yellow apartment block with imposing wrought-iron balconies, enormous urns overflowing with flowers. The fountain in the centre of the courtyard has a leaping fish with a big gaping mouth; the sound of gushing water balm to Jo's ears.

'It's lovely! Really.'

Tim motions upwards. 'Very top. No lift, I'm afraid.' Picking up her suitcase, Mr Robertson's eyes fix on Jo. 'Anna's going to be surprised,' he murmurs, nodding her towards a stairwell.

Mrs Robertson's eyes travel slowly down Jo's tie-dye tee shirt, maxi skirt, take in her chunky open-toed wedge-heels. Under her radar gaze, Jo feels scruffy, unwashed.

The three of them are sitting in the lounge, Tim and Jo at either end of an oatmeal-coloured sofa, Anna perched in a matching armchair looking as if someone's stuck a pole up her bum. Decked out in a pale pink twinset and pearls, a burgundy velvet hair-band keeping her shoulder-length brown hair in place, she looks regal, intimidating. The room, like Anna, is pale and elegant – snobby in an indefinable way – and heady with the perfume of dusky yellow roses. Until Mrs Robertson breezed in, Jo had been congratulating herself, thinking she'd landed on her feet: even posh flats in Dublin were kips in comparison.

'Do you think you'll be happy with us?' Anna's clipped English accent breaks the silence. 'You'll fit in?'

What sort of question is that, Jo thinks, staring out a pair of french windows. At the corner of her eye, she catches Anna shoot an uncertain glance at her husband.

'I wouldn't be surprised if Jo's tired,' Tim explains, 'she's been traipsing round churches all weekend. She's quite knowledgeable.'

Jo blushes, pleased he's taking her side; has a sudden hunch Mr and Mrs Robertson might not see eye to eye on everything.

'She's going to need plenty of energy for our two,' Anna snorts. 'You've never looked after children before, have you?'

Jo's tempted to say you don't have to in Ireland: you grow up with them. Instead, she shakes her head politely.

'The most important thing is to have them up and ready for

school on time. Tim has probably gone over our schedule but you and I can discuss it later. By the way, we like to be informal – our last au pair called us Anna and Tim.'

Jo nods, deciding not to call them anything unless she has to. Although they both look about thirty, Tim maybe a bit older, they seem more like her parents. It's the way they act, Mrs Robertson especially: snotty, used to bossing people. And money, naturally.

Mrs Robertson presses a bell and a tiny woman in a black dress and lacy apron trundles in, pushing a trolley. Jo's horrified: she didn't realise people still had maids; is mortified when the woman curtsies before handing her a stiff white napkin.

'*Grazie,*' she says pointedly, hoping the woman understands she doesn't approve of servants. A pair of cinder eyes twinkle.

'Help yourself Josephine, you must be hungry after your trip.' Anna waves a hand towards several plates of fancy-looking sandwiches, a gorgeous-looking glazed fruit flan, the kind Jo had salivated over in shop windows in Rome. 'There's coffee if you'd like some.'

Jo dithers. Each plate is garnished with some kind of grassy stuff; if she picks a sandwich up, it's bound to get all over the place.

'*Signorina,*' the maid bobs and after selecting a mix and cutting a large slice of cake, she hands the plate to Jo.

Anna tuts, mutters something in Italian. The maid, one eye on Tim, flashes back, gesturing towards the trolley, towards Jo, pulling at her apron.

What's going on, Jo wonders: surely Anna isn't pissed off because the maid helped her? As the diminutive woman runs out of steam, Mrs Robertson snaps open her own napkin, begins serving herself. Making a clicking sound with her tongue, the maid turns on her heel and swans out. Jo likes her instantly.

'Maria comes in every day other than Sunday. She takes care of light housework, does the cooking, that sort of thing. Pretty damn good. Makes a superb Pollo Cachitore – Hunter's Chicken. Unfortunately, the recipe's a family secret.'

And I look after the kids. What do you do? Biting into a creamy egg mayonnaise, Jo silently aims the question at Anna.

As if reading her thoughts, Tim answers, 'Anna rides a lot; we keep a horse. There's a good stables on the outskirts of Pavia. Have you ever ridden?'

'Only once, when I was-'

'They're wonderful animals, extremely intelligent,' Anna interrupts, checking her watch. 'I better go and collect the children. They're so looking forward to meeting you Josephine. As a rule, they have dinner on their own, supervised by you of course. As a special treat I thought we'd all eat together this evening.' With a quick glance in the bevelled mirror above the fireplace, she strides out.

As soon as the front door closes, Jo lets her breath out, begins eating in earnest.

With a little cough, Tim shifts along the couch.

'I should warn you, Anna finds the children trying. I'd be grateful if you could give them as much attention as you can.' He places a hand on her arm, leaving it a fraction longer than necessary.

Jo stiffens, swallowing what's in her mouth. 'I better go and unpack before they get back,' she blurts.

'No rush,' Tim assures her, getting to his feet. 'The traffic's pretty grim this time of day.' 'Care for something stronger?' he asks, opening a cabinet. 'There's Glenfiddich ... Scottish of course. If you don't mind being disloyal.'

"Disloyal?"What's he on about? 'I don't really like whiskey that much,' she tells him, trying not to sound impolite. It's not really true anyway; she just can't afford it.

'Sure?' he asks, holding up a bottle.

Shaking her head, Jo eases off the sofa, eager to get out of the room. Jesus Christ, she's going to have her work cut out with this pair, never mind the kids.

7

An alarm screeches somewhere in the tunnel of Jo's head. Nothing human gets up at this hour, she grumbles, forcing herself out of bed, pulling a sweater on over her nightie. She's only been here a few weeks and already it feels like a life sentence. She's not cut out to be a skivvy, toadying all the time, asking permission if she wants to go out. The whole thing's humiliating!

Oh, stop moaning and start painting, she chides herself, blundering sleepily down the hall. Alright, she promises blearily, she'll definitely start today, as soon as she gets the kids to school.

It's uncanny the way sleep transforms the little monster, Jo muses, looking down at Peter. With one cheek reddened by the pillow and his golden hair, he could be an angel. What a pity she has to wake him! Feeling a right eejit, she leans over, makes herself whisper "cioccolata, cioccolata" the way Anna had instructed.

The six-year old stirs. Awake, he's a dead ringer for his mother although there's a hint of Tim's fishy eyes in his sleepy gaze. Seeing Jo, he pushes her away, yells across at his brother. Mark mumbles drowsily, snuggles under the duvet. Quick as lighting, Peter is across the room, jumping on top of the younger boy, pummelling his chest.

'Stop! Right now! Or no cioccolata. I mean it!' Jo recognises her mother's voice which she's always considered weak, easily ignored.

'I want two cups,' Peter demands.

'You'll take what you get,' she hisses. This time she imitates her father's tone although she's wary of using it; after all she's being paid. 'Get dressed,' she orders, leaving the room.

The kitchen, at the back of the apartment, is in shadow, will only brighten around the time Maria arrives which is hours away. Mixing a couple of spoons of chocolate with milk, Jo keeps an ear open. It's terrible she can't leave the boys alone for two minutes without worrying Peter will get up to something. God, she hates him. She'd give him a good hiding if she thought she'd get away with it.

Wearily, Jo pours the gloop into a pot, turns on the gas. It's hard getting used to being part of a family the polar opposite of the one she grew up in. Even the amount of things they eat – the variety – is amazing. When she thinks of the diet she had at home: mince and overcooked vegetables day in, day out! *Verdura*: vegetables. She's been picking up Italian from Maria, words for food mainly – *soupe di mare* a gorgeous fish soup and of course *pollo* which Marie cooks in unbelievable ways including her famous "Hunter's Chicken". "*Choffee*", a word she kept hearing at the market is actually "*Carciofi*": artichokes, a vegetable she didn't even know existed. Stirring the mixture, she winces recalling the way Tim had sat her down, showed her the proper way to eat one: leaf by leaf, dipped in olive oil, the soft inner part scraped off with your teeth. Cringe-making!

'Jooooo…!!'

Mark's scream carries the length of the hallway. Christ, he'll have the whole house awake! Hurrying to the bedroom, she finds him on his knees trying to piece together several ripped-out pages. The younger child's eyes plead with her.

'He hit me, he hit me,' Peter gets in first.

Mark hides himself in Jo's arms, begins to sob.

'Cry-baby, cry-baby,' Peter taunts.

'Pick up that book Peter and cellotape those pages in.' Or I'll knock your block off, she finishes in her head.

The older boy's eyes lock with hers.

'You heard. And bring it to me in the kitchen when you're finished.'

Taking Mark with her, she sweeps out ignoring the swear word whispered loud enough for her to hear. This job's going to be a nightmare unless she can get Peter under her thumb. But how? Anna spoils them, Peter in particular, then expects Jo to be tough. All it does is make him more demanding. He could do with a taste of her daddy. A week of Mr Nowd would set him straight.

Her nose puckers as they near the kitchen. Shit, shit, shit, she forgot the bloody pot!

Jo grabs the burnt saucepan from the cooker, fans away the smoke. Fuck! This is all she needs.

'Where's my *cioccolata*?' Mark wails.

Why you ungrateful- Jo chokes back the words. Calm, she tells herself: they'll be out of her hair soon and she'll be free!

'I'll put more on. Get your schoolbag ready.'

'Are you a mummy?'

'No, I'm not,' Jo answers, opening the fridge to get milk. 'Want *tostini* while you're waiting?' she asks, grabbing a box of dry toast from the cupboard. "Horse biscuits" she calls them privately but the boys devour them smothered in Nutella.

Mark nods happily. 'I like you better than Fiona. She was always cross.'

'So am I,' Jo laughs, patting his head.

After dropping off the kids, Jo decides not to hang around for a chat with the rest of the au pairs. She's had it up to here with them anyway prattling on about clever little Mario or goody-goody Sofia! They seem to feel it's a privilege to look after spoiled brats. A few of them even regard it as a preparation for marriage.

Eejits!

By now, Jo knows the route to the apartment by heart, could do it blindfold. Today's the day, she tells herself, no more excuses. She'd never expected it would be so difficult to get back into painting. Somehow there always seems to be things she has to do: the boys' beds to make, their room to tidy, school clothes to wash and hang out; after that she usually has coffee with Maria and before she knows it it's midday and time for lunch. Jo's heart contracts. The truth is she's been afraid to start: what if she isn't any good? Doesn't know what to paint. At college they were given assignments; were monitored and marked. Maybe she's been fooling herself! Clive Mullins said she had talent, but lacked discipline. She hadn't been sure if he meant she didn't work hard enough or didn't know how to control her materials and she'd never had the nerve to ask.

As she conjures up an image of herself – pencil in hand, a sheet of blank paper awaiting the first stroke – Jo becomes aware of footsteps; realises she's been conscious of them for a while. A little way back, a man carrying a briefcase is keeping step: a businessman by the cut of his three-piece. Reassured, Jo lets go of a feeling of unease; she'll be home shortly, she's almost at the underpass. As she trips down the steps, the man catches up. Jo slows to allow him pass. He hurries by without looking, disappearing around a bend. Right, Jo reminds herself: straight to her room, no stopping for coffee- A shuffling noise intrudes on her thoughts and she notices the man has stopped, is waiting for her, eyes protruding, tongue hanging out. Lowering the briefcase he's been clutching, he thrusts an erect penis towards her. Jo hears herself scream but the sound stays in her head. Making a funny gurgling sound, he reaches out, touches her. Jo recoils but her legs let her down, refuse to budge. Dropping the bag – which is empty – the man lurches back the way he came.

Jo opens the front door as quietly as possible. As she passes the kitchen, she can hear Maria and Anna talking. Fuck, Anna's the last person she feels like seeing. Closing the door to her room, she throws herself on the bed, leaping up almost immediately. Crossing to the window, she looks out – unseeing – then with a little cry, strides angrily to the dressing-table. Gazing into the mirror, she examines her reflection as if looking at someone she doesn't know. She tries to put a name on what she's feelings. But it's like she feels nothing – annihilated, wiped out – and everything: disgusted, defiled, frightened. Dirty. Why did it have to happen? Today of all days when- The front door closes with a bang giving Jo a start. She stands stock still. A moment passes and there's a knock on the bedroom door.

'Want *coff*? Ees ready. *Pronto.*'

Jo tries to speak.

'You ok?' Maria sounds concerned.

Answer, Jo commands herself. '*Sono bene, Maria. Stanca. Sono stanca.*' For some reason, she can handle it in Italian. '*Sono stanca,*' she repeats, louder this time, half-wanting the maid to believe she's tired; another part of her hoping Maria will realise something's up and come in. As the maid's clumpy shoes echo down the polished hallway, tears slide down Jo's face.

8

'You're going to have to organise yourself a little better Josephine.' Anna plays with a *grissini* before snapping the breadstick in two. 'Peter told me they were nearly late for school today.' Her employer smiles sweetly. 'Perhaps you need to get up earlier. We can't have it happening again.'

'I'm sure it won't,' Tim says affably and Jo has a feeling he's got something up his sleeve.

She puts a forkful of food into her mouth. It's been a week since the guy exposed himself and she's been sleeping badly; struggling to get out of bed in the morning. Not that that gives Anna the right to talk to her as if she's a servant – especially in front of Tim! Jo seethes. Peter's a little snitch, telling tales to his mother. Maybe it would have been better if she'd confided in Anna, extracted a bit of sympathy. Then again, maybe not. She can just hear her: it's not as if you haven't seen one before! Or: try looking at horses! She's probably being unfair. Who cares! The whole episode's upset her more than she'd expected. It's as if a bubble has burst and she feels tainted. Even though it wasn't her fault, the fact it happened reflects on her somehow. That was one of the reasons she decided not to tell Anna: she couldn't bear Tim finding out and she was certain Anna would tell him, even if she promised not to. She suspects if Tim knew, he'd think less of her; as would anyone who found out. Why? Nobody blames a person if they're robbed!

As Maria clears away the plates, Tim, with a conjurer's sleight of hand, produces a startlingly blue box, the word '*BACI*' embossed in gold on the lid. 'I bought these as a celebration. *Baci* means kisses. Mark tells me he's in love with you already.'

'I'm sure lots of little boys fall in love with Josephine.' Anna brushes imaginary crumbs from her skirt. 'There's some show-jumping on television. Enjoy the *Baci*.'

Tim holds out the box. 'Go on, have one before you go. You know you like them.' He turns to Jo. 'The chocolates have sayings inside, a bit like Chinese fortune cookies.'

It wouldn't kill her to let her hair down once in a while, Jo thinks, watching Anna dip her hand in graciously, giggling a little. There's a delicacy, a kind of fastidiousness about the way she does things which for some reason Jo finds fascinating. Her voice is fascinating too, like someone used to being listened to. She milks it though, has to get her own way or someone is bound to pay. Between her and Tim the scales are forever tipping: him nice, her nasty, her nice, Tim nasty. Jo in the middle.

'"*Amore e credula creatura*,"' Anna reads in perfect Italian. She puts on a special voice when she speaks Italian: glossy, silken. 'Love is a naive creature,' she translates with a quick glance at Tim. 'I think that one's for you.'

Jo only half-hears, concerned about Tim who seems to have shrunk. Then he laughs, replies in Italian and the two of them are laughing.

At what?

It's Tim's turn to choose and Jo gets a feeling the couple's relationship is on trial.

'"*Un amante teme tutto quello che crede*."' His voice sounds hurt.

'What does it mean?' Jo asks to fill the silence.

'They're just a bit of fun,' Anna replies. 'Your turn, Josephine.'

Tim refuses to be diverted. 'A lover fears all he believes,' he explains. 'What do you think that means Jo?'

The phone rings in the hall and for once Anna gets up to answer it. There's a skitter of laughter and Jo guesses it's her best friend, Elena. She hears the receiver being replaced, Anna padding along the hallway to the bedroom to continue the conversation, the bedroom door shutting.

Tim makes a ball of the crinkly silver paper, leans back against the wall. He looks old.

Why does Anna have to spoil things? Jo shifts in her chair and Tim looks at her, seems to remember she's in the room. His eyes pierce into hers.

Jo wishes she could comfort him, say something to let him know she understands, sympathises.

Tim pushes the box towards her.

'Go on, let's see what you get.'

Jo plucks one blindly, unravels the tinsel.

The sayings are translated into different languages and opening the wrapper, she scans the tiny sheet for the English version.

'"A complete need should not exist. Love life in common with loved ones."'

It seems badly translated and Jo feels cheated. She'd been hoping for something – she's not sure what – some unmistakeable sign about Eamonn.

'Sound advice,' Tim declares.

Jo reads it again, realises it's true. After she met Eamonn, she'd dropped everything: turned him into her life. Then when he'd dumped her-

'What are you thinking?'

Jo looks away.

'You're homesick, I expect?'

She nods, even though it's not true, not the way he means it. She's homesick for love. She yearns to feel special, have someone look at her ... want her.

Without warning, she sees herself melting into Tim's arms, following through the invitation she sees in his eyes. Mute, trembling, she says nothing.

Leaning closer, Tim strokes her hair.

Jo dabs at her tears with a napkin; watches as Tim picks up an apple, peels it methodically, slowly exposing the moist white flesh. Cutting it into slices, he spears a piece, offers it to her.

Jo shakes her head.

The discarded skin, already browning, makes her want to cry. She's never felt so lonely in all her life.

Making lots of clicking noises, Maria bustles in. '*Dai! Dai!* Go!' she orders, shaking her apron at Jo. Tim has already taken himself off to join Anna and Jo's alone at the table, comforting herself with left-over wine.

'*Madonnina! Ma che cosa?* What is it?' the maid shrieks, pushing back Jo's hair to get a better look at her face.

'Nothing, I'm ok. *Io bene.*'

One hand on hip, Maria sizes her up.

'*Poverina!*'

Babbling in Italian, the maid pulls Jo from her chair, marches her out the french windows. On the balcony, she drags her to the railings, gesticulates.

'*No capisco.* Don't understand.'

'*Guarda,*' Maria pulls at her eyelid. Raising herself to full height, she primps her hair, pats her dress and with a little wiggle, swaggers up and down, waving and smiling as if the balcony's crowded with people.

'I should go out? Go to the city? *Va al Citta?*'

'*Si, si. Vai, vai*, go! *Domani.* Tomorrow. Be happy,' Maria beams, slapping Jo on the bottom before hurrying back inside.

9

Jo's mouth waters: it's impossible to choose, there are too many flavours! And the colours! Nobody in Dublin would believe there are shops in Italy – *Gelaterias* – that sell nothing but ice-cream. Remembering Kevin, she decides to treat herself to Zuppe Inglese but when she asks for it, the man behind the counter indicates an empty container. In the end, she settles for a tutti-frutti.

Taking Maria's advice to heart, Jo has spent the morning wandering round Pavia but so far nothing's gone according to plan. The *Duomo* was closed for repairs and a Romanesque church called San Theodora – famous for its frescos – had turned out to be dark and creepy and she hadn't felt like lingering, especially as she was the only visitor. This really annoyed her as she knew it wouldn't have bothered her before the fuckin' guy in the tunnel; since it happened she doesn't feel as safe. The final straw had come when she'd stood trying to get a good look at a medieval griffon near the top of a *Banca d'Italia* and a couple of nosey women had come racing over to see what she was up to. You'd swear she was about to rob the place!

Meandering aimlessly, Jo licks the remainder of her *gelato*: she's had *abbastanza* of acting the bloody tourist! Maria's wrong: seeing people enjoying themselves makes her feel lonelier. Stepping aside to allow a group of teenagers with brightly coloured backpacks shoot past she spots three slender towers ahead, guesses the university must be close, there was a picture of them in the guidebook. According to the blurb underneath, Pavia's famous for towers, has almost a hundred although these are the first she's come across. There were some in the frescos at

San Teodora, particularly in the largest one: an amazing bird's eye view of the city in the fifteenth century. Turning to look at the towers, Jo realises – not for the first time – that she often prefers paintings to the real thing. It's something to do with the way paintings frame objects or places: bestowing a strange heightened quality they don't have in reality.

Across from where she's standing, students come and go through ancient arched walkways. These passageways are called "*loggias*", she's seen them in paintings by Fra Angelico and other medieval artists; wonders if she'll ever be sophisticated enough to drop a word like that into a conversation.

A bell rings and swarms of young people spill out, jostling each other, talking earnestly. Jo watches, wishing she was there to meet one of them; at the same time aware how their happy-go-lucky confidence scares her. It always has, even the short time she was a student herself. They're a different species, she reflects; different from her anyway. Indulging a vague hope someone might notice she's foreign and take it into their head to talk to her, she dallies. A lecturer in a black gown breezes by and remembering Tim teaches at the university, she takes herself off. He'd definitely get the wrong idea if he discovered her loitering outside looking forlorn, and eager. And she can't afford to give him any more ideas than he has.

'*C'e museo vicino, per favore?*' On the spur of the moment, Jo approaches a woman in a white shop coat. 'Is there a museum near?' she adds in English in case her Italian's not right. It's still too early for the boys; besides she'd like to have something interesting to talk about over dinner – Tim will expect it.

The Italian looks mystified then her face lights up. '*Venga, venga, come,*' she says brusquely, walking quickly back the way she came, signalling Jo to follow. Reaching a traffic island, she indicates a long car-congested street.

'*Dritto*, straight. *Sempre dritto*, always straight,' she sings, making slicing gestures with her hand. '*Capishe?*'

'Si, grazie. *Dritto*, straight.'

'*Brava.*' With a little wave, the woman scoots away, turning a few paces later to shoo Jo on.

"S*empre dritto*," Jo tells herself. 'Keep right on.'

'*E aperto?* Open?' Jo asks the attendant seated behind a counter in a small vestibule; hoping she hasn't got there too late. At some point "dritto" turned into a maze of streets and it had taken her ages to find the place.

Muttering loudly, the man folds the newspaper he's reading, bundles himself out of the chair. Motioning Jo to accompany him, he takes her down a draughty corridor, rattling a bunch of keys attached to his waistband as he walks.

Arriving at a pair of palatial doors, he nods Jo into a vast hall crammed with paintings. Following her in, he plods to the middle of the room, indicates each wall in turn.

Self-consciously, Jo looks at the nearest painting, a Nativity scene by a painter she's never heard of; so dark it's almost impossible to make out the crouching figures. The date at the bottom says eighteen-fifty but already the painting has begun to crack, whole sections black from whatever medium was mixed with the oils. The portrayal of the birth of the Child is run of the mill and Jo would like to move on but the man's presence paralyses her and she stays where she is until she hears the sound of shoes shuffling out. Once she's certain he's gone, she does a quick circuit of the room, waiting for a painting to leap out at her, the longed-for surge of energy to flood her body. No such luck, she thinks, grinding to a halt.

The paintings, eighteenth and nineteenth century, are religious or allegorical, reminiscent of works Jo's seen in countless books and reproductions. To pass the time, she decides to try and identify the century, the school, which painters have exerted an influence on the artist. She makes a game of it but before long it palls; a feeling of futility setting in. What's the point of these mediocre paintings, whatever spark they'd once possessed gone. Why does so much effort in the world seem to be for nothing? For all she knows some of these might be considered masterpieces but she hasn't come across even one that sings to her. Looking at them only convinces her of the rightness of her own preferences. Maybe "love", "like" and "not like" are the wrong words to use about art but compared to paintings from Sienna or early Russian Icons or even lots of anonymous paintings from the Romanesque period, what's on display might as well be wallpaper. Something's missing ... or could she be missing something? How can so many people be wrong? Maybe there's an aspect of art she doesn't understand. Something that would allow paintings such as these fall into place.

As she passes the attendant on the way out, he glances up from his *Giornale* to the clock on the wall, sighs wearily. Like her, he's waiting to go home. Shortly, she'll collect Peter and Mark, turn into an au pair again. If she takes the road along the river, she'll arrive at the school just in time.

Stopping near a line of slender trees rimming the river bank, Jo peers anxiously at her reflection. Is she interesting? Different? Or second-rate like the paintings in the gallery? She knows what she'd like the answer to be. Picking up a few dusty pebbles, she tosses them in, watches the ripples spread across the quivering water, scatter her everywhere at once.

'You are hard to please!' Tim pronounces, reaching for the salad. 'Half of those paintings are probably priceless! I know for a fact there's a- oh, what's his name. . .?'

'What do you know about art?' Anna retorts, topping up her wine.

'Quite a bit as it happens,' Tim replies.

'News to me!' Anna makes a face.

They've having dinner and as Maria's taking an evening off, instead of the usual three courses, they're making do with *bifstek* and *insalata mista*. Peter and Mark are in bed, stuck into comics and not fighting, at least not the last time Jo checked. She notices whenever Tim's home, they behave better.

While they've been eating, Jo's been exaggerating her disappointment at the paintings she saw earlier.

'What *do* you like?' Tim prods.

'Well. . .Byzantine art, Icons, medieval paintings. And I love Siennese art.' She stops, uncomfortable with the attention; besides she hates it when they use her to snipe at each other.

'Which painters exactly?'

'Em . . . Simone Martine, Duccio – they're both from Sienna. Fra Angelico, sort of . . .'

'Fra Angelico, I've heard of him. There you are.' He grins at his wife.

Anna picks fluff off her husband's sleeve. 'Very impressive.' She gives Jo a slant-eyed look. 'I'd have taken you for a modern girl. Can't imagine what you see in all that dreary old stuff. Simpering Madonnas and overfed babies. Whatever turns you on, I suppose.'

'Sounds a bit like sublimation to me,' she murmurs, giving Tim a knowing look.

Half-understanding, Jo reddens; sees Tim glare at Anna, mutter something in Italian.

'You know what I tell my students Jo, there are certain experiences you can't share. They're too personal.' He winks. 'Anna would understand if you compared it to riding a horse.'

Nonchalantly, Tim picks up a toothpick, inserts it in his mouth. A blush creeps up Anna's neck.

Tim extracts the stick. 'The *Certosa*! Why didn't I think of it sooner?'

'*Certosa*? What's that?'

'It's the old charterhouse of the Carthusians. It was founded in the fourteenth century. Montaigne visited, oh sometime in the 1500's, thought it was magnificent. Is that good enough for you? I'll take you myself,' he offers.

Anna, who'd gone quiet, smiles unpleasantly. 'How gallant. I'm sure she can find her own way. As far as I know there's a bus every Saturday. Josephine, isn't that Peter calling?'

"*Josephine, isn't that Peter calling?*" Jo mimics Anna on her way down the hall. It drives her bonkers the way she calls her "Josephine". At the beginning, she thought it made her sound important, adult; now she realises it's Anna's way of putting a distance between them: keeping her in her place.

Reaching the boys' room, Jo peeps in, sees Peter sprawled across his bed, engrossed in a comic. Noticing her, the older boy flings it down. 'The game, the game,' he shouts, pointing at the hump in Mark's bed.

Jo sags. The last thing she feels like is acting the clown for these two.

'Please,' he begs. 'We haven't played it in ages!'

'Oh all right,' she relents, secretly flattered they like it; she'd invented it one evening out of sheer desperation.

'Go out, go out,' Peter commands. 'I'll call you when we're ready.'

Jo does what she's told, waiting outside the door until the signal comes.

'Peter, Mark, where are youse at all?' she calls, rushing in and putting on her best stage-Irishy voice. 'If youse don't come out this instance there'll be trouble for shure, for shure. There'll be the devil and all to pay, I'm warning youse,' she threatens, letting on she doesn't hear muffled sniggers.

'I know youse are in here. Wait until I find the pair of ye. I'll take the backsides off youse.'

Making as much racket as she can, she stomps around the room, crashing open wardrobes and cupboards, pulling back curtains.

Gradually, the tone of her voice becomes more and more panic-stricken.

'Where are my little pets? Holy Mother of Divine God and all the Saints! I hope they didn't go out. What will I do without them!'

The first time they played, Mark had poked his head out at this point, pleading with her not to worry, they were both in bed, safe. No chance of that tonight.

Sitting on each bed in turn, Jo pretends not to feel a squirming child beside her. 'Ochone, ochone!' she wails, throwing in a bit of mock Synge. 'They've gone, they've gone, lost to the sea shurely.'

Keening and sobbing, she promises never to be cross with them again if only they come back safe. As soon as Mark and Peter collapse in giggles, Jo leaps from one bed to the other, prodding and tickling, turning each boy over like a lump of dough, all three laughing and laughing, tears rolling down their faces.

The house is in darkness by the time Jo slips out of the boys' room and into her own. She's going to have to come up with a different game: it took forever to quieten them after all the horseplay. Undressing, she wonders what Anna and Tim were fighting over, she could hear them shouting their heads off while she and the boys were messing. Growing up, she'd always imagined rich people led happy, exciting, fulfilled lives.

Anna's to blame, Jo decides, fluffing up the duvet. If Tim as much as opens his mouth, she's straight in with a remark about not needing to be lectured to or the boredom of living with a *professore*. Worse than that she resents Jo showing any interest in whatever he's talking about. She reminds Jo of the girls she used pal round with when she was a teenager: if she dared bring up anything besides boys and clothes, they'd be on her like a ton of bricks. As for mentioning art! Of course, the fact she had culchie parents didn't help: she'd always stuck out, had always been an outsider.

Anna doesn't have their excuse, she's educated; no one's allowed forget she went to Cambridge. Tim went some place she refers to as a "redbrick". Obviously not posh enough from the sneer in her voice.

Jo checks to make sure the alarm's set before turning off the light. Happing herself up, she lets out a long sigh: she *does not* want to end up like Anna or her mother or any of the women she knew growing up: married for the sake of it or stuck in dead-end jobs. That's what had been in store for her; avoiding it was seen as getting above yourself, as betrayal. Well, she's every intention of getting above herself: she's always been looking for a way out; always hoping her prince would come. Eamonn mightn't have been royalty but he'd opened doors she'd never have been able to enter in a million years. She has him to thank for that. Through him, she'd met famous people, important people, people with interesting jobs: photographers, writers, gallery owners, artists who were still living, not dead and hanging on walls. These people knew other people: could make things happen.

Of course, everything had vanished as soon as she and Eamonn split. Overnight, she'd returned to being a nobody. Nobody but different: out on a limb, her old life no longer an option. Jo pulls the quilt up. Eamonn's world was a man's world: women were hangers-on, girlfriends, wives if they were lucky. Was there no way a woman could break into that kind of world on her own merit? A few Irish women artists had made it, ones who came from well-off backgrounds – Nano Reid, Evie Hone, Mainie somebody but nobody talked about them. Not the way they talked about Jack Yeats or Louis le Broquey or one or other of the up-and-coming male artist. There was no shortage of them.

Work's the solution, Jo tells herself, turning on her side. Women need to try harder. All talk and no action, her father used to say. Like her. She needs to take a leaf out of Eamonn's book. He wouldn't dream of letting anything or anyone get in his way, certainly not a woman. It's etched on her brain the occasion he'd sent her packing: he had a project to finish and she was disturbing his concentration or so he claimed. If only she'd had the same ability to resist him; all it took was a look and she was at his mercy. Still is, Jo thinks: now she'll never get to sleep.

10

'*Certosa di Pavia*! *Certosa di Pavia,*' the driver shouts down the bus.

Jo hurries along the aisle.

Extending a hairy arm, the busman indicates a leafy avenue, gabbles in Italian.

'*Dove?* Where?' Jo asks, puzzled to see nothing but fields and overhanging trees.

'*Kilometre, mezzo kilometre, boh,*' he shrugs.

'*Grazie.*'

'*Prego, signorina, prego.*'

Cloistered in silence, the *Certosa* seems to float above its earthbound moorings. Nothing could have prepared Jo: neither Tim singing its praises nor the extravagant descriptions in Montaigne's Journal which he'd ferreted out for her. Absorbed in its atmosphere, she experiences a sensation of stepping back into the past, can almost see the philosopher, hundreds of years earlier, alighting from his carriage: his soul elated by this miracle of shimmering marble. Involuntarily, Jo holds out her arms, feels an urge to drop to her knees.

It's perfect.

Unbearable almost.

Abandoning the heat, she steps inside the heavy doors; is met by a rush of dank air. The interior is huge, cavernous, lit only by rows of tall candles that dwindle and flicker on the high altar, creating strange shapes on the speckled flagstones. Mindful of trespassing on centuries of silence, Jo tiptoes up the nave, sits at the edge of a pew. An over-powering fragrance of lilies merges with the smell of candle wax and a line from a poem by Yeats drift into her mind: "*purer than a tall candle before the Holy Rood is Cathleen*". Closing her eyes, Jo breathes in, feels herself dissolve, become weightless. Ethereal.

Memories stir: she's fourteen years-old, alone in a make-shift chapel, her body flooded with joy. It's the final day of the annual school retreat and she's just made a General Confession. For three days, she'd sat beside her classmates, witnessed their sullen faces transformed into angelic countenances, sick with the knowledge of her own mortal sin; sullying her soul each time she'd received Communion.

When the visiting priest had mentioned certain sins, she'd felt his eyes upon her, her heart quaking at the threat of everlasting damnation. That afternoon, she'd cracked, confessing in a torrent of tears and repentance, begging forgiveness. Grace had poured into her soul, filling it to overflowing and she'd wanted to die. Die before she could feel ordinary again. Human. She'd thought about becoming a nun, dedicating her life to the service of the Church. Later she'd spoken to Mother Superior about entering.

Bernini's St. Teresa moves to the forefront of Jo's mind: it isn't only ecstasy etched on the saint's face, it's submission, total submission to someone other than herself. The rapture of yielding: of bending one's will to another. Had she thrown away the chance of becoming a Bride of Christ? Could that be the source of her longing? The longing for some unnameable thing that's haunted her as far back as she can remember, that found a sort of refuge in Eamonn; finds an outlet in her painting, in her passion for art.

Longing surges through her now, a longing for passionate union with someone or something. A desire to surrender her body.

As she meditates, the chill in the building penetrates her thin clothing, shivers her back to the present. Putting up with the coldness, welcoming it almost, she nurses her thoughts, remains sitting. Closeted there, away from the outside world, she feels safe. Blessed.

Bubbling with excitement, Jo lets herself in, dying to tell Tim about the *Certosa*; Anna, if she shows the slightest interest. The house strikes her as unusually quiet and as she opens the kitchen door, her heart sinks at the sight of a note propped against the coffeepot. "Taking the children to Nina's, staying the night. Help yourself to whatever's in the fridge. Tim may or may not be back. Anna." A PS reminds her she's having the kids the following day.

'Who fuckin' needs them!' Jo shouts, crumpling the piece of paper and flinging it across the room. She's furious at being left behind; having no one to share her day with. At the very least, Anna could have told her, suggested she come. Energy courses through her. What she needs is noise, music; music loud enough to drown the silence. Stomping through the apartment to the lounge, she roots through the Robertson's' collection, searching for something to give expression to her pent-up feelings.

As the opening notes of *La Traviata* fill the room, goose-pimples climb Jo's back. The opera was one of Eamonn's favourites and hearing the glut of ardour in the voices, an ache worse than loneliness threads her body. Tears glisten. She shouldn't have played it, she isn't ready. Oh, if only he was here, eyes smoky with sex: coaxing, compelling.

From the sideboard, a decanter of whiskey winks. Why not, Jo thinks, glancing guiltily about: if they're off enjoying themselves why shouldn't she? With a toss of her head, she gets out a tumbler, pours herself a decent measure.

Carrying it to the sofa, she gulps the alcohol only to find it tastes hot, like the taste of longing. A tear plops into the glass. So much for being a Bride of Christ, she thinks ruefully.

'You didn't hear me come in.'

Catching sight of Tim in the doorway, laden with shopping bags, Jo almost chokes. Shoving the glass under the couch, she leaps across to the record player.

'You can leave it. Anna's the one doesn't like opera. She pretended to before we were married, hence their dusty state.'

'It's alright, I've had enough.' Jo switches off the machine.

'So,' he asks, turning to go, 'how was your day?'

She follows him to the kitchen, unsure whether to help him unpack or not.

'Was the *Certosa* up to your exacting standards?'

'It was gorgeous- I don't mean gorgeous... anyway, I loved it.'

Fuming, Jo picks up a packet of macaroni, shoves it in a cupboard. Tim must think she's a complete moron using a word like "gorgeous". She loves words, so why is she unable to say the ones she hears in her head? Of course, it's always worse if she's trying to impress someone or is in awe of them. Eamonn was an exception, some of the time. Then again, if she loses her temper, she can usually say what she thinks.

'I intend cooking you a wonderful meal. What do you say to that?'

'You cook?' she asks to hide her astonishment.

'It's something every lecturer has to learn. How else is he to seduce poor starving students?'

'Don't look so shocked,' he laughs. 'I'm not going to seduce you. Unless you want me to.'

Jo can hardly believe her ears; he wouldn't dare talk to her like that if Anna was around! But a bit of her is thrilled: flirting means he considers her an equal. Not that she'd fancy him in a million years. And it doesn't have to lead anywhere.

'I don't.' Her eyes challenge his.

'You haven't tasted my food.'

Tim delves into the fridge, extracts a bottle of champagne. Christ! He must be serious. Jo covers her ears, taking her hands away after the pop.

'A toast to art and beauty.' He hands her a crystal flute. 'The *Certosa*.'

She raises her drink.

'And beauty.'

Realising he means her, pleasure fizzes inside Jo, rises like the bubbles in her glass. Does he really think she's beautiful?

'Away, away, I must work.' He tips her drink lightly.

Jo retreats to the balcony, easing herself onto one of the swing seats so she can keep an eye on him. Strange how things change, she muses, swaying backwards and forwards, sipping her champagne, watching Tim dreamily.

It's funny. She's never seen him look so – so free – as if he's thrown off a heavy overcoat, let loose a graceful dancer. Shirt sleeves up, he seems to glide around the kitchen, turning what he's doing into a performance: a fork here, a ladle there, stabbing like a fencer at whatever's sizzling in the pan; humming and performing little steps whenever he passes the French windows, muttering in Italian, wiping his hands on a check tablecloth tied around his middle.

He insists they eat outdoors and not on balcony furniture, which, he assures her, couldn't possibly do justice to the meal he's prepared. Between them, they carry out two upholstered chairs and a table; raid the linen cupboard for a damask tablecloth embossed with pale pink roses. With infinite care, he selects plates and bowls, holding one up for her to admire: so fine it's almost see-through. A pair of plumped-out napkins quiver like watchful doves in the evening sun.

As an afterthought, he plunders Anna's flower arrangement, selecting a single orchid heavy with scent, the tips of the flower tinged purple, its thick buttery leaves spotted. Ominous.

'Dinner's served, Milady.' Tim bows like an obsequious waiter.

Jo returns the bow, almost trips as she pulls out her seat.

'I'll have the balcony removed,' he teases.

The words strike Jo as unbelievably funny and she laughs uproariously.

'To start, there's *peperoni sott'olio* or perhaps you'd prefer *insalata di carciofi?*'

The banquet sparkles or maybe she's had a little too much champagne, Jo thinks, deciding she'd better be careful. She doesn't want to end up drunk.

'I'll have everything,' she answers flippantly.

'You should never say that until you've seen the full menu.' He's flirting again but this time she feels able for him.

'I can't afford a la carte. Haven't you got a tourist menu?'

'We don't cater for passing trade at this establishment, Madam.'

'I must have come to the wrong restaurant,' she jokes.

'Of course,' he adds in an oily voice, 'we might be persuaded to change our minds.'

Lifting a sliver of something yellow and runny on his fork, he brings it to her lips. Jo opens her mouth, allows the hot, creamy fragment dissolve on her tongue. He watches her closely, a hungry expression on his face. Noticing it, Jo forces herself to focus. He couldn't really be thinking of trying to get off with her, could he? Rubbish! She can handle him. Another morsel of food slips down. No problemo! All she has to do is threaten to tell Anna.

Gazing around her, Jo has no memory at all of coming back to sit on the swing seat. And where's Mr Robertson?

'There you are!' she cries, seeing a rather blurry-looking Tim coming towards her, holding two balloon-shaped glasses.

She reaches to take one.

'First you have to pay for your meal. Move over.'

Jo giggles as Tim's face moves closer. His lips are insistent and as she lets his tongue in, he eases her down, the bars of the seat digging into her back. Above her, stars twinkle a warning. Yes, she tells them languidly, she needs to do something. Soon.

'Got to go to the loo,' she announces, struggling out from beneath him.

'Don't be long,' he implores, attempting to hold onto her. Laughing, Jo zigzags out of his reach.

Queasy and dizzy, she steadies herself against the tiled wall of the bathroom; for some reason the mirror she can see herself in is refusing to stay in the same position. She opens and closes her eyes quickly, tries to concentrate. All of a sudden the idea of threatening Tim with Anna does not appear as simple. What will she say, how will she make herself say it? Her mind wanders: what she really needs is fresh air; even better – to lie down.

Tiptoeing along the hall, Jo notices her bedroom door is open. Slipping in, she locks it behind her.

Stupid, stupid! Go and face him, you're an adult. She doesn't feel like one. She feels like a child. A child hiding from an adult, petrified of being told off. It's as if Tim had conferred significance on her and now twelve o'clock has rung and like Cinderella, she's changed back to her real self. She waits, her hand on the handle, knowing she isn't going to open it. When nobody comes, she retreats to the furthest corner of the room, prays he's fallen asleep.

When a knock finally comes, she's surprised how timid it sounds.

'Jo, are you in there?'

Crossing to the bed, she sits on the edge, holding herself. She should have stood up to him – told him no – instead of getting into this terrible mess.

Jo sinks her nails into her palms. Her body's to blame; is always to blame. This is what she gets for flirting with Tim, without wanting to pay the price.

Who says there has to be a price? Men flirt if they feel like it so why should it be different for women?

'*Amore, carina.*'

Jo puts her hands over her ears.

'Jo, open the door?'

'Leave me alone.'

'I only want to talk to you.'

A blaze of contempt sweeps through her. The thought of his tongue, the memory of his hands makes her skin crawl.

'Go away,' she screams, covering her head with a pillow. 'Just go away.'

11

Sunshine streams through the bedroom window: she must have gone to bed without unfolding the shutters. As Jo raises a hand to shade her eyes, she sees she hadn't taken off her clothes either, her best dress crumpled and stupid-looking in the morning light. Her head is pounding and as memories of the previous evening rear their head, she lets out a long moan. What possessed her to lock herself in! Behaving like a fuckin' idiot! How is she going to face Tim: what will she say?

Noises reach her from the kitchen, furniture being moved from the sound of it. She should get up; get it over with before the others arrive back. Jo makes a tentative move, slumps back down. She can't face anyone feeling like this!

It's Sunday, maybe she can say she's ill, stay in bed. She is ill, is going to die if she doesn't get water soon. A screaming electrical noise whistles through the apartment. Tim must be hoovering. Sleep, if only she could go back to sleep. Turning this way and that in search of a comfortable position, Anna's note flashes in front of her eyes, crushes her. There's no way she can survive a day of Peter and Mark! Fuck! Fuck! Fuck! She still has Tim to deal with. And Anna. What if she suspects- The front door opens and Jo holds her breath, waits for the rush of feet but the apartment falls quiet. It must have been Tim going out.

Jo waits as long as she can before slinking into the hallway, making a dash for the bathroom. Revelling in the iciness of the tiles beneath her feet, she fills a toothbrush mug with water, chucks glass after glass down her throat. When she's had enough, she inches warily to the kitchen. Pushing open the door, she sees the room has been scoured, even the rubbish has been removed. Her mouth twists: it's as if nothing had happened – nothing at all.

'Go to your room and change, both of you.' Jo can hear Anna entreating the boys as they troop in; their whoops and shouts already tearing at her nerves. As Mrs Robertson approaches the kitchen, Jo opens the fridge, pretends to be looking for something; a blast of cold air providing a brief moment of relief from her headache.

'Is Tim about?' Anna asks, lifting the *caffettiera*, pouring herself a cup.

'He went out ages ago. I didn't see him.' Taking out a carton of milk, Jo empties it into a jug. 'Did you have a good time?'

Anna grimaces. 'Cold milk, for goodness sake, Josephine! I must teach you how to make coffee properly.' She pushes the cup away, sits fiddling with a strand of hair.

'I don't know how Tim expects me to cope! Nina's had a whole new kitchen fitted. It's absolutely stunning. So modern. But then, her husband doesn't have his head stuck in a book whenever he's at home.'

Jo mumbles agreement, laughing to herself at what Anna believes she has to "cope" with.

An ear-splitting wail echoes through the house, slices through Jo's head.

She wills Anna to go and deal with it; is surprised to see a look of terror on Mrs Robertson's face.

'Would you mind?' Anna appeals as another scream reaches them.

She's scared of her own children, Jo thinks, clutching her forehead as soon as she's out of sight. At the far end of the hallway, Peter's sitting on Mark's chest, his brother's head gripped in both hands as if he's about to bang it on the floor.

'Get off,' she shouts, lunging at him.

Peter wriggles, pushing Jo away as she tries to pull him off.

'What the hell's going on?' Tim bellows, letting himself in the front door.

Both boys jump up and in the muddle of explanations and accusations, Jo's eyes meet Tim's, anxious to let him know she'll say nothing: is sorry for being such an eejit. His eyes – empty as a blank page – reveal nothing.

'We'll be late.' Anna complains, click-clacking towards them. The three adults stand, staring awkwardly the children. Peter and Mark go quiet.

'Nina sends her love. She says she won't take no for an answer next time.' Anna turns to Jo. 'Tim always finds an excuse whenever we're invited to stay with friends. He thinks it makes him mysterious. Being a boring old *professore*, he likes to create a little mystique. Don't you darling?'

'Some women find me mysterious.' His voice has an edge.

'Tim's students adore him,' Anna prattles on, 'but then age is always mysterious to youth. Don't you think so, Josephine?'

Jo looks through her, hoping her vacant expression passes for whatever Anna's looking for; she'll think about the meaning of her remarks later.

Doling out chocolates, crayons and paper, Jo orders the boys to leave her in peace for the rest of the morning. If she's lucky she'll get half an hour, she thinks, closing the shutters in her bedroom. After swallowing a double dose of Andrews Salts, she crawls into bed. In the unnatural darkness, everything seems unreal: the house, the boys in the next room, Anna's remarks, the memory of Tim knocking on her door. His tongue. Only her headache is real and the ache in her heart which is keeping it company.

What if she'd opened the door, let Tim in, allowed him...? He's here; she can feel his hands fumbling with her clothes. See his face...but it's not his face; it's Eamonn's. The eyes are Tim's though ... cold, fishy. Jo's body goes limp. She would never have let him in. He'd end up betraying her; leaving her even more vulnerable in this swamp of family life.

All the same, there were kisses, touches, soft words; all obliterated without her consent. What gives Tim the power to do that: it's not as if they're his property. Men control things. Women accept. Her mammy had never challenged her daddy. *One day you'll understand*, was all she'd say whenever Jo tackled her. Could that be what she meant: that women don't own their own experiences, have no rights over them? That they're supposed to shut up; pretend things are different from what they are? Is that what Anna does? If she does, Jo despises her; she should confront Tim. If she was in her place-

'Look, look!' Mark bursts in waving a piece of paper, lowers it. 'Why is it dark in here?'

'Time,' Peter announces, turning on the light, dumping his crayons on the floor.

Jo waves the boys away. 'And pick those up,' she yells as Mark stands on one.

'He broke my crayon,' Peter shrieks. Rushing at Mark he grabs his drawing, tears it in two. Mark punches him and they fall to the ground kicking and screaming.

Kill each other, Jo screams silently. How could a house like this produce such monsters? Look at the money spent on them, the best school, toys, clothes. Nobody wants them: that's the problem. They aren't loved. Not properly. Anna's to blame, Anna who showers love on a horse. Tim's a man: nobody expects anything from him. It's Anna's job. Anna who never tires of telling Jo how to handle them: if this sort of thing happens, she's supposed to separate them, punish both. Make no favourites.

Well, Jo decides, grabbing Mark's arm, if Tim can do things behind his wife's back so can she. 'If you stop immediately, you can watch telly.'

The effect is instant. Disentangling themselves, they follow her like trained puppies into the lounge. As if making a huge concession, she switches on the set.

'Sit and watch,' she orders, wishing she could abandon them, abandon the whole day. In the flickering screen-light, the boys' faces turn solemn and serious, like apprentice adults. It isn't fair. She shouldn't be here. She doesn't love them either. Maybe Mark. Maybe a little. It would be better if she left. It's only a little over two months and she's had enough pee pees and paw paws to last a lifetime. Mark turns his head, smiles at her. Guiltily, she smiles back. How can she blame them: they're only kids.

'Cut it smaller,' Peter demands as Jo puts a plate of salami in front of him.

Jo clenches her fists: she knows what she'd like to do with it!

'I'll tell Mummy,' he threatens.

'Go on if you want to!'

'I'm not eating it!'

'Don't then!'

Grabbing the salami, she dumps it in the pedal bin; instantly regrets acting so hastily. If he sneaks to Anna how will she explain? She'll say it was off; this little brat isn't going to get her into trouble. Looking anxiously at Jo and using both hands, Mark stuffs what's left on his plate into his mouth.

'Right, bath then bed, both of youse!' she commands, corralling them out of the kitchen. A layer of hatred flares in Peter's eyes, wanes as she out-stares him. A show of toughness, that's all it takes, Jo tells herself, turning on the taps.

'Paw paw,' Mark yells, dancing up and down. While Jo pulls down the younger boy's pants and deposits him on the toilet, Peter strips quickly, hops into the bath.

'Stand still while I wipe ye,' she orders the younger boy.

Mark squirms, trying to see over her shoulders, a hand shooting to his mouth to mask a giggle. 'What's-!?' Jo spins around in time to see an arc of piss cascading into the bath water; Peter sniggering.

'You filthy little-' Jo hauls the boy over the edge, flings him away from her. He screams and yells as if she's murdering him. She doesn't care. Why should she? No one gives a damn about her.

'Get over there.'

Whimpering, Peter crawls into a corner. Seeing Mark's face turn white, Jo's consumed with shame. And fear. She hadn't meant to be rough.

Trying to think, she lets the water out; runs another bath.

'When I tell your mother what you did, you disgusting ...' She hasn't the slightest intention of saying anything but she has to make sure neither of them open their mouths. 'She won't believe you could do such a revolting thing!'

Peter peers pitifully from under his eyelashes.

'Don't tell,' Mark whispers. 'We'll be good.'

'I'll see. Get in the bath both of you, and no nonsense.'

As he plops back in, Peter gives her a sly look. He's going to tell, she thinks, he's going to tell. He can see she's scared. She should have got angrier. At the end of the day, no matter what anyone else does, she's the one who'll get the blame. That's her role. That's really what she's paid for.

12

Jo battles against opening her eyes but the shouting outside her head wins.

'You didn't set the alarm,' Anna wails. 'You stupid, stupid girl! And look at this place, it's a pigsty. At least open the window once in a while, can't you.'

Her face looms, ugly with anger.

'Fuck off.'

'What did you say?'

All out of fight, Jo turns to the wall. She doesn't want to be fired; without a place to live she'll have to go home and she hasn't even begun to do half the things she'd hoped to.

'You shouldn't have said what you did about the room,' she mutters.

'I forgot you Irish are so sensitive.'

Fury blazes inside Jo. Who the fuck does she think she is! All the same, Jo forces her tongue to stay quiet.

'For the children's sake I'll pretend I didn't hear what you said,' Anna concedes. 'Now get up. I'll take Peter and Mark to school, otherwise they'll be late. I want this room spic and span when I return.'

Jo doesn't reply, hoping her silence conveys what she's actually thinking. Sensing defiance, Anna pauses at the door.

'I'm aware you have some high-falluting notions about yourself. A bohemian artist! I haven't seen your work but let me give you a bit of advice. You're barely educated, you've no money and you're lazy. But you're attractive and your naiveté is . . . ,' she gives a silky laugh, '"appealing". You could do worse than learn Italian and get yourself an Italian husband. That way you might be able to finance your little hobby.'

The air around Jo freezes. In a corner of her mind, she hears the front door slam; in her heart a second door slams. Shamed, she hugs the duvet: Anna's words hitting home like punches. One thing's certain: she can't stay after this.

Having tidied her room, Jo broods over Anna's outburst. She'll show her, she thinks, but even as she gets out her paints, her resolve vanishes. She can't bear the thought of being in when Anna gets back. Grabbing her green jacket, she hurries out and down the stairs, stops when she reaches the doorstep: apart from the Italian class she's nowhere to go. It's somewhere, she thinks, banging the door shut behind her.

On her way to the *Scuola Inglese*, a group of student types bunch past, heading in the opposite direction. Their animated faces compound Jo's misery: the whole world seems to be happy except her. And now she's going to have to put up with all those silly au pairs- Jo halts. From somewhere close by comes the sound of singing.

'*Cosa che?*' she asks a curly-haired girl – showing-off – trying out a phrase she's heard Italians using. Fooled, the girl talks so fast all Jo catches is "*manifestazione*" which rings a bell but not loud enough. Still, the Italian seems to be part of whatever's going on so Jo tags along. Who cares about classes, she picks up as much by listening. As more young people show up, Jo finds herself in a sea of excited faces, watches people kiss and hug, punch the air with their fists. *Manifestazione!* Of course! A demonstration. Still, she couldn't imagine people in Dublin going on one wearing so much white: it looks more like an advertisement for washing powder.

The singing starts up again, a roar rippling through the waiting crowds as wave after wave of marchers appear, voices soaring:

'*Bandiera Rossa si triumphera,*
Bandiera Rossa si triumphera,'

Hundreds of placards reach for the sky and Jo tries to make out what they're demonstrating about. She understands '*studenti contra*': 'students against' – but against what? There's a lull and a woman in a swirling red cloak detaches herself from near the front of the march, unfurling a flag with a hammer and sickle as she dances ahead, her other hand flung up in triumph. The crowd go mad. As the woman falls back in line, Jo catches her eye.

'*Viva le donne,*' the woman screams.

'*Vive le donne,*' Jo screams back, wishing she knew what it meant – something to do with women anyway. The red-cloaked woman laughs conspiratorially and Countess Markievicz flashes into Jo's mind. At school she'd read all about the revolutionary but she'd never been able to picture her. Now she has an image!

More marchers arrive and a sudden surge takes Jo with it. They crush into a narrow street, Jo's heart beating wildly: she's only seen demonstrations on telly, has never participated in one. There's a feeling of organised mayhem: people swarming, cars honking, drivers jumping out to shove protesters off their bonnets. Other protesters, faces concealed by red and white scarves, urge people on.

A contingent of mounted police appear, begin to cut a swathe through the lines of demonstrators. Excitement tingling her bones, Jo wrestles her way back to the pavement. *Caribinieri* aren't like Irish police: they're kitted for action – enormous sticks belted at their sides, guns bulging from holsters. She'd prefer to stay out of their way. Further along, the march is feeding into a piazza, crowds already rallying in front of a makeshift platform, placards and banners dancing above their heads. If there's going to be speeches, Jo would like to be there, especially if the woman in red's giving one. With '*scusa, scusa,*' on her lips, she elbows her way along the path but as she gets within reach of the square, the police block off the entrance, forcing the march to halt.

Frustrated, Jo gauges where she is, calculates if she can make her way back and takes a right down the next street, there might be another way in. Lots of people seem to have the same idea and Jo follows them, barging her way through.

As they reach the top of the street, a second convoy of policemen canter up. Automatically, the demonstrators link arms, form a barricade. A horse rears, its huge forelegs pawing the air. The policemen draw their sticks. Out of the side of her eye, Jo checks to see how people are reacting. Nobody is moving.

From somewhere in the crowd, voices begin to jeer, provoking the marchers in the direction of the waiting *caribinieri*. Jo attempts to stay put but as bodies crash into her she's forced forward. A guy next to her, sporting one of the red and white scarves, bends double. Terrified he might have fainted, Jo screams. A space is cleared and the boy leaps up, a chunk of horse dung in his hand. He squelches it into a ball and with a holler, sends the missile flying through the air. It lands on one of the policemen's shoulder, splatters his spotless uniform. The crowd catcall. Hands reach down.

The policeman, his face distorted with rage, swings his baton. Jo squinches at the sound of a loud thwack, hears a scream. Horses' hooves clatter and high-pitched neighing fills the air as several of the man's comrades join in. Lines teeter, break up, people scrambling in all directions. Jo wheels round quickly, almost falls. Voices shout and roar and Jo hears her own voice as an arm crashes into her face, brings tears to her eyes. She brushes them away and protecting her face with her hand, ducks and dives in the shadow of a spiky-haired boy bulldozing his way through. By the time they make it to the *piazza*, it's already beginning to empty out; a few remaining demonstrators circling the abandoned platform. The boy turns and hugs her, shouting jubilantly in her ear before bouncing off, his fist clenched, a determined grin on his face.

In the distance, church bells strike and Jo counts the bongs – amazed to find its lunchtime. Remembering its Monday, the day Anna picks up the boys on her way back from the stables, Jo realises she's free until four. Relieved, she attaches herself to the tail end of a bunch of marchers. One of them, a pale-faced guy with John Lennon glasses, gives her an enquiring look. Jo blushes, '*Straniera*,' she mumbles, which she's nearly sure means "foreigner".

'*Brava*,' the guy claps her back, says something to one of his companions, a gorgeous-looking Italian with a rose pinned to her hair. The girl hugs Jo like an old friend, offers her an arm.

'*Dove andiamo?*'

'*Universite. Capito?*'

Jo nods, dismissing the thought of bumping into Tim. So what! And even if she's a bit scared, she's never felt so alive. Who'd have thought tearing down streets yelling your head off could be this exciting! After a short walk, the girl nudges Jo, indicates the campus. How different it seems from only a few days ago. Completely different, Jo thinks, avoiding eye-contact with the mounted *caribinieri* who seem to be itching to get loose. Ignoring them, students saunter past, chatting and laughing, passing cigarettes to one another. One couple stop and kiss. Long and slow. The crowd suddenly swells and in the confusion Jo's gets separated from her new friends. Before she has a chance to look for them, a loudhailer crackles and a woman's voice fills the courtyard. It's the woman in red and as she starts to speak silence descends.

Jo listens barely understanding, noticing the run in the woman's tights, how shabby her cloak is. She isn't good-looking either, her face too mobile, her kohl-rimmed eyes screwed up against the sunlight. *Non importa*! What does it matter? The passion in her voice, her belief in what she's saying is mesmerising. When she stops, protestors scream applause, leap up and down, throw hats in the air. Jo taps a guy in a brown cord jacket.

'What's the name of the woman- *Come ti chiama la donne nelle...*' she pats her own jacket – she doesn't know the word for cloak – '*rossa*, red? Her? *Lei?*' she points.

'*Camilla Rossi*. You don't know her? *Non conosche ...?*'

Jo doesn't hear the rest of what he's saying. "*Camilla Rossi*", she repeats. What a fabulous name!

A hand tugs her. '*Parla Italiano?*'

'*Un poco.* A little.'

'*Da dove?* Where you from?'

'*Irlanda, Dublino.*'

'*Sorella, sorella.*' The man seems overjoyed.

A sister? Could it be because Ireland's Catholic?

'*Camilla e un'amica.* A friend. *Venga, venga.* Come. You like to meet her no?'

'*Grazie, grazie,*' Jo squeals, unable to believe her luck.

Sitting in the bar next to Camilla, Jo's tongue-tied. Not on account of her lousy Italian, Camilla speaks good English. And she's friendly. When they were introduced, she'd kissed Jo on both cheeks, invited her for coffee and Jo sensed an instant empathy between them. It's just the questions she'd love to ask seem stupid, personal. Especially in front of Camilla's friends who are all gathered around two tables, celebrating the demo, arguing and shrieking and laughing. What she wants to know is how Camilla got to be the way she is; how can Jo get to be like her? What does it take?

'*Altra caffe per piacere,*' Camilla calls to a passing waiter to bring Jo a coffee. 'What are you doing in Italy?'

'I'm an au-pair-'

'Au-pair! *Stronsa*! The bourgeoisie are parasites – they always get someone to do their shitwork.'

Jo marvels. That's exactly what she thinks although she hasn't the words – isn't clued in enough – to put it like that. She doesn't even know what "bourgeoisie" means – something to do with the French Revolution if she remembers her European history. Inwardly she sighs. Anna's right about one thing: there's so much she doesn't know but then she left school when she was barely seventeen.

'I'm going to give in my notice,' Jo confides, wanting to impress her. 'It's like being a servant. Do this, do that. She can hardly butter her own bread.'

Camilla bursts out laughing, says something in Italian to the others.

'I'm explaining "butter her own bread!" That's good.'

It's actually something Mr Nowd said about Jo and she feels a stab of guilt. Still, it's just as true about Anna.

'*Simpatico*!' a friend of Camilla's pronounces.

'*Molto*. Very,' Camilla responds.

'And her husband tried . . .' she falters.

'*Poverina*. Men are, how you say, "pigs"!'

'*Porco Dio*,' Jo ventures. She's heard the phrase several times, has been waiting for an opportunity to use it.

Everyone laughs.

'*Porco Dio*!' a boy splutters.

'"*Porco Dio*" mean's God's a pig. You must be careful where you say it,' Camilla explains. 'So who are these Italian pigs, we'll go and sort them out.'

'They're English-'

'English! How can you work for an English family?'

Jo's saved answering as a waiter arrives with a tray of coffees.

'Your country's at war with them. We should be too. An

economic war. They come here and buy up all the farmhouses, steal land from the *contadini* – the peasants you understand – pay them nothing! *Mi fa schifo*! Makes me sick!' With a shrug, Camilla sticks an amaretto in her mouth, chews it before launching into a long speech. It flows over Jo's head but she notices that whenever she hears the word '*Inglesi*' "English", everyone smiles at her sympathetically.

Jo isn't sure. The Robertsons are English but despite Anna's rant, she's never thought of them as the enemy. If anything they're snobs, imagining themselves superior because of where they come from; looking down on her, especially Anna. And she hated the way she'd called her room a "pigsty"; when the British ruled Ireland they were always comparing the Irish to pigs. But she doesn't think the way the Robertstons treat her has anything to do with what's happening in the North; of course there could be a connection: she's not absolutely sure what's going on there herself. Her daddy who's from the north was always blaming the southern Irish for being "West Brits", "standing idly by". But she's a "southerner" and so are her brothers and sisters.

'You can tell us about the war?' a girl with glasses asks earnestly.

Confronted by their eager faces, Jo feels ashamed. She ought to know more. She remembers writing an essay about the heroes of 1916 when she was at school but no one talks about them anymore. And the truth is until today, she's regarded politics as men's business.

'It's not that simple, lots of Irish people live in England, ye know, they're married to English people.' Some of her own relations as it happens and once her daddy had refused to go to a cousin's wedding; but that was because the man wouldn't convert and not because he was English. Jo decides not to mention that; the whole thing's complicated enough as it is.

A spotty-faced boy says something and Camilla rears, begins to lecture him. Jo's able to make out words like "*capitalismo*", "*oppresivo*", the rest escapes her. The Italian woman stops in the middle of a sentence, turns to her. 'My friend asks why we are involved in this demonstration, what are the connections? Also what are the connections with what is happening in Ireland? Some of them are not politically advanced. I am explaining that education is one of the ways to keep power and wealth in certain hands. It should be free, not only for the rich. Here in Italy, the working-class are dependent on the ruling class. Oppressed people are always dependent on the oppressor. So the Irish go to England to work, they marry and have children. That way they are divided among themselves and the revolutionary *potenziale*, you say 'potential'?'

Jo nods.

'. . . that potential is,' she searches for a word, '*ridutta, capito?*'

'*Si, si,*' Jo answers. 'Reduced.'

Camilla nods.

Jo takes a sip of coffee, aware she's giving a false impression. Her own political understanding is next to nil. What would be the right impression? She might not be political now but who's to say what she'll become? At this very moment, she could be outlining the shape of the person she'll turn into – like doing a sketch in pencil before starting to paint. She'd give anything to be like Camilla. There's a buzz about her, a sense of possibility which reminds her of the first time she met Eamonn: as if a window had been opened, a gust of fresh air let in. And the people she's friends with seem interesting. Of course, they probably imagine she thinks like them, shares their ideas. Well, she likes their ideas; they make more sense than a lot of people's. It's not totally new either. She's always been conscious of rich and poor: growing up the way she did it would be impossible not to be. She just never thought you could do anything about it. Camilla's right: universities should be for everyone. Given half a chance she'd have gone but it was never an option. Worse: it had seemed natural people like her didn't go. Why? She's as intelligent as anyone.

Camilla raises her cup. 'We must fight to change things. Destiny is in the hands of young people.'

Jo wishes she could throw her arms around her. To be able to say things like that – to be able to be that serious.

'We all have a role to play. *Lotta continua*.'

"*Lotta continua* ..." Jo had seen the word on lots of placards earlier. '*Lotta* ..?'

'It means "struggle" – "the struggle continues". We must fight.'

Jo's not sure she's a fighter; hopes there's some kind of role for artists. When she knows Camilla better, she'll ask. Then again, who knows what might happen once they become friends.

'*Andiamo*. We go. We have a train to catch.'

'You don't live here?'

'I live in *Firenze*. These two *a Roma*- '

'But ...'

'How you say, we are ...?' Camilla suddenly shakes with laughter. '"Outside agitators".' Her fist goes up in a salute. Several others follow. Jo looks at the clenched fists, feels her heart clench, the glow inside wane. She wants to go on talking, get to know Camilla. Both of them want more from life; they have that in common. And Jo can tell from the beautiful coral necklace she's wearing she likes nice things.

The Italian talks rapidly to a man with buck teeth; they appear to be making plans. Turning, Camilla kisses Jo on both cheeks. 'Luigi, look after the Irish girl. She is lonely.' With a grin, the guy moves into the seat vacated by her.

'You are with friends,' Camilla whispers. '*Civediamo*. We will meet again.' With a nod to the others and a little wave, she heads for the door.

Seeing the red cloak disappear, Jo's tempted to run after her.

'*Parla Italiano?*' Luigi asks.

'*Poco,*' Jo answers listlessly. 'Speak slowly please. *Lentemente per favore.*'

'*Questa querra in Irlanda del Nord, seconda lei-*'

'*Non capisco*, I don't understand,' she pretends, even though she knows full well he's asking her opinion about the North. With Camilla gone, she's not interested in talking about Ireland or anywhere else.

'For you, this war in the North ...' Luigi persists. Jo listens half-heartedly as he lapses in and out of Italian using the same words as Camilla – "*oppresivo, imperialismo*". This time, the words reverberate dully in her head.

Shit! Why didn't she think of it! She'll give up her job, move to Florence-

'*Scusa, lei ha* "address" *per Camilla?* I would like to go to Florence. *Mi piace andare a Firenze.*'

'*Indirrizzo*: address.'

'*Si, si, di Camilla, grazie.*'

'*Non importa.*'

What does he mean "it doesn't matter"? '*Perche?* Why?'

'*Camilla va ...*' Luigi stops, speaks to one of his friends.

The friend bows. 'I explain. I speak more English a little. Camilla-'

'I just want her address-'

'Yes, but she leaves the country *presto*, soon, *settimana proximo*-next week. She goes to the camps in Palestine, *capito? Lei e una dottore ...*'

'Camilla's a doctor?'

'*Si, si. Lei capiche Italiano, brava.*'

'She's going to Palestine?' Jo's heard of Palestine but she hasn't a clue what he means by "camps"; wonders if he's using the word wrong?

'Is she going to work there? *Lei lavora aqui?*'

'Yes, many *rifugiati*. She is brave, no?'

Jo feels totally out of her depth. "*Rifugiati*" sounds like refugees but what have refugees got to do with Palestine? Palestine's the Holy Land, the place where Jesus was born. And Camilla a doctor?! Haranguing people on marches, dancing in the street; she's the weirdest doctor Jo's ever met.

'You go?' Luigi holds out a hand.

'*Devo andare.* I have to go. *Tarde*, I'm late,' she explains. '*C'e bambini a casa.*'

'We drink here, *Sabato,* Saturday. You like come?'

Jo gives him an ambiguous smile. Maybe she'll come, who knows.

Walking across the square, she notices a sliver of sun – vivid red – suspended above the turrets of the university, as if the tail of Camilla's cloak had caught in a cloud. Or maybe Camilla's left a sign in the sky, a sign for Jo to follow.

13

'*Scusa signorina, hai momento?* Moment please.'

Turning, Jo sees a smartly-dressed Italian guy hurrying towards her. He looks vaguely familiar: maybe she saw him on the demo or in the bar. All the same, Jo gives him a wary look, starts to walk away.

'*Non ti preocuppata, sono amico di Camilla. Mi chiamo Massimo. Ma scusa!* I speak English. Do not worry, I am a friend of Camilla. My name is Massimo.'

Jo slows down and he smiles, displaying gleaming white teeth. 'You are friends? I see you talking.'

'Yes, well, I only met her ...'

'It is good. I know Camilla. Many years. May I walk with you?' he asks.

Jo does a quick reccy – she's found herself doing this since the shitbag in the underpass thing – is glad to see a young couple on the other side of the road, a woman with a dog in the distance.

'Sure. *Va bene.* I'm in a bit of a hurry.'

'You stay in Pavia?'

'Yeah. I'm an au pair.'

'You are living with Italians?'

'They're English.'

'Aahh! They know you are on demonstration?'

'Are you joking! I tell them as little as possible.'

The woman with the dog, a large Doberman, has almost caught up with them, the animal tugging on its lead. Without warning, Massimo lets out an angry flurry of words. Whatever he says seems to infuriate the woman and she turns on him, sticking her face into his, letting him have an earful; the dog growling, straining to get at Massimo. When the dog-owner's had her say, she whacks the side of one hand to the crook of her elbow then stomps off, pulling the animal with her.

Massimo glares after the retreating figure. 'I hate to see dogs on leads. They should be free. They have as much right as human beings. Yes?'

Jo nods although she's never thought about it. Dogs on leads has always seemed normal; a bit like her not going to university. Maybe it's not.

'It's like being an au pair,' she jokes. 'Except you're on a lead the whole time.'

Massimo laughs. As they continue walking, he asks questions, eager to know her thoughts on the demo, what she thinks of Camilla; where she comes from. He seems interested in everything she says; looks especially pleased when she tells him she's Irish.

'What do you do?' Jo asks in a lull.

'I am engineering student at the university, in my first year. My heart is not in it. It is my parents!' Grimacing, he makes a money sign. 'That is all they are interested in.'

'What are you interested in?'

'Animals. I should have been a *veterinario*. And you?'

'Art, although I . . .' Jo trails off as they arrive at the underpass. Descending into the tunnel, she registers a flicker of anxiety. Glancing at Massimo, she tells herself she can trust him; that people who care about animals are trustworthy, kind.

Emerging into the open, Jo points to the apartment block; has a sudden sinking feeling as she recalls the fight with Anna. 'That's it. We're at the top.'

'You like we meet again? For *caffe*? Wednesday or Thursday *pommerigio,* afternoon, at the university? You can come to the *mensa,* "canteen" you call it, I am there. There is something I would like to speak to you about.'

'Mornings are better. I have to pick up the kids in the afternoon. Wednesday's best. What's it about?'

'I will tell you Wednesday.'

'O-kay.'

'*Civediamo, ciao*.' Massimo bows.

Jo watches him walk away, curious what he wants to talk to her about; she doesn't think he fancies her. Maybe he wants to practice his English. One way or the other, it'll be a contact. Who knows: Camilla might come for a visit.

Jo climbs the stairs slowly: she'll ignore Anna as much as possible, act as if she doesn't care. As she sticks her key in the door, she realises she won't say a word about leaving. Not yet. She has to wait for the right moment.

That evening, Jo swallows her pride, quizzes Tim about Palestine. It's the first time they've spoken about anything other than the boys since the night he made her dinner. He seems astonished at how little she knows but what has people being displaced or refugee camps got to do with art? Most artists don't concern themselves with world events, at least not in a straightforward way. A few like El Greco and Kathe Kollwitz have and Picasso painted Guernica about the Spanish Civil War although you wouldn't know that from looking at it.

Jo says none of this to Tim, just sits and listens. When he excuses himself to correct essays, she goes to her room, sits in thought. Is she ignorant? Anna seems to think so and Tim implied it. The idea cuts her to the quick. She's always thought of herself as special, singled out; wonders if growing up means discovering you're ordinary, one of the crowd. She'd hate to think that was true: she *is* special and one day she'll prove it.

All the same, discovering Camilla is going to work in a refugee camp, under the conditions Tim described, while she – the great Jo Nowd – can't even screw up enough courage to talk to her employers about quitting is a blow to her pride. She owes it to Camilla to leave but the very thought of provoking the Robertsons' anger paralyses her. Her father's to blame. As a kid, if she needed something – money for school books or a school trip – she had to wait for him to be in the right mood. Even then, she had to sit on the couch in the living-room, wait until he noticed her, asked her what she wanted. If he was actually in a bad mood, he'd had a fit, shout and accuse her of thinking he was made of money. Everyone in the house was afraid of him, including her mother. Not that he'd hit them; he didn't have to. Living with the threat all those years had left its mark; so other than packing her bag and sneaking off in the middle of the night, she's not sure how she's going to leave. It wouldn't matter so much if she was getting any of her own work done but the longer she stays the more she feels she's shrivelling up, not expanding.

Jo hopes whatever Massimo wants to talk about is interesting – exciting even! As she skips up the steps of the university, she silences a voice reminding her she should be using her time to paint, not bunking off. She hadn't mentioned the rendezvous to Anna or Tim, she likes the idea of doing stuff they don't know about. Still, it might be a teensy bit awkward if she bumps into the *professore*! The canteen's easy to find but Jo has to circle the room twice before spotting Massimo who's tucked away in the furthest corner; absorbed in an official-looking document, a pot of coffee on the table in front of him.

'*Ciao!*' he says, looking genuinely pleased to see her. 'I was hoping you would come.'

'I said I'd come, didn't I?' Jo teases, as she sits down.

'*Caffe?*' he offers, indicating a second cup on the table.

As he hands it to her, he looks at her intently. 'I need to ask you a favour. A big one. First, I must ask if I can trust you?'

'Of course you can. What kind of favour?'

'I tell you I love animals-'

'There's no way I can have a dog if that's what you're hoping, no pets-'

'No, no. *Aspetta*. Wait. I explain. I belong to a *gruppa ci ciama-Non importa,* the name is not important. It is a small group, we are concerned about animals. Do you know many big companies, our government as well, carry out very bad experiments on them?'

Jo shakes her head; another thing she knows nothing about.

'For what purpose? Cosmetics! *Scusa* but it is true. And medicine. *Molto peggio*! Much worse! Often animals die or are killed deliberately.'

'You want me to stop wearing make-up?'

Massimo laughs. 'No, no, not all are bad.'

'I don't think I could go out without my face!'

'"Without your face?" *Ah capito*. But you do not need to wear make-up. You are beautiful. I mean it, a compliment.'

'Flattery will get you everywhere. What's the favour?'

Massimo leans across, lowers his voice. 'When we find experiments, we go and set the animals free – "liberate" them, you say? There is one of these laboratories *vicino* – near – Pavia, a short journey on the bus. We would like you to go there. All you must do is find out if the gates are locked. *Molto simplice*. Very simple.'

'Why don't you go?'

'I am known by the *caribinieri*. We are old friends. *Scherzo*! I joke. It is more easy if a *straniera* – a foreigner – goes. You are a tourist. Looking. You think it's a museum.' He waggles his shoulders, makes a silly face. 'Why not?'

'You want me to go all the way out to this place to see if the gates are open? Sounds a bit daft. Are you sure that's all?'

'*Niente eh*? Nothing! If you don't like to do, it is ok. I am talking to Camilla, I mention you. The Irish girl.'

'I thought she'd gone to Palestine!'

A look crosses Massimo's face. Reaching for the *caffettiera*, he pours them both more coffee.

'She has trouble with her papers. She is communist, *capito*? Like half of Italy. But all is well. She is going soon.'

'Are you a communist?

'Berlinguer!' Massimo makes a spitting noise. 'They are capitalists in disguise. Like my parents. *Ricca, ricca*. Rich! Not all of course. Camilla is ... how you say? The real thing? That is an expression?'

Jo nods: it's what Kevin said about her.

'So you will do this?'

'S'pose so. I can probably go next Friday.' Jo shrugs like an Italian. At least she'll have something to talk to Camilla about if they ever meet again.

14

Jo ticks off a church which looks Romanesque. She'll nip in on the way back, see if there are any frescos; the bus only took twenty minutes so she has plenty of time. Massimo's directions are spot-on, she thinks, as she passes a gas station. A car parked at one of the petrol pumps beeps her. Men are incurable, Jo fumes, glaring at the hippy-looking driver who beeps again, grins.

According to the map, the laboratory's about a quarter of a mile outside the town and as Jo trudges along the verge of what seems to be the start of a major road, she begins to regret letting Massimo talk her into it. Something feels fishy about the whole thing although she can't put her finger on anything in particular. Still, it's vile what they do to animals; it needs to be stopped. As apartment blocks give way to sad humpy fields, a large building comes into view.

The laboratory, a sprawling complex protected by high walls, looks bleak, uninviting. Just the sort of place to carry out secret experiments, Jo thinks, eyeing the words '*NON INGRESSO*' in bright red at the top of a metal sign. The meaning's pretty obvious but to ram it home a pair of iron gates with lethal-looking spikes are not only locked but barred. Jo gives a half-hearted push anyway, peering in through the railings to see if she can make out the rest of what's written on the notice-board. It's mostly gobbledegook but the words '*militare*' and '*pericoloso*' don't need translating.

A screech of brakes sends Jo's heart leap-frogging to her mouth. Swivelling around, she sees a uniformed officer jump out of a police car.

The driver leaps out after him leaving the car door hanging

open. As the pair hurry towards her, the first man who's tall and skinny, puts a hand to his gun. A voice in Jo's head warns her not to move.

As they get nearer, both men start shouting.

'*Non capisco, non capisco. Non sono Italianna,*' Jo screams.

'*Carta, carta?*' the tall one demands.

'*Sono Irlandaisa, au pair a Pavia, casa* Robertson.' Jo tells him, fiddling through her bag for her *Permesso di Soggiorno*. Breathing a sigh of relief, she hands it to him. He scrutinises it; tosses the Residence Permit to the other officer.

'*Irlandaisa?*' Both men look her up and down. '*Perche?* Why?' The driver indicates the building with his head.

'*Far passeggiata*', Jo explains, which she thinks means "going for a walk". '*Penso era Museo*', she adds, remembering Massimo's suggestion. '*Mi piache l'arte.*'

The Italians make faces, shrug and shake their heads.

'*Vienne con noi. Ora. Subito,*' the driver barks. '*Capito?*'

Jo understands: she has to go with them. Right now!

The tall guy, who seems less suspicious, puts an arm to her shoulder, guides her towards the car while the other shouts into some kind of walkie-talkie.

Jo drags her feet, resisting as much as she dares. '*Machina, machina!*' the policeman bellows, pointing to the car, ducking her in roughly when they get there.

They couldn't arrest her, could they? For what? All she did was look. Besides, she has to be in Pavia in a couple of hours to pick up the boys.

Jo racks her brain for a way to say all this. '*Devo … prendere i bambinis da scuola presto,*' she cobbles together, praying he'll understand. '*Sono tarde.*' "I'm late," she pleads, even though she isn't. Not yet.

'*Capito, capito. Lei parla bene l'Italiano. Brava.*'

'*Grazie,*' she answers, trying to butter him up. Italians are like us, she thinks, they love anyone who makes an effort to speak their language!

He smiles and Jo realises he's young, not much older than she is. The smile switches off as soon as the driver arrives.

Minutes later, they pull up outside a police station. It's next to the bus station and Jo has a vague memory of noticing it earlier. Talking over her head, they usher her inside and down a long, grim corridor. The driver throws open a door. '*Resta qui,*' he barks.

Not much choice, Jo thinks, as they slam the door. The room's empty except for a bench but when she plonks herself down she realises she's too agitated to sit. To calm her nerves, she walks up and down, wondering if she should stick to Massimo's story – going for a walk, thinking the building was a museum – not that the stupid gink had warned her there was the slightest chance of getting arrested! If she'd known that! Before she has time to make up her mind, the two policemen arrive back accompanied by a man in an open-necked shirt.

'*Hai il numero di telephono del Signore* Robertson?' The man hands her a pen and paper. '*Scritto!*'

Jo writes down the number and they go out, leaving her alone again. She's in big trouble now: the Robertsons will do their nut. It suddenly dawns on her the police might ask her why she'd gone there in the first place – it's hardly a tourist hot-spot. She can always say she hopped on the first bus that came along or she could say she thought she recognised the name- Before she has time to decide, the tall *caribinieri* comes back in.

'*Va via!*'

In case she's misunderstood, Jo hesitates.

'*Via, via*! Go!' he dismisses her. Ushering her out of the room, he showers her in Italian – the word "*stupido*" repeated more than once.

Jo goes straight from the bus to collect the boys. When they arrive back at the apartment, she finds Tim and Anna waiting. Snapping his fingers, Tim orders Peter and Mark to go straight to their bedroom and do something useful. Once they're out of earshot, the Robertsons marshal Jo into the lounge and shut the door.

The last time the three of them had sat in the lounge was the day she arrived, the day Anna had interrogated her about her suitability, not for the job, but for living with them. Now they've got their answer!

'What on earth were you up to?' Tim thunders. 'I got a call at the university from the *caribinieri*. Maria got one too. She was terrified – she thought you'd had an accident.'

For a moment, Jo considers telling the truth then changes her mind. It's not worth the risk: they mightn't be sympathetic; might feel obliged to march her off to the police.

'I'm sorry, I really am. I felt like going somewhere and I got the first bus that came along. I miss being in the country.'

'Where you were was hardly countryside! According to the police you were trying to enter some building.'

'I was not. I was only looking. I thought it might be a museum.'

'It's a military establishment. I would have thought that would have been pretty obvious?'

Jo shrugs. The less she says the better.

'For goodness sake Tim, it was a silly mistake! The *caribinieri* are over-reacting as usual!'

As Anna rushes to her defence, Jo can hardly believe her ears.

'You know what they say? They have to go round in twos: one who's able to write and one to keep an eye on him for subversive tendencies!' Anna laughs and Tim joins in half-heartedly.

'What did they say to you at the station?'

'Nothing much. They called me stupid, I think.'

'It was stupid. There are dangerous elements in this country. Coming from Ireland you should know all about that. You could have got yourself into a lot of trouble.'

Involuntarily, Jo recoils; is aware of Tim noticing. He tries to catch her eye but she keeps them fixed on the floor.

'Go and see what the boys are up to, they're too quiet,' Anna changes the subject.

She can't bear anyone else being the centre of attention for long, Jo thinks spitefully.

'And consult one of us before you go wandering off again,' Tim calls after her.

Jo fumes. Wait until she sees Massimo – look at the shit he's landed her in!

Jo makes a beeline for the *mensa*. There's no sign of Massimo and after ordering a coffee she carries it to one of the tables; the canteen's pretty empty so she has her pick. As she lingers over her drink, students begin to drift in. They all seem to know one another and call or wave, a few stopping to chat to those already seated. A tall guy wearing a Che Guevara berry shouts something across to a woman whose head is stuck in a book and everyone laughs. A joke, Jo guesses; and it suddenly occurs to her what had seemed odd: not one person had spoken to Massimo the whole time she was with him or even nodded to him. And why the hell had he hidden himself in a corner when the obvious thing was to sit near the door so she'd see him as soon as she came in.

Jo drains her coffee. She'd passed a sign for "*Dipartimento di Ingegneria*" on her way in. All she has to do is go to Administrations. Could she? Why not? If Massimo's an engineering student they'll know.

Finding a door marked *Segretario*, Jo knocks politely.

'*Avanti*,' a voice calls.

A youngish woman with Titian-coloured hair looks up sympathetically from behind a typewriter.

'*Scusa. Io non parla molto Italiano. Me piache parlare* — I like to talk — *con Massimo Buda. Molto importante.*'

'My English not good.' '*Massimo Buda? Momento.*' Opening an official-looking register, she scans it, reaches for the phone. Jo tries to eavesdrop but the woman lowers her voice so all she catches is Massimo's name.

Shaking her head, the secretary puts down the receiver. 'No Massimo Buda … *Altro dipartimento? Capito?*'

'*Sicuro?*'

'Certain, yes. I ask.' She spreads out her hands, palms up.

'*Molto grazie.*'

'*Prego, signorina. Mi dispiace.* Sorry.'

He must have been lying, Jo realises, as she walks back across the quad; he definitely told her he was in first year engineering. What else had he lied to her about? Suddenly aware of being watched, she looks up: half-expecting to see Massimo.

'What are you doing here?' Tim demands.

'Nothing.' Christ, she'd forgotten all about him.

He checks his watch. 'Come with me.'

Crossing the courtyard, he escorts her into one of the older ivy-covered buildings; down along several badly-lit corridors.

Taking out keys, he opens one of the offices – his name's in silver on the door – motions her inside.

'Sit. And don't give me that wide-eyed look! I had a feeling I saw you here last week. You were with someone. Might I ask who?'

Jo tries to think quickly. It goes against every bone in her body to squeal on somebody, especially to an Englishman. Besides, all she knows is Massimo's name-

'If you're mixed up in something you need to tell me.'

'I'm not involved in anything.'

'No? Well, I'm afraid I didn't buy your "going for a walk" excuse. For argument's sake, let's suppose you did go there for some perfectly innocent reason – now you know it's a military establishment, has it occurred to you that whatever you were up to might not have been so innocent? There have been several atrocities … I presume you know about them?'

'Are you mad! It's got nothing to do with-'

'So what's it to do with?'

Jo says nothing, plays for time.

'When I saw you, you were coming out of the Engineering Department. I only have to make a few enquiries.'

'Alright, I did meet someone – you don't have to know their name. He belongs to an Animal Rights Group. I bet you didn't know experiments are carried out on animals in that "military establishment"! All his group do is set the animals free. It's not right torturing them.'

'What was your role?'

'It wasn't a "role"! He asked me to check if the gates were left open. That's all.'

Tim leans back on his chair, studies Jo a moment.

'I don't suppose this so-called group were going to liberate animals in broad daylight. So gates open or shut are immaterial. It's much more likely they were trying to find out how long the police took to get there.'

'They came almost immediately.'

'Precisely. Have you arranged to meet this person?'

'No. I was hoping I might bump into him.'

'And?'

'He told me he did engineering. The secretary said they didn't have ... anyone registered.'

'You'll probably never hear from him again. It's more than likely they had someone watching the whole thing.'

Jo remembers the car at the petrol station; remembers thinking the driver wasn't the usual type who beeped.

'I don't have to tell the police, do I? I don't know anything. Honestly. He probably didn't even give me his real name.'

Tim takes his time before answering; seems to be debating something in his head.

'I'll think about it. In the meantime, I need you to promise me something. Two things, actually. One – not to get involved in any more "escapades". Two – if this person or anyone else approaches you, you are to come to me immediately and we'll go to the police together. I want you to swear.'

'Ok, I swear. I promise.'

'You're getting off lightly. Now go! I have students to teach. And by the way, I agree with you about animals.'

Jo takes her time going back to the apartment. What Tim had said made sense. She'd been suspicious herself; had really only agreed to go because of Camilla. Wanting to impress her. That's her problem – wanting to impress people. As she nears the bridge a flock of seagulls wheel and swoop. Jo leans over the parapet to watch. Seagulls look the same everywhere, she thinks, she could be looking at the Liffey. Below her the water barely moves — going nowhere. It's hard to believe a guy like Massimo could be involved in something dangerous; in one way he seemed genuine, thoughtful. Are things in society that bad? Camilla seems to think so and Jo wonders if her and Massimo are really friends or was that another lie? It's hard to know what to believe. The thing that surprises her most is Tim not insisting on going to the police: it's the kind of "proper English" thing she expected of him. Sitting in his office he seems a completely different person to the one who'd made a meal for her, kissed her. Maybe he's trying to make up to her. Or maybe, she thinks, dipping into her newly acquired cynicism, he's still worried she'll spill the beans.

15

'Josephine, are you there?' The bedroom door opens and Anna comes in, a phoney smile on her face. She's been friendlier than usual these last few days and Jo suspects she wants something.

'As you know I'm having a small dinner party tomorrow night. I was wondering if you might help serve the entrées? Maria will be preparing the food, with my assistance of course. And her sister's coming over to lend a hand.'

Although she'd love to refuse – the idea of bowing and scraping to guests is embarrassing – Jo nods.

'You're welcome to join us for the main meal. One or two people your own age are coming,' Anna continues, making an obvious effort not to look around the room.

'Thanks.'

'I can count on you then.'

'Yeah.'

Jo's eyes follow her out. Camilla's right: unless she learns to open her mouth, these people will make a servant of her.

The following morning, Jo and the boys are in the middle of breakfast when Maria charges in – all flap – her sister and her sister's youngest daughter Giulietta in tow.

'*Mange, mange!* Eat!' she shrieks, throwing her hands in the air. Clicking her tongue, she bustles around, pulling open drawers and cupboards, throwing utensils and gadgets onto the work surfaces, bossing her sister who's *oohing* and *aahing*, holding things up to admire.

The little girl, a finger in her mouth, gazes solemnly as Peter and Mark slurp their way through bowls of sticky cereal. Peter pulls faces when he thinks no one's looking; the child, more fascinated by the mess they're making, pays no attention.

The bell rings, and Maria hooshes Jo out to answer it.

Two men are waiting on the doorstep, one shouldering a ladder, the other carrying a pair of heavy silk curtains that had been sent for cleaning. Barging past Jo, they manoeuvre into the lounge and she hurries after them, worried she'll be blamed if any of Anna's precious ornaments are knocked over.

Hearing the racket, Peter comes rushing in; places himself near the window, his arms folded across his chest like a miniature foreman. As the men move a sofa out of the way, they play along with the boy, consulting him, pretending to take his opinion seriously. There's a tentative knock and a woman clutching an armful of long, flat boxes, demands to know where the '*cucina*' is. Nipping out, Jo points her in the right direction. Returning to the lounge, she finds Peter perched at the top of the ladder, smirking at her, basking in the workmen's approval as they fuss and pet him, calling him '*bravo ragazzo*', "good boy".

'Get down, get down!' Anna shrills from the hallway. 'Josephine, what on earth is Peter doing up there?'

Before Jo has time to respond, the doorbell chimes and Mrs Robertson rushes to get it.

Tapping his nose, one of the men winks at Peter: '*La mama?*' Peter snickers.

Anna opens the door wide and two men in bleached aprons shuffle in bringing with them a tantalising aroma of food.

'I don't see any truffles! *Gli tartufe speciale, dove?*' Anna wails; attempting to inspect the trays they're carrying. The men shrug, hoist the food out of her reach. As they proceed down the hallway, Anna lets fly in Italian; Maria's voice joining the hullabaloo as soon as they reach the kitchen.

'Jo, Jo!' Maria appears a moment later, rubbing her hands on her apron, grinning wickedly. '*Gli tartufe speciale non arriva. Madame pooff!*' She makes a sort of exploding noise and grabbing hold of Peter, frog-marches him out of the room. With her free hand, she beckons Jo to follow.

'*Jo, cucina.*'

'*Gioca con la piccolina,*' the maid orders Peter when they get to the kitchen, pushing him towards Giulietta. Behind her back Peter sticks out his tongue but he does what he's told – picking up a wooden block and handing it politely to the girl. Maria's the only person in the house he's afraid of.

The odd-looking boxes the woman had been carrying are spread across the table and Jo sees they're packed with dozens of long-stemmed roses. Holding up a vase of last week's flowers, Maria plucks out the faded blooms, thrusting the empty jug at Jo.

'*Tutte la casa …*' Maria waves her arms to imply the whole house.

'Ok. *Va bene.*'

Maria twigs Jo's ear. '*Madame pooff!*' She laughs again.

Jo dawdles as she collects the vases, dumping the old flowers whether they're dead or not. She takes even more time swilling out the stale water in the guest bathroom; starting guiltily as the door's pushed open and Giulietta stares up at her.

'What – *Che cosa?*'

The child pulls at her to come and Jo takes her hand, charmed by the tousled head, the determined walk; things might be different if she'd had this little angel to look after. In the hallway, the familiar rumpus of Peter and Mark's squabbling can be heard.

Thrusting open their bedroom door, Jo finds them tussling over a giant bag of peanuts. Giulietta points, her baby eyes glued to the nuts. Peter's distracted by Jo's arrival and grabbing his chance Mark yanks the bag which splits open, spewing the contents everywhere.

'Now look what you've done!' Jo yells.

The boys fall on one another. Ignoring them, Giulietta scrabbles on the floor, grabbing peanuts, shovelling them into her mouth. Jo tries to pull the boys apart.

'What's going on?' Anna barges in, sliding on a peanut, almost tripping. 'For goodness sake! Can't you keep those two quiet? Do I have to do everything myself! Peter, Mark!' The boys stare up at her.

From the hallway, Maria and her sister, laden with mops and buckets, glance in. Seeing them, Giulietta stuffs handfuls of peanuts into the pockets of her dress and waddles out.

'Maria!! The truffles! *Gli tartufi-*' Anna explodes. 'Behave,' she screams at the boys before hurrying after the maid.

'It's a madhouse,' Peter says unhappily. 'Mummy's always like this whenever we have dinner parties.'

'I bet. C'mon, we'll go out.' She's had enough of the mayhem herself.

'Again, again,' Peter and Mark beg in unison as soon as Jo stops.

They've been playing a running game along the river path and she's winded. She must be getting flabby from all the spaghetti.

'Once more, once more!'

'Ok.' Holding Peter's hand in her left hand and Mark in her other, Jo begins to sprint. 'All in together boys, this fair weather boys', she chants, gathering speed, hauling them towards each other so they almost collide; waiting until the last minute to fling them apart.

The boys shriek and giggle. 'Again!'

'I'm jacked. We can skim stones instead.'

'What's that?'

Picking up the flattest stone she can find, Jo takes aim. Both brothers watch: following the missile as it sails through the air, clips the water, bounces and bounces again. Jo smiles with relief; it doesn't always happen.

'I can do that. Easy,' Peter sneers.

Jo hands him a stone and he stands, concentrating.

'Throw,' Mark urges.

Letting out a low whistle, the older boy releases the stone, his face twisting into a scowl as it plops into the water.

'He put me off'! He put me off!' Peter wails.

'Oh shut-up. He didn't. You have to learn. You don't just throw it. You have to-'

Grudgingly, Peter watches as Jo demonstrates the knack and her second stone skites the water.

'My turn, my turn!'

With a grin, Mark flicks his, cheering it on as it hops and skips on the surface before sinking.

Peter glares at his younger brother and carefully selecting a thin, oblong stone, takes a second shot.

Let him get it right, Jo prays.

Once, twice, three times the pebble brushes the water, jets of spray shooting into the air.

Peter's face is bright with joy and Jo hugs him to her, pulling Mark to join them. Her heart warms. Keeping her arms around both of them, she propels them to a bench. For once Peter doesn't protest and Mark's chubby little arm winds round her waist. Snuggling against her, they seem happy, content almost, for the first time since she came.

After lunch, Jo takes the boys to one of their friend's houses;

Anna had arranged for them to stay overnight so they won't "spoil" the party. Arriving back, she pops into the kitchen to get something to drink; finds Maria wading through a mountain of vegetables.

'*Dove Anna?*'

'*Mal de testa*,' Maria taps her head, chuckles.

"Headache," Jo translates, but Maria shrugs, chuckles again.

'*Posso aiuto?*' she offers to help

Maria shakes her head, turning down the sides of her mouth like a clown. 'You trouble.'

Jo fills a glass with orange juice, raises a toast. Maria tosses her head and forming a hole with her thumb and forefinger, rams a carrot in and out. Jo laughs. With a grin, the maid pulls at Jo's skirts, winks; then resuming her usual serious face begins scraping again.

Smiling at the crudity; the 'crudité' Jo jokes to herself, she realises she hasn't thought about Eamonn for a while. Immediately, she feels an ache. The pain hasn't vanished, she thinks, it's lying low. Not even that: part of her is pretending the relationship isn't over, that in some imaginary future when she goes back to her real life he'll be waiting for her. If she met someone else it might help but as long as she'd holed up here with the Robertsons the chances of that happening are pretty slim! Them and their silly dinner party. What must Maria think – all the preparation, the enormous expense. It probably costs more than a year of her wages; she's seen the price of truffles, a small fortune! What she'd give to have a peek inside the Sicilian's head.

As if Maria's forgotten Jo's presence, she begins to sing, at first to herself then louder, the words and melody hypnotic, laced with grief. Moved by the sadness of the air, Jo sways.

Noticing, Maria sets down her knife and taking a step back,

stands poker stiff as if she's mounted a stage. Holding Jo's attention, she begins a song, her face impassive, the harsh discordant notes piercing her heart. Jo smiles as she listens: perhaps she's getting a look into Maria's head after all.

Abruptly, the maid stops.

'*Boh!*' she spits, flicking a hand off her chin before going back to the vegetables, hunching over, her face hidden.

The two of them sit companionably, Maria working steadily, the clock on the wall ticking quietly. The spell's broken as Anna shambles in, trailing a silky dressing gown and rubbing her temples, a morose expression on her face. Without a word, she pours a glass of mineral water. Jo and Maria exchange glances as Mrs Robertson downs a couple of pills, pads out again.

On her way to her room, Jo passes Anna in the hallway screaming down the phone. The truffles are still missing, she gloats: who says everyone doesn't have their own problems.

Jo smiles as Anna offers her delicately rouged face: the gold torque at her neck sparkling a welcome to the aged gentleman who bows elegantly, leaning in to whisper in her jewelled ear. Whatever he said must have pleased her, Jo guesses from the way Anna's eyelids dip, her cheeks dimple happily.

Jo follows the old man into the lounge where early arrivals are nibbling and drinking, eagle-eyed at each new guest. Maria and her sister, decked out in smart uniforms, glide noiselessly among them, jiggling glasses of champagne, offering silver platters overflowing with appetising nuggets of food.

Without explanation, Anna had changed her mind about Jo serving. Observing the guests, Jo almost envies the maids; at least they don't have to socialise. Despite her best dress, she looks like a poor relation next to the polished gathering of shimmering women, lacquered hair whipped into elaborate meringues, necks dripping with jewels; eyes hard as coals as they smile. The men at their sides appear every bit as formidable; a veneer of politeness gluing their limbs together.

Jo skirts the room, avoiding Tim who's holding court in front of the fireplace: witty and charming, not the fumbling drunk knocking on her door, whispering love-words.

The whole charade suddenly sickens her and Jo decides to eat by herself in the kitchen. The idea of spending the evening making stilted conversation with a bunch of stuff-shirts isn't her idea of a good time; that's if they condescended to speak to her.

Nicking a cigarette from an ivory box, Jo escapes to the balcony. You need to be someone or have pots of money for those kinds of people to notice you, she scoffs, lighting up behind one of the earthenware urns. She's an au pair, what does-

'Boring old farts aren't they?' 'Sorry, I didn't mean to startle you.'

Seeing someone young – a slightly chubby blond guy – Jo relaxes, takes the cigarette from behind her back.

'Rupert's the name. Don't laugh,' he begs.

Jo makes a feeble attempt to swallow a giggle, almost chokes on smoke.

'How can anyone take me seriously with a name like that!' the young man complains in a plummy accent. 'I blame my parents. I'm sure they did it deliberately.'

'Your mother probably liked Rupert Bear when she was little. I'm Jo. I look after the kids.'

'You're Irish,' Rupert pounces, as if he's come up with the solution to a difficult crossword clue.

'Yip. Where are you from?'

'All over really. Born in Egypt, educated- truth is I've been thrown out of more schools … Sorry, I don't suppose you want to hear any of that drivel.' His face lights up. 'Looks like food's up. Are you going in?'

Jo makes a face.

'We could always eat al fresco. It's bound to be more fun.' With a click of his heels, Rupert strides off.

That's definitely her last fag, Jo decides, stubbing out the cigarette. She doesn't even like them; it's the idea of smoking that attracts her. Peeping through the window, she can see Rupert pile food onto plates, unconcerned what Anna or anyone thinks. And the way he boasted about being thrown out of school; where she comes from that would be considered a disgrace. One law for the rich.

Moments later, Rupert wobbles back, plates balanced precariously.

'Afraid it's all rather mixed up. Same when it gets in your tum I suppose. Drink?' he asks, producing a bottle from one of his pockets.

Extracting the loosened cork, Jo puts it to her head.

'Good to see a gel who can drink.'

Eejit! Jo thinks, as Rupert hunkers down beside her.

As they gorge themselves, Rupert picks food off her plate like an old friend, offering titbits from his, chatting idly. Pity he's not her type, Jo thinks, spooning a sort of custardy desert that tastes *molto* alcoholicy. Definitely not her type, she decides, catching him staring at her.

'Wow! Someone went a bit mad with the marsala!' he exclaims, muscling in and helping himself to hers. 'I'm sure you're far too young to be eating this *zabione*,' he adds, digging in again.

'I'm not much younger than you so stick to your own,' Jo

protests.

'You like it here? What do you think of good ol' Tim? Made a play for you yet?'

Jo's too gobsmacked to answer: is that a normal question?

'You don't have to say a word, I can read it on your face,' he continues. 'Not your scene. I'd get out if I were you.'

'I would if I could but it's not that simple. What would I do?'

'Something will turn up, it always does. It pays to force the issue. Take my parents, super really but one-track. Desperate to get me into the family business. Banking! Can you imagine anything so dreary? I didn't fight them. Wouldn't have stood a chance. Got on a plane and here I am. Been here almost a year.'

'Where are you living?'

'We have a place near Florence. Mummy bought it when they were going for a song.'

Jo scrapes up the last of the cream. Got on a plane, the family business, a place outside Florence; she might have guessed. Christ, do these people never listen to themselves! Still, it's a pity she doesn't fancy him, she could ask him to wave his magic wand.

'What's so funny?'

'Nothing. I was thinking about someone I met, she's from Florence.'

'Who, maybe I know her?'

'I don't think so.' What would Camilla say if she saw her chatting up the enemy!

Rupert frowns. 'You've no idea the stick I've had to put up with.'

And you've no idea what life's like, Jo wants to tell him. How could he? Easy to say something will turn up when it's already there. The Ruperts of the world haven't a clue!

'I've got an idea. Why don't you come and stay? Mummy isn't

arriving until next week; there are oodles of rooms anyway. Come for a few days, a few weeks if you like. Who knows, I might find you something. Florence is so much nicer than Pavia. It's full of artists. I bet you're into art.'

'How can you tell?'

'Educated guess. Most people who come to Italy are.'

About to launch into her "becoming an artist" speech, Jo stops herself. She's been here ages and done fuck-all. Maybe if she lived in Florence things would change. *Firenze*! Is it possible this eejit could find her a job? If he did, she'd be able to rent a place. A room of her own! She'd definitely paint then. Living with the Robertsons has given her an insight into what Virginia Wolff was getting at.

'One of my favourite paintings is in the Uffizi.'

'Which one?

'Madonna and Child. It's by Duccio.'

'Can't say I like that sort of thing. Mummy's a bit of a fanatic, rather puts one off. I design posters. Op, pop, a touch of Dadaism for the cognoscenti. I've got this fabulous little printing press; you'd be amazed what it can do.'

Jo sighs. With his hippy hair and clothes, she might have known they'd be the kinds of things he'd be into! Posters! What a let-down.

Unearthing a piece of grubby paper from his pocket, Rupert scribbles something, then hands it to her. 'That's the phone number of the gaff in Florence. Have to make tracks. I'm meeting some friends in Milan, acquaintances actually. Bit of a bore. You know how it is.'

Jo hides her disappointment. She knows how it is alright. People like Rupert fly around the world: dinner in Pavia, supper in Milan, breakfast who knows? And people like her clear the dishes. Suppose she was stupid enough to chuck in her job and go to Florence, only to discover he'd gone to a party in London! Where would that leave her?

16

As weeks roll by, Jo re-lives her conversation with Rupert; on good days convincing herself he really meant it when he said that if she ups and leaves she's welcome to turn up at his door; at other times telling herself she'd be an *amadán* to rely on anyone with a name like "Rupert" who uses words like "oodles". Still, it doesn't stop her fantasising, picturing a light-filled room, an easel, the *Duomo* shining in the distance. If she moved to Florence, Sienna would be nearer and she'd be able to visit her beloved art. Ravenna would be closer too: San Vitale with its extraordinary 6th Century mosaics created especially for the Empress Theodora is high on her list. If you mentioned mosaics *casa* Robertson, Anna would think you were talking about bathroom tiles! If only she was her own boss, could go where she liked. Had money! Anything over from the pittance they pay her – pocket money really – has to be kept for emergencies. No wonder she can't paint! If her body's not free, how can her imagination be?

Getting Peter and Mark ready for school or helping with their homework, Jo dreams of ways to "force the issue" as Rupert suggested. She's convinced Anna senses her rebelliousness, is unsure how to handle it. It simply isn't cricket, she can hear her whinge.

The thought of upsetting Anna pleases Jo but her feelings around Tim are more complicated. Despite what happened, their evening together had created a bond of sorts. If only he'd found a way to let her know she mattered, acknowledged the meal he'd cooked for her, the fact he'd tried to get off with her, said the things he'd said, even if he hadn't meant them. If he'd done anything other than act as if nothing had happened …

Some chance! At the end of the day, he's Anna's husband, shares her belief in their God-given right to have everything their own way. Both ways! Even Maria has begun to irritate her. Jo would love to shake her, get her to mutiny.

Daily, she rehearses a litany of grievances, hoping to kick-start her courage. Like a wound-up time-bomb, she stalks the apartment: waiting for the wrong word, the wrong action to set her off. In the meantime, she collects the boys, brings them home, feeds them, entertains them, gets them ready for bed. Gets herself to bed.

Another fifteen minutes and she can realistically start slopping out dinner. Jo and the boys are surviving the terrible in-between time after they come home from school and before supper; Peter jangling her nerves more than usual.

'You have to,' he yells, tugging at her arm.

'No I don't,' Jo answers. 'Find your own airplane, you lost it.'

His eyes spit.

'You find it, my mother pays you.'

The words unleash Jo's pent-up anger. 'Who do you think you are, you bloody spoiled little maggot!'

Peter raises a hand to strike her, lowers it, his expression faltering. Turning, Jo finds herself face to face with Anna.

'Go straight to the kitchen, Josephine. I'll talk to you in a moment.'

Humiliated, Jo slinks from the boys' bedroom. Waiting for Anna, anger and fear battle inside her.

'I heard every word. How dare you speak to Peter like that,' Anna storms in, her face chalky-white. 'I'm not paying you to verbally abuse my children.'

'What about the way he talks to me?' Jo retaliates.

'You're the adult, although you don't behave like one.'

And you do? Jo looks Anna up and down: this woman who doesn't look after her own kids, employs someone to cook and clean is accusing her of not being an adult! It's the last straw. Without bothering to reply, she stalks out of the kitchen.

Back in her room, she pulls down her case. She's not going to give Anna the satisfaction of throwing her out. She'll leave now, get a train to Florence. If Rupert's away or was only being polite, she'll stay in a hostel. He probably imagines she's loaded; is au pairing to pass the time between "fun things". So what! Fuck him, fuck the lot of them, she'll just go- Hearing a rap on the door, Jo freezes.

'I want to speak to you,' Anna calls in a placating tone.

As her employer marches in, Jo busies herself folding clothes.

'What are you doing for heaven's sake?' Mrs Robertson enquires. 'Come now, there's no need for that.' She touches the pearls at her neck. 'Look, I realise the children are difficult. I'm sorry I flew off the handle.'

An apology, Christ! Jo's mouth opens and shuts, second thoughts seeing their chance. Making herself homeless and jobless isn't exactly what she wants to do. Not right this minute.

'You can't leave a job every time there's a little ... unpleasantness.'

Rocking on her heels, Jo fiddles with the clasp on the case.

'Why don't you take the evening off, go to a film. We'll say no more about it.' With a wan smile, Anna retreats, shutting the door firmly behind her.

Apathy sets in. Powerless against it, Jo allows it suck her under. Most days, returning from dropping the kids at school, she shuts herself in her room, pretends to be doing something; not that anyone pays much attention. She doesn't even bother going through the motions of taking out her paints; just mopes feeling sorry for herself, entertaining daydreams of confronting Anna, storming out. On really bad days she imagines being back in Dublin, bumping into Eamonn, their lips meeting as she falls into his arms.

One morning, as she lies daydreaming about her first exhibition in Florence – with Rupert's help of course – she realises it's not only her inability to face the Robertsons that preventing her leaving. Setting herself adrift in a strange country terrifies her. What if things go wrong? She can't bear the idea of having to go home with nothing achieved. Even if she doesn't like where she is, it's a safe haven. And although she's doing nothing, she's doing it abroad, not faffing around Dublin, drinking her head off. Things will change, she assures herself. They always do.

Arriving back the following afternoon, Jo's surprised to find Tim in the kitchen drinking coffee. He makes a rule of never setting foot in the house until evening.

'I'm taking you two to Piero's,' he tells the boys. 'You can stay the night, if you behave.'

Jubilant, Peter and Mark rush to change out of the old-fashioned smocks they wear to school, Mark running back in to give Tim a hug.

As soon as his youngest has left the room, Tim turns to Jo. 'Piero telephoned earlier to say his latest batch of oil is ready. He likes to make an occasion of it. Want to come for the drive? We won't be staying long. Anna's invited some people over later.'

Jo picks up Peter's school bag from where he'd dropped it, puts it away. Piero lives in an old farmhouse halfway between Pavia and Milan. She and Tim would be alone on the way back. Is that why he's suggesting it?

Mark comes back in, shirt buttoned skew-ways, waving his new shorts.

'I was going to do some painting,' Jo excuses herself, bending to help the boy off with his school trousers.

'You seem to be doing a lot of painting recently, not that we've had the privilege of seeing any of it. Mark, you're well able to dress yourself.' He looks her in the eye. 'Avoiding us rather?'

Now, a voice urges, now, say you want to leave. Instead, she stands aside as Peter — wearing a cowboy hat and waving a gun — gallops in on a make-believe horse.

'All right Peter old chap, steady on.' A hand presses her arm. 'Are you sure?'

Jo nods, holding her nerve until she hears the front door shut. Instinct urges her to run after him, say she's changed her mind. She could use the time on the way back to tell him; it might be easier away from the apartment. She wavers, then with a shrug, retreats to her room. What a coward she is! Furious at herself, she storms back to the kitchen, hoping to find Maria, scrounge a "*coff*".

'I thought you'd gone with Tim.' Anna seems surprised to see her.

'I have stuff to do.'

'Fine. We're having some old friends over for dinner. If you'd prefer to eat earlier let Maria know and she'll leave something ready. I'm having my hair done so I'll be away most of the afternoon.' She turns to go. 'As you are here Josephine, would you mind doing me a favour? Be a darling and sort out the drinks cabinet. Maria hasn't time. If there are any bottles with small amounts left you can put in a bag and give them to her. She takes them home. There's probably quite a few after the dinner party.'

Why don't you do it, Jo thinks, as she smiles yes.

Jo lines up several bottles, sherry, grappa, something she's never heard of called Noilly Prat. Most have only a few dregs in them and she hopes Maria appreciates this kind of charity. Reaching further in, she pulls out a bottle of whiskey from the back of the cabinet. It's half full or half empty – depending how you look at things – and she wonders if she should include it?

Why not? "The labourer's worthy of her hire," she misquotes Luke's Gospel to the empty room. It's a bottle of Glenfiddich, pure malt, *Scotch whisky*, spelt without an 'e'. That must be what Tim was referring to the day they'd sat on the couch and he'd put his hand on her arm. It seems so long ago now.

Never too late to toast old times, Jo thinks, pouring a little drop into a glass, saluting the man in scarlet and green on the label. Who's to know? As the liquid reaches her stomach, Jo feels instantly cheerful. Maybe she should hang onto it: she deserves it as much as anyone. On her way to the kitchen, Jo makes a little detour, stashes the bottle under her bed.

'For you. *Per lei* …' Jo hands Maria the bag of booze, blushing suddenly at the thought she might have seen the Glenfiddich, be expecting it. Taking out one of the bottles, the maid eyes it disdainfully and with a grimace of distaste, shoves the lot in the small cloakroom where she hangs her coat. With a scornful shrug, Maria goes back to doing what she's doing, cutting up something – fish by the smell of it. She's probably making her incredible *soupe de mare*, Jo thinks, sloping away guilty. If only Maria wasn't the maid and she wasn't the *au pair*, they could sit and get tipsy together. Or as they say in Dublin: if you had fish and I had chips, we'd have fish and chips.

Just one more sip, she assures herself as she hauls the whiskey from its hiding place, puts it to her lips. Catching sight of her reflection in the dressing-table mirror, she salutes. Tim was right: it is good.

Maybe she should kiss the rest of the day goodbye, get pissed instead? She'll have to be careful though, not give the game away.

After all she stole it. Shure ye know the Oirish would do anything for a drink. Shtole it your Honour. Ah but who did she steal it from – that's the question? Did she steal it from the English robber barons, the right dishonourable Robertsons or from the poor betrayed servant woman Maria? Jo swallows a mouthful; this time the whiskey goes to her head. You'd need the whisdom of Sholomon to answer a question like that or maybe the Pope himself. What is she talking about: isn't she in the Pope's back garden! She could go and ask him personally. A tap on the door interrupts her reverie.

'*Sono occupata*,' she calls, although she thinks "*occupata*" is only used about toilets.

'*Coff pronto*. You like?'

'*No grazie*,' she answers. '*Lavoro*.'

'*Lavoro*' she repeats, 'I'm working. As the man said, "nice work if you can get it." "And you can get it if you try," Jo sings. All the same a coffee would sober her up. What does she need sobering up for? It would take more than a drop of Scotch to make her drunk. Isn't this the life, she toasts: what has she got to complain about? A little whiskey and everything's easy-peasy! *Molto simplice. Molto, molto, simplice!*

The sound of knocking jolts Jo awake. Addled, she tries to shake her head clear.

'Is everything alright Josephine?' Anna asks through the door.

'I'm working,' she calls, reddening at the thought she might come in. The room stinks of alcohol.

'Maria says she hasn't seen you all afternoon. You're not sick?'

'I'm fine. I'm drawing.' Shitbags, let her voice sound normal.

She hears Anna hesitate then the sound of her high-heels receding.

When Jo stands up, her head spins. She needs air. And quick!

Cracking open the door, she peers out. She can hear Anna and Maria gossiping in the kitchen. If she can get as far as the balcony without being seen, she'll be alright. The conversation becomes animated and seizing the moment, Jo shoots along the hall into the lounge. Noticing several new bottles on top of the drinks cabinet, including a bottle of Glenfiddich, she curtsies. Nice drink!

Out on the balcony, she feels light and airy, as if she might blow away. Holding her head to the breeze, she takes lungfuls of air, giggles.

'What's so funny?'

Turning, Jo sees Anna in the doorway of the lounge, a canteen of cutlery in her hand.

'Just remembering something.' 'Your hair's lovely,' she comments, counting on Anna's vanity to distract her.

Anna swivels so she can see her reflection in the mirror. 'Janni's a pet. He knows exactly what I want. Oh and thanks for sorting out the bottles. If you'd like a drink, help yourself,' she suggests, clip-clopping out, taking the knives and forks with her.

Gliding back into the lounge, Jo opens the new bottle of Glenfiddich, pours half a glass. See, she rebukes herself: she's not such a meanie.

'Here's to you Mrs Robertson,' she sings. "Robinson", she corrects herself. Robinson, Robertson, what does it matter? Humming the tune, she waltzes back to her room.

Hearing someone trying the door handle, Jo curls up. Leave me alone, she mutters irritably into the pillow. What does she want now?

'We're about to eat if you'd like to join us.'

Eat? But it's only ... Jo struggles to locate the clock. It's somewhere – she can hear the ticking. Nine o'clock! It can't be!

'Coming, coming,' she calls, heaving herself up. Better have another drink before facing them, the hair of the dog. Not that she's in the mood for eating with strangers, never mind drinking with them! Draining the bottle, she laughs. She's definitely feeling a little drunk. A leetle drunk and a leetle, leetle crazy.

Glass in hand, Jo enters the dining room, surprised at how slidey the floor is: you could skate on it.

Anna glances up.

'Josephine this is Clio and- Are you alright?'

'Josephine's fine,' she answers, holding up her drink. "*Here's to you Mrs Robertson. Heaven holds a* ..." Her voice warbles off. But where? One minute it was in her mouth, the next it had vanished. Like a wisp of smoke into the never never. What an amazing discovery! She must tell someone before she forgets.

'Did you know my voice disappeared...'she trails off. That isn't what she meant to say.

'Are you drunk?'Tim's words cut into her.

'Why not? It's a free country, isn't it?'

Holding her glass like a microphone, she booms: 'Anyone for peepees or pawpaws before we start eating?' She attempts to go from face to face but everyone's features keep shifting and a woman with jewellery up round her forehead is staring daggers. Jo's never seen her before, perhaps she should explain.

'Did you know we have to go peepee-'

'That's enough!'Tim shouts. 'Sit down immediately or leave.'

Jo frowns. Strange how they all look as if they're swimming. And the table is floating. Or maybe the floor's moving? Smiling blithely, she drifts towards her seat, reaches for the chair. At the last moment, she changes direction, dumps herself on Tim's knee.

'What do you think you're doing?' he protests, throwing her off.

"Open the door Jo," she mimics. '*Amore!*'

'I'm warning you!'

'Tim, do something,' Anna pleads.

'*Oscail an doras*,' Jo shouts gleefully, 'that's Irish. *Apri la porta amore mio. Mia … mia …* I'm a girl.'

'She is drunk. Go to your room,' Tim orders. 'This minute.'

'Not "go to your room", "open the door",' Jo corrects him.

'Let's get on with our meal,' the jewelled woman whines.

'How can you eat, I wanna dance,' Jo bellows, 'I wanna dance.' They aren't going to ignore her. She won't let them. Steadying her chair, Jo hops up on it. What is she doing? She's not sure but she has to do something. With a flourish, she opens a button on her blouse. She's got too many clothes on, that's the trouble.

'*Italia, Italia …*'

Something hits Jo's face: rain slides down her cheeks. Rain! Just what she needs, what she's been missing. A bit of Ireland. It's too bloody hot in this country. Far too hot for the likes of her.

Firenze

17

As Jo pushes in the heavy embassy door, a woman with glasses perched on the end of her nose, glances up from behind a mountain of newspapers. Sunlight glints on the scissors she's wielding, snip-snipping as she clips out an article, places it on top of a small pile.

'Mrs Goodwin,' Jo enquires, reading the laminated sign on the desk. 'Sorry to bother you.' She neutralises her voice, trying not to sound too Irish. 'I'm looking for work. Someone at the youth hostel told me to try here.'

The woman sniffs, continues what she's doing, a frown creasing her forehead. Jo hopes they won't throw her out on account of the North: a crowd had set fire to the British Embassy in Dublin a few years earlier; danced in the street as it went up in flames.

'What sort of work? Do you speak Italian?' Mrs Goodwin removes her spectacles, rests them on her chest.

'A little,' Jo answers; mentally apologising to Camilla as she gives the English woman an ingratiating smile. What choice has she, she's almost out of money and this is the only lead she's had all week.

'Simon,' the woman calls to a bearded man struggling with a typewriter. 'We've got another one. Not much Italian, can you think of anything?'

The man, who is only using his index fingers, suspends them above the keyboard while his eyebrows merge. 'There's always Vanda's,' he says at length. 'The last girl's bound to have done a runner by now.'

'What's Vanda's?' Jo asks.

'Vanda runs a *pensione* near Santa Spirito. I can give you directions. She's always looking for help. Making beds, cleaning, that sort of thing. It's live-in. She's a bit of a terror, mind you. And the hours are long.'

Jo can't believe her luck! Not only a job, but a place to live. She can move out of the hostel before they throw her out. And put off getting in touch with Rupert: she can't bear the idea of going cap in hand. She watches the pen as it scratches its way across headed notepaper; "enemy" or not she could hug both of them.

'Thanks, thank you.' Jo stuffs the address in her bag. Real work at last, not kow-towing to brats: she won't do a runner.

Pensione Vanda, *Pensione Vanda*: the neon sign scrawls the words across the bedroom wall relentlessly. In less than two minutes the alarm will go off. Not that Jo needs an alarm, her own unique one arrives at five o'clock each morning as a horse and cart clatters down the cobbled laneway outside the B&B.

The first time it happened, Jo had leapt out of bed and rushed to the window: it sounded as if an army of tanks was thundering down the street. Leaning out, she'd watched the metal gates of the next door yard fly open, an old-fashioned wagon with canvas covering crash through. From out of the shadows, men had appeared, begun unloading barrels from the cart, hurling them through a trapdoor. When the same thing occurred the following morning, she'd tried convincing herself it was romantic: the hunched back of the driver gripping the reins, the sound of steel on stone, the shouts and profanities of the workers. A sight to inspire her. But when she couldn't get back to sleep, she'd cursed her luck, cursed Vanda. The room she's been given is not a proper bedroom, just a storeroom in an extension shared with mountains of towels and sheets, enough toilet rolls to wipe the whole of Italy. She's tried everything to block out the racket, covering her head with the duvet, stuffing cotton wool in her ears; nothing works. As soon as the din wakes her, the neon sign kicks in, the illuminated words branded on her brain like a signpost to the Hell she once believed in. If God exists, He's teaching her a lesson: life with the Robertsons had been a piece of cake. Compared to Vanda, Anna was a paragon of virtue, at least until the nightmare time waiting for the new au pair to arrive. If "elegance" is the word Jo associates with Anna, 'glitter' sums up her new employer. Vanda glitters. Sparks fly off her, from the top of her sequinned hairnet to the gold high-heels which clack-clack even when she's stationary. A sheen of sweat coats her fleshy arms and face but it's her eyes which unnerve Jo most. They seem to have a life of their own: no matter where Vanda is, an insolent stare, a corner cut, and she's on it like a bloodhound.

"Time to get up, you lazy good-for-nothing!" Vanda's high-pitched voice shrills as Jo drags herself out of bed. In Jo's imagination, Vanda speaks perfect English; in reality she has only a few words; screams in Italian to compensate.

Peeling off her tee-shirt, Jo runs water into the cracked sink, splashes herself before throwing on the scratchy shift her employer insists she wears. Shutting the door behind her as quietly as possible, she hurries down the stairs, tiptoes along the corridor connecting the extension to the rest of the house. In *Pensione Vanda* there is only one golden rule: never, on pain of death, disturb one of the stupid guests.

'*Bon giorno*,' she mumbles, glancing to see if Vanda's father – Babbo – is up yet, squatting in his ratty armchair. The old man spends his days leering at her from behind one of the dirty magazines he slobbers over. Jo had been shocked the first time she'd noticed what he was reading – if you could call it reading – had blushed, not just for herself but for the statue of Our Lady in the alcove above him. Magazines like that are banned in Ireland and so they should be. If he was her father she'd burn them! Him too! Seeing his chair empty, Jo gives it a kick.

Without turning, Vanda spits a gob of Italian, her operatic movements implying some unspeakable tragedy Jo's responsible for. She searches the room for a clue: she'd done the washing up before going to bed, put the *sugu* away as per instructions, stuck tee-towels and serviettes in the washing machine...

'*Panini?*' Jo offers.

'*Va, va,*' Vanda dismisses her with an angry wave.

Maybe Babbo's had a heart attack, Jo exults, releasing the lock on the heavy front door, delighting in the breath of freedom caressing her face. '*Sono sciave,*' she informs an uncaring world. And she might as well be a slave, the way Vanda treats her.

Outside, the street has a dusty yellow look, pockets of night lingering in doorways, down shadowed laneways. A faint rumble can be heard in the distance, as if the world is creak-starting. The sun hasn't got into its element and as she strides along, Jo revels in a sensation of feeling warm and cool at the same time. Doubling back, she ogles a pair of orange high heels in a posh shoe shop before hurrying on, terrified of giving Vanda any excuse to end these precious excursions. As she ploughs through early morning workers, Jo keeps an eye out for the road-sweeper; she can usually judge how early or late she is by where he's got to. This morning, he's parked in front of the hairdresser's – *la parrucchiera* – puffing contentedly on a cigarette, his arms propped on the rim of his smelly cart as he gazes soulfully into space. Jo waves and he waves back, a sloppy grin on his face: maybe some jobs aren't as bad as they look.

Reaching the *panettaria*, Jo stops for a quick look in the window. Even after a month, it still amazes her. In Dublin there's bread: batch, sliced or turnover; here it's patterned, plaited, stretched and curved into all sorts of shapes. Italians can turn anything into an art!

Pushing in the door, the smell of freshly baked bread makes her light-headed; her own breakfast has to wait until the guests have vamoosed. Standing in the short queue, she can watch the bakers through an archway as they knead and twist lengths of dough, fling it into the air; their tall hats and floor-length aprons making them look as if they've stepped out of one of the nursery rhymes she read as a kid. As usual the way the work's divided strikes Jo as odd: men doing the baking, while women, rosy-cheeked from the heat, rush around feeding enormous trays into the roaring mouths of furnaces, their feet making patterns in the floury dust. For some reason, she'd have thought it would be the other way round.

'*La bella Irlandaisa!*' Marco, the owner, greets her when it's her turn, wiping a pair of large hands on his apron. '*Come sta questa matina?* How are you this morning?'

'*Bene, grazie.*'

'*Que bella journo, si?* Beautiful day, yes!'

'*Si, molto bello.*'

'*Quanto panini questa matina?* How many?'

'*Trente per favour.*'

'*Trente?*' He flashes his hands three times. 'Turty?'

'*Si, si, grazie.*'

Every morning, Marco repeats the same thing and every morning Jo digests his words, savouring them: like manna from Heaven they nourish her. The owner seems to have adopted her, waving like an old friend if he sees her hurrying past on messages, sometimes beckoning her in, getting her to sample freshly-made *biscotti*, hovering anxiously for a smile of approval as she samples a biscuit. The previous Sunday, she'd bumped into him ambling hand-in-hand with a little boy in a velvet coat and had hardly recognised him. In everyday clothes and without the hat, he'd looked small, insignificant.

On her way back to the pensione, the moist bread smells of sleep and Jo wishes she could curl up in bed, eat the rolls one by one. Some hope! *Paninis* are reserved for guests and each morning Vanda orders exactly the right number, counts them as soon as Jo returns.

Jo places a roll by each serviette and an extra one for each guest in a little plaited basket at the centre of the table. She takes her time: relishing the peace before the ravenous hordes descend and madness begins.

'Jo! Jo!' Hearing Vanda shout, she races out, colliding with the landlady in the hall, getting a noseful of perfume and sweat.

This time she's ready.

'*Lenzuolis,*' she says into Vanda's sweaty face not giving her time to open her mouth. '*Vite, vite!*' Vanda pushes her towards the patio. It's one of Jo's jobs to take the sheets down so Vanda's flower boxes can be seen in all their glory.

While she pulls the *lenzoulis* from the line, the sun, making its way over the higgledy-piggledy rooftops of Florence, warms her back. Vanda likes them folded in a particular way and after a couple, Jo gets into her stride, stacking the crisp laundry on a large patio table. Hearing footsteps, she glances over her shoulder, sees Babbo's almost toothless mouth grimacing at her, his eyes slithering all over her body.

Bastard, she thinks, turning away but he shuffles over and

before she can stop him, grabs one end of the sheet she's holding.

'*Fatto io,*' Jo tells him, tapping her chest to emphasise she's doing it but he ignores her, raising and dropping his shoulders as if he doesn't understand. Jo glowers.

'*Molto piu veloce,*' he sucks on his gums.

Quicker my arse, Jo thinks, trying to wrench the sheet out of his grasp. Instead of letting go, the old man waltzes the length of it and with a rapid movement doubles his end into hers, his hands coming to rest on her breasts. Furious, Jo stamps on his foot and the old man howls, his wet eyes glaring at her.

'*Mache! Cosa c'e?*' Vanda bustles out, snatching the sheet out of Jo's hands.

'*Domanda lui*, ask him!' she snaps back, pointing at Babbo. Vanda hisses, curling her tongue round the sound, tugging her father's ear until he screams.

'You in, serve' she commands Jo.

Hiding a smile, Jo skips past.

'Good morning,' she parrots, stepping back to allow a pair of frumpy-looking English sisters into the dining-room.

'Another beautiful day, not like home,' the older of the two croons.

'Lovely,' Jo agrees. Dirty bitches, she mouths behind their backs, wishing Anna could see the state of the room they leave behind: she'd know what a pigsty was then!

'Do you think we could have some toast? The bread here ...,' the younger sister whispers conspiratorially. 'Would you mind awfully?'

'Of course not,' Jo replies politely. I hope it poisons you, she curses, knowing Vanda will mind and she'll get the brunt. She sighs. Another day has begun at *Pensione Vanda*.

Taking her hands out of the greasy water, Jo picks up a towel, dries her fingers one by one. Gazing out over the rows of freshly laundered sheets, she's able to catch a glimpse of Giotto's bell-tower in the distance. "*Campanile*" the Italian for bell-tower seems to describe perfectly the delicate pink and white marble structure with its sugar-candy lightness. It's where she'd been going the previous Sunday when she'd bumped into Marco and his nephew. Although she'd intended spending the day on her own work by the time the weekend came she'd been suffering from a major dose of cabin fever. Besides, Florence was begging to be seen.

Jo could cry at the thought of the fourteen en suites she has to clean by lunchtime. The idea of clearing up after people's fucking and shitting and God-knows-what makes her want to pull her hair out! Why is she the one charring when everyone else is free to enjoy themselves without lifting a hand! She could scream thinking of people doing the things she'd love to be doing: visiting the Bargello or the Uffizi, wandering round the Convent of San Marco admiring the Fra Angelicos. Most of them only passing the time: they could be anywhere.

When she can put it off no longer, Jo climbs to the third floor. By now, the *pensione*'s deserted, has the gloom of an empty railway station. Heart sinking, she lets herself into one of the twin rooms at the end of the corridor, is confronted by the usual mess. Her eyes light on a half-eaten apricot. What's the point, she asks a non-existent jury, of eating in bedrooms being forbidden in six languages on the back of every door when no one pays a blind bit of attention! Dropping the offending item into a wastepaper basket, she crosses to the bathroom: she might as well get the worst over first. Grimacing, Jo uses one end of the guest's toothbrush to yank a wad of hair clogging the sink, flushes the gunk down the toilet. She's tempted to send the brush with it;

instead she takes her revenge on a pair of discarded underpants, kicking them out of the room, laughing as they land on the dressing table. So much the better, she'll leave them there: see if anyone has the nerve to complain! Don't they realise it's another human who has to clean up after them!

'Jo, Jo!' Vanda's screech reaches her from the bottom of the stairs. '*Dov'esse, dov'esse?*'

"Where is she!" Where the hell does she think she is! Hearing Vanda's voice getting closer, Jo grabs the toothbrush and levering the underpants off the table, flicks them under one of the beds.

'*Venga, venga,* coming!' she calls. Shit! How much longer can she stick this dump!

18

'Where are you?!' Rupert yells into the phone.

'Near the *Duomo* ... *Piazza di San Firenze*,' Jo reads the street sign, registering the welcoming note in his voice. Dialling his number, she'd been scared he might be offhand, even pretend not to remember her.

'I'll be there in twenty minutes. Grab a coffee in ... oh, go to *Piazza Della Signoria* and sit outside somewhere. Watch out for me,' he adds.

Walking round the corner, Jo stops a moment to look at the David. It's always puzzled her why Michelangelo made the figure so big: Goliath was the giant. Maybe he was trying to make the point that when you defeat someone you take on their attributes? Or maybe he didn't think anybody would believe that somebody ordinary, somebody small, could do something extraordinary.

'She sounds a real dragon,' Rupert exclaims when Jo finishes telling him about Vanda.

Naturally, she'd embellished her account; suspecting drudgery wasn't Rupert's thing: too removed from his own experience.

'How long have you been in Florence?'

'Just a while,' she answers vaguely.

'What happened with the Robertsons? Took my advice?'

'I got a bit drunk one night,' Jo proffers, making a face. She'd rather forget the whole saga, her skin prickling at the memory. The shenanigans at the dinner table may have put the kybosh on her job but the Robertsons had got their own back, insisting she stay until her replacement arrived. Christmas was looming which meant the girl wouldn't be coming until after the holidays. A week before the big day the whole family had skedaddled to England to visit grandparents, leaving Jo high and dry. She thought she'd die of loneliness until Eamonn took up residence in her head, then she thought she'd die of grief.

'I expect you told them a few home truths!'

Jo shrugs, wishing Rupert wasn't quite so nice. All the same, she feels weirdly at home with him, as if she's known him forever or he's some long-lost relative. A rich long-lost relative. Sitting beside him in the square, she feels normal – free – for the first time in ages. Maybe that's what "*simpatico*" really means: being in tune with someone without understanding why. It doesn't change the fact she has to go back to the B&B, work endless bloody hours, get shouted at for no reason, deal with other people's shit. But it's something: all she has for the moment.

'I've been thinking,' he announces, 'you can't possibly stay at Vanda's.'

Jo bursts out laughing at the serious tone in his voice.

'What's so funny?' He sounds hurt but Jo can tell he's putting it on.

'You haven't a clue! "You can't possibly stay at Vanda's," she repeats. 'The problem is I have to unless I find another job. Unlike some people, I don't have parents who can bale me out. I bet when you say you've no money all you mean is you haven't been to the bank. When I say it, I mean it.'

'Don't lecture Josephine, you sound like Mummy.'

'You're an eejit! Idiot,' she translates in case he doesn't understand.

'Ok, I take your point. I'll find you another job, how does that sound?'

'That's more like it.'

'Now, Jo, I'm going to order more coffee and I want you to

tell me all about your terrible background.'

Jo eyes him suspiciously: the last thing she wants is him feeling sorry for her.

'I'd like to know. Honestly. How can I understand how the other half lives if no one tells me?'

Jo hesitates. She suspects that deep down she has enough rage to blow the place up. It would be a release to open her mouth, spill it all out.

'Fuck off.'

'What a relief.' Rupert mimes mopping his brow. 'For an awful moment I thought you were going to make me feel guilty.'

Jo looks across at the David, realises how close she'd come to shooting herself in the foot. The wrong decision could have ruined everything.

'I know,' he brightens, pointing at a glass case on the counter. 'Why don't we have some of those yummy pastries?'

Jo had noticed the cakes while she'd been waiting; could only imagine what they cost.

'I can't decide which one to have.'

'Let's try one of each.' Rupert's eyes twinkle greedily.

The seesaw of life, she thinks, a feeling of ease washing over her. As Rupert almost empties the stand, Jo enjoys the look of consternation on the waitress' face. She was right. Her life's going to change: she can feel it in her bones.

19

Even though it's Sunday, her only day off, Jo gets up at the crack of dawn. She's been invited to lunch at Rupert's and wants to look absolutely "spiffing" for the occasion.

'I'm so lucky, I'm so lucky, I'm lucky and plucky and wise!' she sings, prancing around the room. Things are even beginning to improve at the pensione! The first time Rupert left her back, Vanda had been waiting, hands on hips, eyes on red alert.

'I have to see her in the flesh,' Rupert had begged as they drove there.

She smiles, remembering the look on Vanda's face as she clapped eyes on his porsche, then on Rupert. Smelling money, her flashbulb smile had illuminated the street. After that, she'd begun treating Jo a little better. When Jo reported this back to Rupert, he took to bowing formally to her employer, tooting his horn cheekily before driving off. Vanda had fallen for it, pinching and poking at Jo whenever she comes back from a night out, insinuating all sorts of carry-on.

How wrong Vanda is. Rupert's a friend, that's all. At the sound of an engine slowing, Jo goes to the window but the car cruises past. A friend not an equal her mind taunts and she remains where she is, staring out. Money's the problem: he has it and she doesn't. In subtle and not so subtle ways it changes things. Having it means he's free to do what he likes. Of course, he's more than willing to treat her but that's not the same thing. Besides, she doesn't like it. The fact she's fun to be with, is always coming up with interesting things to do or see, levels things a bit. Rupert's hooked on whatever it is she offers; seems to need it. Need her; he can't see her often enough. They must have eaten in half the best *trattorias* in Florence and last Sunday he drove her out to San Gimiano ...

Jo feels a stab of guilt: despite all her avowals about the amount of work she'd do once she got to Florence she hasn't done a scrap; she's either slaving at the pensione or out with Rupert enjoying herself. It doesn't help she's on her feet from six in the morning until nine o'clock at night with only a few hours off during siesta when she's too exhausted to even think. Real artists work themselves to the bone, starve in attics if they have to, a voice rebukes her. All right, she bargains, if he suggests going somewhere next Sunday she'll definitely say no.

Delving into the battered wardrobe, Jo pulls out a lacy top she'd bought with her first wages, holds it out. It's a bit OTT and she'd not sure if it's really her. Rupert had chosen it. He likes to think of her as wild, untamed – compared to him – and she encourages it, afraid he wouldn't like her as much if she were totally herself. So what if she revs things up; at least she knows she's doing it. And it's not as if the way she behaves is completely false although sometimes – afterwards – she feels as if she's betrayed herself.

With a shrug, she shoves the top back in its bag, takes out a pale flowery dress, one of her old favourites. The thing is Rupert prefers people who are sure of themselves, who expect things, don't ask politely. He loves her to complain – the more off-the-wall the better – as long as she does it in a funny, sarcastic way; he doesn't like it if she's too serious or God forbid gets upset. The last thing he wants is to have to actually deal with the things she says. Of course, it doesn't help that Rupert's own lifestyle is part of what pisses her off: designing posters instead of working in the family business hardly makes him a rebel. Not to mention the generous allowance that finds its way into his account each month!

Jo changes her mind – the dress is too pretty, makes her look young. She'll wear the new blouse and lots of kohl, go for mysterious. A horn toots – Rupert never honks – and Jo leans out the window. Seeing her, his face lights up and he waves and calls and she waves back, trying to kid herself, pretending not to notice what's sticking out a mile. Grabbing her bag, she takes the stairs two at a time, as if she could leap over the problem. Don't let Rupert be in love with her, she begs. Don't spoil everything.

'This is the pile.'

Jo sensed Rupert had been trying to prepare her for something; assumed he was feeling a bit nervous about introducing her to his mother. Looking in though the wrought-iron gates, she understands.

'I should have warned you. Can't stand the place personally.'

At the far end of a tree-lined avenue, the sun-kissed exterior of a large house – the kind with columns and porticos – glows in the soft morning light.

'I know what you mean. It's just like home.'

Rupert chuckles and Jo joins in, her laughter fading as a uniformed servant appears to unlock the gates. With a casual nod, Rupert drives through, proceeding slowly along an avenue lined with busts of haughty-looking gods and goddesses that eye Jo suspiciously. Manicured lawns on either side look as if they've been cut with a pair of scissors. Fucking hell! Jo thinks, as they pull up in front of the entrance, this isn't a house: it's a mansion. A sharp-nosed woman, reclining on a sun-bed, props herself up on one elbow.

'That's Mummy. She'll try to terrify you but she's a good sport really.'

Jo gulps. Whenever Rupert had mentioned his mother –

which was fairly frequently – she'd imagined her looking a bit like her own mammy only more elegant, a kind of older Anna. The person staring at them, in nothing but a skimpy bikini with the straps pushed down, bears no resemblance to any mother she's ever met.

Jumping out, Rupert trots around to opens Jo's door.

'Don't leave that eyesore there,' the woman complains brusquely.

On the point of getting out, Jo shrinks into her seat, convinced his mother had used the double-meaning word deliberately.

'Don't worry Mummy, I'll move it,' Rupert replies; throwing Jo a puzzled look as he ducks back in.

'She's not all that bad,' he assures her as they cruise past a tennis court and a large blue oblong that looks like a swimming pool.

'She likes the Irish. Her people have a place outside Cork. Bandon House – a bit of a folly from what I gather. I've never been myself.'

Jo cringes. Why is life always dangling things in front of her then whipping them away? What made her think there was any possibility of friendship – any common ground – between her and Rupert? He probably wouldn't even understand why she feels offended. If she had the nerve she'd tell him to turn round and drive back to Florence.

Once they've parked, Jo asks to see the garden, realising too late that "grounds" is probably the correct word. Acting the landed gentleman, Rupert ushers her around, very much at home as he names the exotic-looking shrubs and trees on display. After clearing drifts of leaves clogging a drain, he points to a field of leafy plants, explaining animatedly about a drainage system he's having installed. Pleased to see him serious for once, Jo feeds him questions, feigning more interest than she feels. If only his mother could be as easily fooled, she sighs, regretting having accepted the invitation. A sixth sense had warned her but she couldn't resist. She knows Rupert's expecting her to wow his mother but she feels cowed already; she'll never manage to be outrageous in front of a woman like her. Jo could kick herself. By the end of the day she'll be friendless and since Rupert hasn't found her a job she'll be stuck at Vanda's. Now she's gone and mucked things up, Jo begins to feel a little bit in love with Rupert.

Something prickles the side of her face. As Rupert weaves a tiny pink flower into her hair, Jo cheers up: maybe things will turn out all right. He's mad about her, so his mother can look down her nose all she likes!

'A penny for them.'

'Wouldn't you like to know,' she teases.

He reaches to take her hand but she pulls away. 'Catch me if you can,' she calls, racing off and darting into a field staked with tall poles, startlingly green nets draped loosely over them. Crisscrossing to avoid furrows, she screams with laughter whenever Rupert gets close. Catching up, he topples with her onto the ploughed ground. They lie a moment side by and she can tell he's happy.

'I haven't run like that since I was at school. I'm puffed.' He walks a finger up her arm.

Jo turns her head away. Couldn't she try? See what happens? He's the perfect candidate for her 'woman-of-the-world' plan. If she's serious about getting over Eamonn, she has to start soon. And Rupert's nice, really nice, so what's stopping her? She doesn't fancy him, that's what. Isn't that the idea? No – the idea is not to fall in love. She still has to fancy the person. Besides Rupert's in love with her, she'd be using him.

Leaning across, he kisses her cheek. 'Dear Jo.'

'Are you a virgin?' he asks shyly, opening out her hand with his. 'I suppose most Irish girls are, catholic and all that.'

Jo nods in a non-committal way.

'I know you'll laugh but sometimes I wish I were you. Everything about you is so … I don't know – fresh. It's like you're doing things, seeing things, for the first time. I feel so ancient. I'm glad we've met.'

He pulls her to him and feeling her resistance, whispers, 'A kiss?'

Jo lets him kiss her, surprised at the softness of his lips. If this sort of thing came naturally to her, she'd allow him make love just to give him something: a present of herself. She knows he wants her, his face slackening as he turns away. They don't speak and Rupert concentrates on blowing smoke rings that catch each other's tails, hover in the air above them. She can't force herself to have a relationship with someone because she likes them and the trouble is – despite their differences – she likes Rupert, really, really likes him.

'Do call me Margaret. Rupert's been telling me all about you. What part of Ireland are you from?'

Rupert's mother turns the full force of her brittle, enquiring eyes on Jo. The question seems harmless – asked as Margaret ladles a thin cold soup into Jo's bowl – but Jo's certain the woman intends making a meal of her.

'I hope the soup's all right. It's been in the fridge all week. Taste it, there's a good boy.'

Frowning, Rupert obeys. 'It's fine. I should warn you, Mummy's a real miser. She can't bear throwing anything away.'

'I hate waste. Where was it you said, Jo?'

'Dublin. The south side,' Jo answers, omitting it's the 'wrong side' of the south side; imitating, as best she can, the throwaway note in Margaret's voice. Hoping to pass.

'We have some wonderful friends over there. Con Dunne. You don't happen to know him? He has a practice in one of those streets near the Four Courts. Married one of the Fitzgerald girls. Imogen. Pretty little thing. Dim, but plenty of money.'

'Don't be silly Mummy, why would Jo know them?'

'It's such a dear little place, everybody seems to know everybody.' Margaret gazes frostily at Jo.

Anybody who's anybody, Jo thinks, trying to picture her own mammy cross-examining a visitor or letting them know they were being served week-old soup.

'It can't be that small.'

'Well darling, whenever I go over for the Horse Show it's impossible to get a moment to oneself. I'm sure I've met half of Ireland by now.'

'All the old fogies … Jo's not interested in those kinds of people, are you Jo?'

Jo shakes her head.

'What are you interested in?'

Jo's mouth dries. 'Art … painting,' she manages.

'Splendid. So we do have something in common. I like to think I get on with Rupert's chums. He has such a wide variety, don't you darling? Who was that funny boy you brought home … what was it he did?'

Jo stirs the soup round and round a turquoise Majolica bowl, darts a glance at Rupert; relieved to see he's gone bright red.

'Tell Mummy about Vanda. Jo works for this perfect ogre. You'd adore her, she's such a character.'

Jo makes an effort to describe Vanda and life at the pensione but it doesn't sound very funny and she's relieved when a girl carrying a tray interrupts. If nothing else there's food, she resigns herself, realising she's ravenous. Without speaking, the girl places a large serving plate on the table with a kind of dirty-looking jelly on it alongside an enormous bowl of salad.

'Tongue in aspic, Mummy's favourite,' Rupert announces.

Jo stares at the pinkish-brown mess lurking beneath the jelly, thinks she'll be sick. 'I'll have salad, I'm not that hungry.'

'More for us!' Margaret's eyes shine gluttonously.

On the verge of tears, Jo pushes a pink radish around her plate. This isn't at all how she'd imagined her visit! As soon as lunch is over, she'll suggest a drive; get Rupert to take her back into Florence. They can go somewhere, have a proper-

'I better go and pick up Phil,' Rupert announces. Release, Jo thinks, readying herself but with a 'back soon' in her direction, he wipes his mouth perfunctorily, drops the linen napkin on the table and with a jangle of keys is gone.

To cover up her disappointment, Jo finishes off her wine, folds and unfolds her napkin, then remembering Rupert's casual attitude, crumples it.

Two girls enter noiselessly, begin to clear the table. Jo wishes she could help; being waited on, having to act as if the maids aren't there is excruciating. The fact they're her own age makes it worse; at least Maria was older. As they pile dishes on top of one another, Jo realises she can't even tell which girl came in earlier.

'Coffee?'

It takes Jo a moment to realise Margaret's addressing her. She shakes her head, ransacking her brain for a witty remark but nothing obliges. Rupert's mother doesn't seem bothered by the lack of conversation, giving off an air of having plenty to think about. Surreptitiously, Jo studies her, wonders if anyone has ever got the better of her.

'You look tired my dear. The young don't seem to have half the energy we had in my day. We could dance until dawn for nights on end. What do you say we go native and have a siesta? Such a sensible idea, especially after a good lunch.' Turning to one of the maids, she addresses her in fluent Italian: for a few moments becoming a totally different person.

'Rafaela will show you to your room. There's hot water if you feel like a bath.'

Jo follows the girl upstairs; glad they don't speak the same language – somehow it helps. Peeking at Rafaela's blank face, Jo wonders if she despises or maybe envies her. It's weird being suddenly treated as if you're important and she's not quite sure how to behave. Not wanting to give the impression she takes this sort of thing for granted, Jo smiles benignly, as the maid, having opened the door, stands aside to let her in. As she squeezes past, a shrewd expression creeps into Rafaela's face and Jo blushes.

The room is dark and cool, slats in the shutters throwing beams of light across the polished wooden floor. Jo flops on the four-poster, dangling her feet over the side in case she dirties the pristine cover. Rafaela knows I'm not one of them, she thinks, as the maid's footsteps die away: we can smell each other out.

Away from Margaret's hostile gaze, Jo's bursting with energy, wishes she could go for a walk. Sliding off the bed, she wanders into the adjoining bathroom, sits on the edge of an old-fashioned, free-standing bath, making a face at the fat lion-faced feet bearing the weight. A padded kimono hangs invitingly on the back of the door, a pile of fluffy white towels on a small tiled table. Why not, she thinks, turning on the taps. On a shelf above the bath, bottles of fancy-looking bath oils are begging to be used and Jo chooses a pale green liquid that smells heavenly, hoping she's chanced on the most expensive. Drizzling it in, she uses twice as much as she would normally, giggling as the steaming water froths. Slipping out of her clothes, she sinks into the foamy bubbles, lets out a long slow sigh. What a relief to be on her own! Luxury, pure and utter luxury!

Remembering the insult of the week-old soup and Margaret's dislike of waste, Jo drips in more of the green stuff, swishing and splashing the water; the heat flushing her pink, the perfume making her heady. Adjusting her neck on the perfectly placed headrest, she catches sight of her bloated reflection in one of the gold taps. That's how she'd look after a few years of high living, not skinny as a rake like Mummy. What must it be like owning a place like this: no wonder Margaret's arrogant. She'd be arrogant if it was hers. And this is only their holiday home, Jo scoffs as she heaves herself out; wrapping herself in enough towels to dry a family.

Curled up on the bed, Jo begins to drift off. Out of nowhere, the story of Hansel and Gretel slips into her mind; it was one of Mark's favourites. On the verge of sleep the meaning of the fairy-tale seems crystal clear.

20

'We're going for a swim, c'mon lazybones,' Rupert's good-natured voice calls through the door.

Jo groans. She doesn't want to leave the warm wonderful place she's found.

He knocks lightly.

'Coming! Down in a sec.'

After pulling on her clothes, Jo smoothes the bed and hurrying into the bathroom, hangs up the towels, conceals the almost empty bottle behind the others. Racing downstairs, she runs her fingers through her hair to untangle it. By the time she reaches the front door, Rupert's words sink in. Shit! Now she's going to have to confess she can't swim. Oh God, she prays, let whoever Rupert went to meet not be able to swim either.

When she arrives at the pool, Jo finds only Rupert and his mother; Rupert already splashing about, Margaret soaking up the sun on a flowery beach chair.

'Get changed,' Rupert shouts, seeing her. 'The water's wonderful.'

His mother smiles wearily from her colourful perch.

'Give the girl a chance, Rupert. Poor darling, he gets so enthusiastic about things. Thank goodness for everyone's sake they die out quickly.' She throws Jo a pitying smile.

Jo's antennae rear: what a wagon! Does this woman think she's trying to steal her precious son? Meeting Margaret's eyes, Jo realises it's exactly what she thinks and she wants Jo to be under no illusion what her attitude is. So she isn't good enough?

'Maybe he's never found what he likes,' Jo counters. 'Rupert was telling me-'

'I think I know my son well enough,' Margaret cuts in.

'That's what my mother says about me.'

Ignoring her remark, Margaret turns attentively to Rupert as he wades towards them.

'What are you two talking about? C'mon Jo.' Expertly, he arches his body, dives in. Moments later, he surfaces, water spinning from him like shiny coins.

'You should have told me,' Jo protests, 'I didn't bring a swimsuit.'

'Oh Mummy, aren't there some at the house?'

'I don't think so. Who needs a swimsuit?'

As Margaret blithely unknots the sarong she's wearing, Jo looks away: she's never seen an older woman without clothes; would rather not. The thought scares her.

'Young girls and their modesty,' Margaret laughs.

Abandoned by the poolside, Jo watches as Margaret and Rupert cavort, pitching water over each other, dodging and play-acting as if she wasn't there. Now she's been exposed as an interloper, the two of them can get on with being themselves. For a second time, she wishes she hadn't come, wishes the ground would open up and swallow her.

'Philip! There you are!' Rupert bounces up in the water.

Turning, Jo sees a slim, tall, dark-haired man strolling down the path. Nearing her, he doffs an imaginary hat.

Rupert hops out and after shaking himself off like a dog, bounds towards the stranger. 'Where did you get to? I waited ages.'

Christ, he's like a Greek god in jeans, Jo thinks, observing the visitor's chiselled face, the line of his jaw, the perfect proportions of his body.

'I changed my mind, that's all, decided to walk.' A nasal

American accent tickles Jo's ears.

Covertly, she watches the newcomer peel off his jacket, drape it across a chair. The white shirt he's wearing is tight-fitting; his narrow denims show off his long legs, his hips, his- Jo swivels her eyes away as Rupert's mother emerges from the water, one gracious hand extended. Philip presses it to his lips, an amused expression on his face as if it's the most natural thing in the world for a middle-aged woman to pop up naked in front of him.

'Silly boy, walking all that way in the heat!' Margaret's magisterial voice booms. In a flash, Jo understands Rupert's mother doesn't need to be dressed: money clothes her. If anyone's naked it's Jo.

'At least I have the decency to wear something.'

'Fetch me a towel.'

He tosses her one and Margaret makes a show of wrapping it around her, flicking her hair seductively, her eyes sweeping the American from head to toe.

She's flirting, Jo realises.

'I don't think you two have met-' Rupert suddenly remembers her, 'Jo Nowd, this is Philip Stegner.'

'Hi,' he grins. 'You wanna watch the sun …'

'Sorry?'

'Skin like yours. I imagine it burns easily. Where are you from?'

'Ireland. Have you ever been?' she asks lamely.

'If the girls all look like you, I intend making it my business.'

"In Dublin's fair city, where the girls are so pretty …" Rupert begins to sing.

Jo wishes she could join in: swap 'shitty' for 'pretty'; if she were alone with Rupert she would but in front of his mother and this stranger she's scared no one would find it funny.

'Anything to drink?' Philip asks.

'I think that's the only reason you come and see us,' Margaret makes a pretence of minding. She's donned a bikini, is standing in a yoga position – hands joined above her head, one leg bent against her thigh.

'Can you think of a better one?'

Unfolding herself, Margaret places a hand on his shoulder, her red nails digging in.

A shock of jealousy takes Jo by surprise.

'Why don't we go up to the house, we'll all be more comfortable.'

Jo allows the others to walk ahead. Don't be so obvious, she warns herself; gorgeous or not, he's at least thirty, older maybe; probably thinks you're a kid.

'Phil likes to insult us, don't you darling?

'You love it,' she hears him respond.

The banter continues as they wend their way back. Since Philip's arrival everything is charged: as if someone pulled a switch and they've all come to life, discovered a reason to be together.

'We'll sit on the patio. Jo, see what state those chairs are in,' Margaret barks. 'I must have a word with Giorgio about leaving them out.'

'Allow me,' Philip offers, brushing past and hoisting several interlocking chairs effortlessly. While he's untangling them, the French doors open and Rupert appears, jiggling bottles.

When they're all seated, Philip selects one, holds it out. '*Est!Est! Est!*' he reads from the label. 'Know where the name comes from?' He directs the question at Jo.

She shakes her head.

'That's what I love about Florence; you get to recycle all the stories.' The wickerwork creaks as he settles back.

'It was like this,' he continues, 'once upon a time, this guy, who's rolling in money, wants to find the best wine in Tuscany so he sends his servants to all the vineyards, all the little mountain villages, all over the goddamned place. They spend years, a decade, sampling wine, investigating rumours, waiting for harvests to ripen. One day,' Philip raises a bottle, 'they stumble across this. The message they send back has only three words. *Est! Est! Est!* Here! Here! Here! And that's what it's been called ever since.'

Jo laughs out loud; Margaret and Rupert more dutifully.

'Guess they were drunk,' he adds, pushing the bottle aside.

They laugh some more. Fascinated, Jo watches as Philip chooses a different bottle. As the wine tinkles into their glasses, she sees in a future memory, four people sitting on a patio in Florence on a summer's day, laughing and talking. Perfect. For a moment.

'How's the painting coming along?' Rupert asks nonchalantly.

Jo almost chokes: he's an artist?!

She sees him tense, a muscle at the side of his face twitch. 'Now this is a good story,' he drawls. 'You know old Claude who paints those wonderful luminous male nudes. Well, some of his students wanted to know the secret: what he mixes to get that quality. Guess what he told them? Olive oil! Can you believe it? Olive oil!' Philip shakes with laughter. 'Olive oil,' he chortles. 'Wait, I haven't finished. Then he gives them the name of the most expensive kind – what's it called? – and they're off buying gallons of the stuff, thinking they'll turn out little Michelangelos. Or McAngelos as we say back home'

He undoes the top button on his shirt and Jo gets a glimpse of dark curly hair.

'What a naughty man,' Margaret scolds. 'Those poor students.'

Philip scowls, anger darkening his eyes. Then he snorts. 'Assholes! Most of them wouldn't know a good painting if it hit them in the face.'

'Who do you think is good?' Jo asks. 'I mean painters.'

One of Rupert's eyebrows arch and Jo's face flames. What made her ask such a ridiculous question!

'How much time have you got?'

'Phil's a wonderful painter but he can get a little touchy on the subject, can't you darling?' Margaret re-fills his glass.

'Painting's like any other goddamned work. The last thing an artist needs is a shrine. It makes me want to throw up, all these mini-gods prancing around Florence with their palettes and penises.'

'Now Philip, there's no need to get carried away. We know who you're talking about and Stefano's a good painter, whatever you say.'

'I'm not just talking about that creep; the whole damn lot should be boiled in oil.'

Margaret angles her body to catch the remaining sun. Once she finds a comfortable position, she wags her sunglasses.

'You're not doing yourself any favours. You know as well as I do you're one of the best painters in Florence. It's up to you what happens ...'

Jo's pulse goes into overdrive: "one of the best painters in Florence"! And what does Margaret mean it's up to him what happens? She checks to see the American's reaction but he's staring into the distance as if he hadn't heard, the tick in his cheek more pronounced.

After a moment, he tips his glass, knocks it back in one go.

'Staying for supper?' Margaret enquires without moving.

Please, Jo prays, please.

'Thanks for the offer. Guess I'll mosey on down the highway. Grab a bite later.'

'Don't be an idiot. Rupert will run you in.'

And I'll come, Jo adds silently.

'No sweat man.' Rupert's on his feet.

'I prefer the exercise,' Philip asserts. 'I'm sure we'll meet again,' he bows slightly to Jo then with a curt nod, walks down the drive and out of sight.

A warm wind whistles past Jo's ears, whips at her hair. She half-stands as Rupert accelerates, the low-lying car hugging the verge on a sudden bend. Wow! It's like living the speed, being part of it.

Below, Florence sparkles like a jeweller's display case: all she has to do is reach out and help herself. Anything's possible. Rupert plus money ... make things possible. Jo feels light, dizzy. God, the amount she drank to hide her disappointment after Philip left. It's not as if she even knows him; she might never see him again. At the thought her heart flips.

'Why are you slowing?' she asks crossly.

'Jo, sit down, the *caribinieri* don't like foreigners taking liberties.'

'Who's afraid of the *caribinieri*? Poor little Rupes,' Jo jeers.

'Come on Jo, don't be a pain.'

To annoy him, Jo grabs at the windscreen, hitches herself up further.

'Look at me!'

'You're crazy!'

Jo braces herself, feels her stomach heave. Why is she doing this: she'll make herself sick. She flops down.

'Be a bore then.'

'You're white as a sheet.'

'I'm fine, just drive.'

She can see Rupert watching her out of the corner of his eye. Suddenly, she feels sober, empty. Why did Philip leave and ruin the whole evening?

'What did you think of Phil? He seemed to like you.'

So she wasn't imagining things! Jo hides her delight; Rupert mightn't appreciate her thoughts about Philip.

'How do you know him?' she asks.

'Mummy bought a few of his paintings. Actually, he reminds me of you.'

'Me? In what way?'

'He's angry at things although he makes more of a joke of it.'

'Thanks, you mean I'm a moan.'

She pretends to sulk knowing Rupert hates being misunderstood: being liked is vital to him. That's one thing they have in common.

'I love it when you pout,' Rupert teases.

'I don't pout! Silly English girls pout,' Jo blazes then bursts out laughing. Rupert joins in, squeezes her hand.

'How would you like to go to Sienna on Sunday?'

'*Mi piace molto, molto, molto*!' Jo beams, conveniently forgetting her intention of staying in and working the following weekend. Besides, one more week won't make much difference; she'll get stuck in the following Sunday. Definitely.

'Is he that good a painter?' Jo fishes.

'Pretty good. I think so and so does Mummy which probably means he is. There's one little problem.'

'What?'

'He hasn't finished anything for yonks. He starts canvases then stops before they're finished.'

'How does anyone know he's good?'

'He had a one-man show when he came to Florence, a few years back. It was a complete sell-out, took the art world by storm.'

'Maybe he's dried up?'

'I don't think so. I think he rather fancies the idea of the struggling artist. Not that he starves, he lives off a legacy, investments, nothing much. Came to Mummy once for a little advice. Daddy might be the banker but Mummy's the brains especially when it comes to money.' He stops. 'I don't think he wants to be successful. According to Phil that's for creeps like Stefano or Michele. I remember him saying – of course he put it in a rather funny way – that once an artist's work starts selling, you know he's producing shit.'

'That's stupid. What about good books or films, no one says they're shit because people like them.'

'Maybe art's different. Mummy thinks it's oedipal, his mother's a painter; quite famous in the States, has a huge reputation. You'll have to ask him.'

Jo hopes she'll get the chance. The more she hears about Philip, the more intriguing he sounds. Different anyway: someone who makes his own rules. There's an air of mystery about him too that attracts her.

'He's full of stories isn't he?' Jo asks to keep the conversation going.

'Want to hear a good one about him and Mummy?'

Jo's not sure she does, has an awful feeling he's going to tell her they had an affair.

Rupert laughs at the memory.

'It must be about two years ago, she decided to buy a painting from him before he'd completed it. She'd called to his studio one day and saw it, paid quite a bit. I think she thought it would force his hand. You've met Mummy – she likes to get her way. A few months later, he arrives up to the house with the canvas, still half-finished – hands her back half the money.'

Rupert hiccups with laughter and Jo wonders if she could ask – casually – where Philip's studio is. Although what she'd really like to find out is whether he has a girlfriend? He could be married for all she knows, although he didn't seem married.

'Your mother likes him?' she angles, risking disappointment.

'I don't think they've slept together,' he says after a pause. 'But from what I hear, he goes through women like wildfire. Mamas fall for him, then daughters see him as a challenge. He can be charming when he wants to be.'

Realising she's already begun to spin a story about Philip – one in which he lives an ascetic existence dedicated to art, despising women but prepared to make an exception for her – Jo's sorry she asked. Discovering he has the same effect on lots of women is not what she wants to hear.

'Don't say you haven't been told,' Rupert jokes although Jo detects a cautionary note in his voice.

'Why do I need to be warned?'

'You might bump into him in your travels. He lives near Santa Croce.'

'I'm going straight there tomorrow.' Jo pinches Rupert's arm playfully; secretly wondering if she'd dare.

'Would you like to go for a coffee or a nightcap, it's early?'

Glancing out, she sees they're almost at Vanda's. She doesn't have anything left to say; would prefer to be alone so she can sift over everything that's happened. Besides, after that kiss, it's important to make clear only friendship's on offer.

'Have to get up early. Work, remember that four-letter word?

But thanks for today. I had a great time,' she fibs, although it's partially true. 'A change from this dump!'

'I nearly forgot,' Rupert exclaims as she moves to get out, 'well I didn't, it's more I'm not sure if it's your thing.'

'What?'

'Remember I said I'd find you a job? Well, I have. Modelling at the *Nuova Scuola dell'Arte*. It's one of the best-known art schools in Florence for foreign students.'

Jo's face drops.

'I didn't think so. Especially after the episode at the swimming pool. Pity. It's good money.'

Jo remembers the models at college: nobody batted an eyelid.

'You think I'm an eejit don't you?'

'It's not like stripping. Look at mother – she'd take her clothes off in front of a bishop. Probably has.' Rupert giggles. 'Besides, where would all the great painters be if they didn't have models?'

Rupert's right, nudes are taken for granted, have been for centuries. She can remember coming across a curious painting of a young woman sprawled naked on a sofa, her head tossed back, an enigmatic smile on her face. The pose was slightly shocking and Jo had been amazed to discover the model was an Irish girl from Cork. It didn't tally with anything she'd been led to believe about Irish women, especially Irish women in the nineteenth century.

A light goes on in one of the downstairs windows and Jo can see Vanda looking out. 'Mind you, I don't know how much longer I can hack it here. I better go in. She's probably waiting to scream at me over something.'

For once Rupert doesn't get out. Leaning across, he brushes his lips against hers. 'I enjoyed today too.'

Jo gives him an ambiguous smile. 'Give us a ring,' she shouts as he drives off.

As she tiptoes into the pensione, Vanda scuttles into the hallway, a towel round her head, her skin damp and mottled after showering; the silky dressing gown she's wearing clinging to her body, exposing rolls of bulging flesh. Jo grimaces. With a figure like that you'd think she'd put on a few more clothes.

'*Ancora l'Inglese?*'

'*Si.*'

'*Ricca, ricca,*' she rubs her fingers.

'*Amico,*' Jo insists, knowing from the gleam in Vanda's eyes what she's getting at. '*Sono stanca,*' she adds, yawning spontaneously.

Vanda stands aside but as Jo passes she grabs at her skirt, hoists it up.

'*Basta, basta,*' Jo shouts, wriggling to get out of her grip.

'*Poverina,*' Vanda laughs scornfully, pinching her thigh.

Freeing herself, Jo scrambles upstairs, followed by peels of raucous laughter.

From where she's standing at the top of Torre del Mangia, Jo can see the whole of Sienna. She'd always assumed the reproductions she'd seen were touched up but if anything the reality's more vivid: it's like looking at a living painting.

'Did you know the city went into a grand decline when the Florentines took over? They didn't even allow them run a bank. That's what preserved the place.'

Jo nods at Rupert, surprised as usual by the titbits he knows; things to do with banking, she thinks, a little disdainfully.

'Jo,' Rupert whines, waving his arms in front of her face, 'you promised.'

'I know. But doesn't the view make you glow inside?'

'Yes. With hunger! When I said I'd take you to Sienna I didn't expect to be punished.'

'I thought that's what public schoolboys loved. And shut up, we've hardly begun.'

'Apart from the five hundred and five steps you've just forced me to climb, I've been dragged round the Palazzo Publico as well as three churches and I haven't even had my mid-morning coffee.'

'Alright we'll go for coffee, after that we'll visit the Cathedral then the Museo. It has these wonderful paintings by Duccio.'

'I don't know how you can tell one medieval painting from the next,' Rupert grumbles. 'They all look the same. It must be a Catholic thing.'

Jo ignores him. It would probably be better if they split up and she went to the museum on her own before going back to the Palazzo. She definitely wants to see the Maestas again: allow herself wallow in it without Rupert fidgeting. Simone Martini is – was – an absolute genius! How could anyone look at that fresco and not be astounded! Even remembering it makes her shiver.

Reluctantly, she trails Rupert down to the foyer, out into the sun-blown square. Tourists, ensconced beneath umbrellas, shoot sympathetic glances as the pair of them bumble past chairs and tables scattered appealingly in their way. From habit, Jo's about to check the prices when she remembers Rupert's doing the honours. Shaking her head with amusement, she watches him gauge the best cafe and a moment later they're sitting in comfortable chairs, fat cups of coffees steaming in front of them.

'Let's have some panforte.' Rupert licks his lips as he scans the menu. 'Scrumptious. Sienna's famous for it, you know.'

While he orders, Jo studies his plump boyish face, a lock of blond hair over one eye, his crumpled but expensive linen suit, a pale silky scarf setting it off. All week, she'd day-dreamed about being here but in her fantasies it was Philip who accompanied her, Philip whose hand held hers, whose breath she felt on her neck as they went from painting to painting.

'We'll come again when the *Palio*'s on,' Rupert announces, pushing a strand of hair away.

'The what?'

'The *Palio*. It's a horse race, Italian style. They have it twice a year. The riders dress up in all this medieval gear and go tearing round the Campo. It's pretty spectacular although Mummy thinks it should be abolished. I suppose horses do get injured occasionally. As far as I know there've never been any fatalities.'

'Sounds awful. What's it for?'

'To commemorate the battle of *Monaeaperti*. And to live dangerously. You should try it sometime Jo. All these museums will turn you into a dull old gel.'

Jo sighs. Rupert's definitely the wrong person to have come here with!

'Here we are!' Rupert's eyes brighten as a waiter appears with a plate of goodies.

Jo breaks off a piece from a thick slab of cake, takes a bite. It tastes spicy, fruity, like hard Christmas pudding.

'Now try the *copate*, they're superb!'

'These?' she asks, picking up a wafery-looking cake.

'Eemm. Now, this is what I call getting to know Sienna,' Rupert laughs. 'Better than any old painting.'

'I suppose this is your idea of living dangerously?'

Rupert taps his midriff. 'You bet.'

Jo giggles. It's impossible to stay annoyed at Rupert for long.

The following morning, Jo sleepwalks through the bedrooms and as soon as they're done, she hurries to the kitchen. Vanda's been entrenched there since breakfast, poring over an accounts ledger; receipts and invoices strewn across the table. Babbo's out playing bowls, so Jo plonks herself in front of the range, waiting for Vanda to tell her if anything else needs doing. Ignoring her, the landlady carries on totting figures, cursing and muttering as she jots down calculations. Tell me I'm finished, Jo begs silently. She feels giddy: if she doesn't lie down soon she'll expire. Next time she's out with Rupert she mustn't let him keep her out so late. Or ply her with alcohol. It's alright for him; he's probably still sleeping it off.

'*C'e un uomo teleponarci,*' Vanda mutters as she turns a page, almost as an afterthought.

'When? *Quando?*' Jo is suddenly wide awake. What man could be telephoning her?

'*Ieri pomeriggio.*'

Yesterday afternoon! But she was in Sienna with Rupert. Her insides churn, '*Che telephonarmi?*' " L'Inglese?" She uses Vanda's nickname for Rupert.

'*Non lo so,*' Vanda shrugs.

You don't know! Jo doesn't believe her for a second. Her thoughts race. The only other man she knows in Florence is Philip. Could he have phoned? It would be easy enough for him to find out where she works.

'*Era un Americano telephonarmi Vanda, un uomo Americano?*' Fuck her Italian, she should learn to speak it properly. Vanda puckers her crimson lips, points with her pen towards an overflowing bin.

'*Io?*' Jo responds indignantly. Since when did it become her job to carry out bins?

'*Subito*! Now!' Vanda orders.

Jo would like to tell her what she can do with it but she hasn't the words or the heart; besides she'd rather not antagonise her employer right this moment. Trying to ignore the stench, she makes a feeble attempt at lifting the bin but the pong makes her want to retch and she lets go. Emitting a string of curses, Vanda rushes across the room.

'*Cosi, cosi,*' she indicates to Jo to put her arms round it.

Jo looks from the bin to Vanda: there's no way she's going to embrace the rotten smelly thing. 'Do it yourself!' she explodes. '*Non sono sciave!*'

The words stop Vanda in her tracks. Her eyes narrow.

'*Sciave, sciave,* slave, slave!' Jo goads, all caution gone.

Letting out a shriek, Vanda flings herself at the girl. As Jo leaps to avoid her, her foot slides. Hoping to save herself, she grabs at Vanda, pulling the landlady with her as she falls, the bin following in slow motion, a tidal wave of weeping rubbish oozing out over the brightly-tiled floor.

21

Jo peeps through a slit in the Chinese screen. The classroom's beginning to fill as more and more students crowd in. A few are already at work, legs visible beneath easels. Pinning up her hair, Jo thinks of the little mermaid in the fountain at the front of the school; wishes she could borrow the immobile curls covering her breasts, the long scaly fish tail. Opening the buttons on her dress, her hands fumble. She knows from experience that none of those drawing her will give a damn what her body looks like — in fact the less "normal" the better — but she does. Always has. The first time Eamonn had undressed her she'd closed her eyes — afraid to see — afraid of him seeing; petrified of what lay beneath her clothes. He'd got her to stand naked in front of a mirror: made her look, made her touch, made her say words out loud. To please him she'd mouthed the words, faked touching. Beautiful, he'd pronounced and she'd rushed to agree, relieved it hadn't seemed that different from bodies she'd scrutinized in art books and galleries. She'd kept her mouth shut about the repulsion she felt at the puckered skin around her nipples, the gash between her legs. Terror coated the surface of her skin, was etched into the curves of her body. It couldn't be otherwise! All her life, everyone — nuns at school, her mammy — had taught her to fear it, hate everything to do with it. Mortify the body, they'd urged, deny its existence. In a funny way she'd only ever felt free of it when she and Eamonn …

A rising hum on the other side of the screen alarms her. Quickly, Jo pulls off her dress, slips out of her underwear; quells an urge to put everything back on and run out of the room. She should never have let Rupert persuade her — he's not the one posing. Why is she always ending up in situations where not doing something is as difficult as doing it?

Blank your mind, she urges herself, edging out, grateful for the little bit of cover an uncomfortable-looking chair offers; choosing a sideways position so as much of her body as possible is hidden. A few students glance up; others are preoccupied sorting through pencils and charcoal. One or two drift around the room, looking vaguely in her direction. The moment she's been dreading comes and goes. When her heart stops pounding, it dawns on Jo nothing's going to happen: she's just another prop to measure and explore as if she were a basket of fruit. She feels stupid – in some weird sense outraged – like the time she'd lost her virginity and expected the whole world to come crashing down. It had hurt, that was all, and not that much. Naturally, no one had warned her the real pain comes later. "Don't," is all you got told. Not why.

Inviolate. The word was in one of the hymns they sang in Special Choir at school. Is her body no longer inviolate? Most likely not, if it means what she thinks it does. Squinting down, she's aware how detached it seems, as if it belongs to someone else.

The would-be artists study her – faces screwed up – trying to pick an angle; an easy one she imagines. A smiley girl with a chiffon scarf holding back long mousy hair, abandons her easel, sits on the floor in front of the platform. Time ticks by and Jo forgets she's not wearing clothes. Their probing reduces her to something abstract and she begins to feel a kind of power over them as they labour to produce an acceptable image. A few of them seem as nervous as she is; hearing their sighs and coughs she's back at mass on Sunday morning, all eyes on the altar as the priest holds up the body of Jesus Christ. This time it's her body on the altar: a woman's body.

'Jo, could we change the pose after break?'

Looking up from her coffee, Jo smiles at Lia, notices she's wearing a pale green scarf with splodges of red this morning; she must have a drawer-full.

'Sure, how would you like it?'

Lincoln, one of the American students, struts forward, cupping his hands to his chest, 'How about this?' he sniggers.

There are a few forced giggles.

'Very funny, prick.'

As soon as the words are out, Jo regrets them. Lincoln might be a bastard but he's a rich bastard whose father's made some kind of endowment to the college. According to the grapevine, he's forever in the director's office, grassing on anyone he doesn't like. Jo's in his bad books already. At the end of her first week, he'd asked her out and she'd refused. She doesn't like him, has no idea why he's there: all he draws is the same caricature over and over, all exaggerated breasts and distorted bum.

He glares at her, furious in front of the other students.

'This one can talk, remember the last one? Boy, was she dumb.'

'You mean she didn't fall for your cheque-book.' Tony, the youngest guy in the class makes a pretend swipe at Lincoln's baseball cap. 'Aaww!'

'Aaww,' everyone joins in.

Lincoln's neck reddens. 'Scholarships can be rescinded,' he smirks at the younger boy.

'Up yours,' Tony hisses, giving him the finger.

A bell rings. Slipping out of her dressing gown, Jo offers a series of turns and twists, contorting her body until they agree a pose. This one's not too demanding, she thinks, at least she can rest her head on her arms. She's only been modelling a few weeks but already it's driving her crazy. Most of the students are alright but there are a few toffee-nosed Brits and pain-in-the-ass Yanks she'd like to hang and not in a gallery! And she's bored, bored, bored: it should be her on the other side of the dais. The monotony of sitting has much the same effect as working at Vanda's did. After hours of posing, all she's in the mood for is gorging herself in some trattoria with Rupert or lounging with him outside a cafe … hoping Philip might show up, a voice in her head completes. Okay, she hushes it, that's definitely at the back of her mind although it's still hard to admit she fancies someone. Even to herself. Not that she's in love! Eamonn- her mind snatches at his name although she senses something's changed … is changing. Not that the pain's gone away – it's there, the ghost of it anyway.

'If you could turn slightly, stare out the window,' Lia whispers. Jo nods. She doesn't mind doing what the English girl asks; she has talent and unlike most of the others, she's serious. Jo's caught sight of her a couple of times in the Uffizi or out on the street sketching. She envies her ability to sit so self-contained, a box of pencils and crayons at her feet, heedless of traffic or passers-by stopping to gawk. Maybe she should suggest going for a coffee, it would be nice to have a girl to talk to. Mentally, Jo traces Lia's aquiline nose, full lips, slightly hooded eyes, the long wispy hair gathered in a scarf as usual. Changes her mind. There's something too posh-hippy about her: like the world's one great big adventure playground. Probably is for her. Rupert knows her vaguely, remembers meeting her at some diplomatic bash. Jo had filed away his remark. What was it, oh yes, "she's rather jolly". "Jolly"! God, Rupert's an eejit sometimes.

A cramp brings Jo back to earth; as she adjusts her leg, Lincoln sighs impatiently. Gee whiz, I hope I didn't spoil your masterpiece! Jo smirks inwardly. Oh no, now she has an itch on the inside of her thigh. She allows the tickle go on as long as she can bear it then inching a hand along, scratches. Lincoln slaps down his pencil. Jo reddens.

'Would it be too much trouble to go back to the original pose?' he asks.

Fuck you! Try sitting like this, Jo seethes. Damn, there has to be easier ways to earn money. Marry a rich man like Rupert. She would – if only she could fall in love with him.

It's Saturday and Jo lazes on her bunk. She's the last one left in the room but then unlike her all the others are on holidays. Time to make herself scarce, she thinks, hearing the cleaners' chatter in the next dormitory. Mingling with a group of Americans, she sneaks down the stairs to the reception area, hoping Paolo isn't on duty. He's already spoken to her, several times, about overstaying her welcome. This morning she's in luck: there's someone new on the desk and she gives the woman a quick wave before stepping into the sunshine.

It's not that she doesn't want to move; she'd love to have her own space. If she can swing another month, she should have enough saved for a deposit on an apartment or at least a room in one. Provided she doesn't eat! When she thinks of all those rich kids at the school, it really bugs her. She could always ask Rupert, he'd be only too glad to lend her money, give it to her if she'd take it. But she's too much in his debt already.

Standing on the Ponte Vecchio, Jo toys with the idea of going to see the Giottos at Santa Croce. Aware her motives are anything but pure, she's been putting it off, half-afraid of bumping into Philip, half-wanting to. Not this morning either, she resolves, turning in the direction of the Uffizi. She'll spend her time with the Ducios and Martinis. Be good.

Dodging in through the revolving doors, Jo dawdles in the foyer. She loves the moment of arrival: the grandeur, the possibilities, the expressions on visitors' faces.

'Hi,' a voice calls and Lia trips over, all starry-eyed. 'I've just been to see the *Primavera*,' she thrills. 'It's sooo beautiful!'

That definitely puts paid to coffee, Jo decides. How can anyone rate Botticelli and his pretty pictures, the Primavera most of all! She might have guessed it would be the kind of painting Lia likes.

22

Not much longer, Jo calculates, steeling herself to hold the pose. Two more days and the whole school's off to Switzerland for a week to paint mountains and ski. Get pissed on the piste, lucky bastards! Naturally, she isn't invited. And Rupert won't be around; he's gone sailing with his parents. Someone lent them a yacht. Just like that. Along with a cook, a masseur and God knows what else. Oh, well, she'll use the break to find somewhere to live; even if they don't throw her out, she'll go bananas if she hears another drawly Yank saying they're "doing Europe".

Bent over in an awkward position, she watches upside-down as a flock of birds fly across an empty sky. They could be on their way anywhere, Ireland even. She'd give her right arm to be going home for a few days: meandering up Grafton Street, heading into Keoghs for a drink. She can almost feel the fuggy atmosphere, see the excited faces of her friends as she walks in. "Look who's back, the arse tit! Jaysus! How's it going with the Hightalians?"

She couldn't risk it: one glimpse of Eamonn, a mention, and she'd be back at square one.

The birds – or birds that look like them – double back as if they'd gone the wrong way or changed their minds. What would it be like if humans could fly? More and more, Jo feels she has no control over anything. She does things or goes places because she has no other choice. Maybe free will is something the Catholic Church- Her reverie's interrupted by shuffling, someone whispering, and Jo checks to make sure her pose hasn't slackened; a couple of afternoons ago she'd fallen asleep. No fear of that today: the position is a killer. As soon as the holidays are over, she's going to insist on more breaks; she could sit until the cows come home and most of this lot wouldn't improve.

A boy, just in front of her, exhales, his face creased with effort. Jo looks at him sympathetically. It's not their fault, half of them are only putting in time before going to college; taking the course because their parents think it's the "right thing". In the long run, they'll end up lawyers, accountants, married with –

Clang, clang –

Whipping on her dressing gown, Jo feels a twinge of excitement. At the hostel the previous evening, she'd got talking to a French girl – after noticing her diary had a reproduction of Mona Lisa on the cover – and the girl had agreed to sit for her. Jo hopes she'll show up: having a model will give her the boost she needs to get going again. As she steps down from the platform, she's suddenly aware of someone hovering at the back of the class. Fucking hell! What's he- Jo's about to call out but Philip is already leaving the room.

The American is standing by the little mermaid, talking to a couple of older students. Catching sight of Jo, he raises an eyebrow. The girls turn, give Jo the once over before drifting off.

'Hello.'

'Hi there.'

He bursts out laughing. 'You sure look solemn!'

'No- em – I wasn't sure you knew it was me.' Jo blurts the first thing that comes in to her head. 'And no jokes about not recognising me with my clothes off,' she adds.

'Touchy, aren't you?'

'That was meant to be a joke. Anyway, I thought you were supposed to be the touchy one!' Jo could kick herself. Why is she being so uptight?

'Do you come here often, the school ... I mean.' Great! Clichés now!

'I used teach here occasionally – if that's the right word. Let's go. For an original line like that, the least I can do is buy you a coffee. There's a half-decent joint on the next block.'

'I wouldn't mind being asked.'

Philip makes a play of scratching his head. 'The formal type! I'd never have guessed. Would you care to join me for a beverage?' Without waiting for an answer, he lopes off. Jo remains where she is.

'What now?' he demands, turning round.

'This isn't Japan, ye know.'

He scurries back, bowing his head, rolling his arms round one another, mock oriental. 'Real touchy.' A hand flicks her chin. 'Coming?'

Jo searches the distance. One part of her is kissing him; another part is getting as far away as possible. Who does he think he is, turning up like this, thinking he can snap his fingers?

'Have I said something to upset you?'

Jo turns on her heel but he catches her arm.

'Why don't you stop playing games?'

'I don't know what you're talking about.'

'I think you do.'

He looks into her eyes and Jo flushes.

'I get it. C'mon. We'll tell each other our life stories over a cup of coffee and then we'll go back to my apartment and fuck like hell. How does that sound?' He grins. 'We could skip coffee?'

Jo can't decide whether to laugh or cry.

Philip links her arm. 'Just my luck, the kind who needs the life story.'

As Jo's steps match Philip's, she remembers a newspaper story about a man who'd walked twenty yards with a knife in his chest before keeling over. His brain had taken all that time to register he was dead. Any moment now, she's going to fall flat on her face. But before that happens, she's going to walk away from this madman. Why? Because he'd spoken her thoughts out loud, thoughts she's ashamed of, would rather pretend she doesn't have?

An arm winds its way round her neck. 'Let's go back to my place.'

Jo studies the ground, tears stinging her eyelids.

A hand raises her face to his. 'I make the best coffee in Florence.'

Church bells ring out as Jo accompanies Philip up the stairs to his apartment and she crosses her fingers it's a good omen. He ushers her into a large light-filled room and she reads it quickly: the objet d'art littered everywhere, an Eastern-looking hanging covering an entire wall – the sun picking out threads of gold – a bookcase crammed with art books. She feels intimidated, out of her depth and has to suppress a feeling she's on the verge of making a terrible mistake. On their way there, she'd stolen glances at Philip, bowled over by his looks, aware of heads turning as they passed; aware too of what Rupert had said about him going through women like wildfire. She definitely fancies him: is that a good enough reason to sleep with him? Wasn't that the plan? Theoretically yes, but now she's here, now he's taking off his jacket-

'Come here.'

Jo stumbles across the room. As she gets closer, he reaches for her and gripping the back of her head opens her mouth with his tongue. The kiss ignites and she folds herself into him.

'Not so fast.'

Taking her by the hand, he leads her to the bedroom. The bed has been made and she wonders if he made it for her; was so sure she'd come?

'You have five minutes,' he tells her, lying flat-out.

Mortified, awkward, Jo scrambles up beside him, bends to kiss him.

'No kissing.'

She freezes. Whenever she and Eamonn made love they were usually half-pissed; he did everything anyway.

'Don't tell me you're a virgin?'

'Sort of,' she mumbles.

'I can see you're gonna need a few lessons. Hey, hey, I'm only teasing,' he soothes, as redness creeps up Jo's neck. Turning her towards him, he kisses her hairline, her forehead, burrows into the neckline of her dress. 'Lie on top, I want to feel your weight.'

Jo rolls over. Maybe she should explain: he probably doesn't understand what it's like growing up in Ireland, being brought up catholic.

'No talking,' he warns, putting a finger to her lips. In desperation, Jo bites it and he yelps.

'I knew I had a little tiger,' he jokes, slipping a hand under her dress. 'Now let's see what we've got up here.'

Naked to the waist, Philip stands near the window gazing down at the square. Freshly showered and dressed, Jo nestles into him, her whole body basking in the afterglow of having finally done it.

'Something up?'

'Nope.'

Breathing in his smell, Jo idly watches the tourists below. A few seem to have called it a day, are planted outside one or other of the myriad cafes, looking tired and bored, their battered guidebooks off-duty. How cool to have an apartment this close to Santa Croce! The church, at the far end of the piazza, glimmers in a late afternoon haze. Giotto's frescos spring into Jo's mind – vanish as her bare arm meets Philip's. It's a year since she slept with Eamonn, since anyone touched her; not counting the silly episode with Gino. As Philip pulls her closer, she nuzzles his warm skin. Without warning, a drizzly feeling of guilt dampens her spirits. It's stupid, Eamonn has no claim on her; probably never gives her a second thought. Their relationship is over. That's not the problem, she realises: it's her own feelings she's being unfaithful to: feelings she'd thought unchangeable. And they are, she tells herself: it's not as if she's in love with Philip; or there's the slightest chance he could take Eamonn's place...

'Could I see some of your work?' she asks, anxious for something objective to cling to, to exonerate her.

'Another time. Throw on your jacket and we'll go rustle up a drink.'

"Another time." So it isn't going to be a once-off!

Jo follows Philip back into the bedroom. Whistling, he picks a shirt with a pattern of tiny flowers from his wardrobe. As he buttons it, Jo notices a small painting, icon-like, on the wall above the bed. It's a woman's neck seen from the back; her hair done up in a French pleat. The skin tones are translucent as if it's just been painted; an incredible serenity pervades the study. Jo wonders if it's one of Philip's; wonders who the woman is?

'Ready?' he asks, slinging a leather jacket over his shoulder. Jo's heart misses a beat. As they trip down the stairs, she congratulates herself. Who needs to be in love! Maybe she'll turn into a woman of the world after all.

Goodbye to this dump, Jo thinks, humming as she folds her clothes, squashes them into a new holdall. Hallelujah! No more being woken up by someone climbing into the wrong bunk.

'Going somewhere?' Rupert sticks his head round the door before sashaying in. He looks great after his sailing holiday, tanned and healthy, a little thinner. Seeing him, Jo realises how caught up she's been with Phil.

'I called the other day but there was no answer,' she gets in quickly, leaving out how relieved she'd been; wonders if he's heard. 'You've been away ages, were you sailing the whole time?' she babbles on, wishing he'd say something if he knows, make it easier for both of them.

'Very busy, very sorry,' he pipes in a silly robotic voice.

'I'm moving out.'

'So I see.' He gives a wave. 'Can it wait? Have you time for a coffee?'

Jo nods, realising that after today things might be awkward for a while. Something tells her the happy threesome she'd pictured isn't going to happen. She senses sadness behind Rupert's nonchalance as he chirrups on about the life of a sailor lad, larding it on, for once trying too hard. Well, she's sad too: for his sake she wishes it was anyone but Philip.

The street's crowded and she waits for Rupert's arm to snake her shoulder but he trails at her side, arms hanging. Up ahead a busload of sight-seers are blocking the street outside the Bargello and it's on the tip of Jo's tongue to tease him about the pretendy row they'd had the time they went there, a silly argument over Donatello's David: Rupert insisting it was a masterpiece, Jo refusing to agree. He'd almost got them thrown out, imitating a sculpture of Mercury they'd seen, giggling and acting as if was about to topple over. The sombre tower of Palazzo Vecchio looms and for the first time Jo feels as if Florence has lost some of its magic. Stubbornly, she digs her hands into the pockets of her tweed jacket. As she does, her fingers touch the miraculous medal. Stroking it, she remembers her desperate plea the day she arrived in Rome; realises a miracle of sorts has occurred: it would be greedy to expect perfection.

Rupert pulls out a chair and Jo realises they've ended up in the same cafe they met in all those months ago; wonders if he chose it on purpose. Back then as they'd sat stuffing themselves with cake, she'd had a feeling her life was going to change. Now it's about to change again.

'You're smoking a lot,' she says to break the silence as they wait for their order to arrive. He stubs a cigarette out, lights up another.

Why doesn't he get it over with?

'Mummy's gone back to England. She asked me to give you her regards.'

I bet she did, Jo thinks, slicing into her pastry; wishing they hadn't ordered torta Brasilianas, they're too rich and her stomach's queasy enough. For once, Rupert seems to have lost his appetite.

'Fancy a walk?' he suggests, leaving his cake uneaten.

The Arno is almost dried out, smelly; the water mark on the wall like a dirty ring on someone's neck. As they mooch along wordlessly, Jo spots an umbrella belly-up in the mud, recalls the two of them sitting underneath one in Sienna sharing panatone when Philip was nothing but a pipe-dream. Voices carry and she sees three women in skin-tight dresses and high-heels loitering in the entrance of a *palazzo*, their eyes gliding towards each passing car. She thinks of Gino, wonders if he's still hanging around the hostel, chatting up foreign girls? And Kevin, if he ever got off with any of those German women? Probably all spoof. Feeling nostalgic, she tucks her arm into Rupert's, squeezes it, angles her head towards the rickshaw clutter of Ponte Vecchio. Once she's moved in with Philip – not long afterwards anyway – she'll invite Rupert for dinner and slowly, slowly, things will go back to normal.

'This view is the only thing I'll miss,' he says without looking at her. 'And you of course. Goes without saying.'

Jo feels an icy trickle down her spine, hopes Rupert doesn't mean what she thinks he means. 'What are you talking about! You're not leav- That's stupid! You don't have to!'

'Afraid so, old gel. Phil's a dear but ... male pride, you know how it is.'

'No, I don't know how it is. We can still see each other. I'm not going to prison.' She can't bear the idea of his going. She needs Rupert. Without him, things are too – real.

A hand closes over hers.

'I hope you'll be happy.'

'Piss off. Just piss off. Don't always be such a fuckin' gentleman!'

'You haven't seen my mind.'

'Bastard!'

They laugh, Jo's laughter turning to tears as she buries her head in his shirt.

'Are you really going? Where? Home?'

'Greece actually. For a few months. Would you like to come? You're welcome.'

Jo looks into his face, sees he means it.

'No strings, I promise. Cross me heart and hope to die,' he adds in an Irish accent.

Jo's lip quivers, she feels she really might cry. Without Rupert as ballast, moving in with Philip takes on a different slant: she's not sure she's ready for it. There are things about Philip-

'If you're worried about filthy lucre, there's bags of it.'

Jo looks away, afraid he might be able to read her thoughts. From what she's gleaned from Philip, Rupert's family isn't just rich: they're stinking, connected to royalty. Hers for the taking. It's not as if she doesn't have feelings for him. He's a mixture of all the English characters she's ever read about, envied in some weird way. Rupert Bear, Christopher Robin; there's even a touch of Winnie the Pooh. Most of all, he reminds her of someone called

Ralph Reckness Cardew, a schoolboy in a Christmas annual belonging to one of her brothers. She'd fallen madly in love with Ralph the year she'd turned twelve. If only she could step into the fairy-tale …

'He's not right for you.'

A wall of resistance rises inside Jo. Doesn't he realise it doesn't matter if Philip's right for her or not. Having met him, she's no choice.

'I can't go. I'm sorry.'

'I had to ask. By the way, I've got something for you.'

He pulls out a small carved box and after pressing a tiny button, hands it to her.

A ring embedded in red velvet glints up at her.

'It's antique. The stones are genuine. If you're ever in a jam it'll get you home, a little further even.'

'What do I do, rub it?' She looks at him through wet eyes then she's in his arms, his soft mouth brushing hers.

'I love you,' he whispers.

23

'You haven't told me where we're going,' Jo grumbles, trying to decide if her hair looks more sophisticated up or down.

'State secret,' Phil answers, 'c'mon we'll be late.'

'Like?' she holds out her dress.

'As long as it's for home consumption.'

'Jealousy will get you everywhere,' she laughs. 'Maybe I should have worn the green? If I knew where we were going? Go on, a hint …?'

'You look fabulous. Women!' he snorts, opening the door and pulling her with him.

As her heels tap-tap down the stairs a memory of women walking up the aisle at mass surfaces: how she used dream about making that sound.

'What's wrong with women? You can't get enough!'

'The only damn thing they think about is how they look.'

'You're just as vain.'

'I've got something to be vain about.'

'Yeah, me!'

He pulls her into the shadows, kisses her.

'Sassy aren't you?'

'Sexy you mean.'

'Very…'

'Wanna go home?'

'I promised Te-'

Jo pounces. 'We're going to Ted's! Ha-ha.'

'Hey, you gotta act like you don't know. I'm supposed to tell you I'm dropping in to collect something. He's cooking dinner, wants it to be a surprise. Don't ask me why.'

Jo's disappointed; an evening of buddy-buddy with Philip and Ted isn't what she had in mind. Phil had introduced her to him shortly after she'd moved in and since then they've bumped into him in a couple of bars, visited his apartment at the top of hundreds of worn slippery stairs. It annoys Jo the way he tries to look young, wearing denim, his stringy grey hair pulled back in a ponytail; he must be at least fifty. He's told her the exact same story several times: about giving up a career in real estate, leaving New York and coming to Florence to paint. To follow what he calls his "heart's desire". "That's my motto," he's repeated each time, "follow your heart's desire, no matter what age you are."

She finds him a bit patronising and when she saw the canvas he was working on, prominently placed in the centre of his living area, she'd secretly thought he should have saved himself the trip. He seems in awe of Philip, always referring to him as an "artist", falling over everything he says.

'How come you know him? He seems old.'

'I admire him,' Phil answers. 'He has cancer. As soon as he found out, he sold everything, settled with his wife financially and came here. That's between you and me. He's not looking for pity.'

That probably explains the radiators on full-blast whenever they'd called.

'What d'you think of his paintings?'

'They're crap!'

Jo walks along silently. She's always finding out stuff that changes the way she looks at something. Even so, it annoys her Ted's work isn't up to much. She wants all Philip's friends to be like Rupert – not necessarily rich – but at least brilliant at what they do. Ted's mediocre. Strange the way it doesn't bother Philip, especially as he's always having a go at people who can't paint.

When Ted answers the doorbell, he puts on a big 'surprise to see you' number. 'Look who's here! Well, well. Come in, come in!'

A smell of cooking wafts from the kitchen.

'We've dropped by to collect that … book you borrowed.' Phil winks at Jo.

'C'mon in,' Ted repeats, louder this time.

The hallway's dim but as soon as he opens the living room door there's an explosion of light.

'*Happy Birthday to you, Happy Birthday to you, Happy Birthday dear Philip, Happy Birthday to you*!' Bellowing at the top of their lungs people spring from behind couches and curtains. They mob Philip, clapping him on the back, holding out beautifully wrapped presents.

'Ted, you son-of-a-bitch! You told me it was to welcome Jo!'

Ted puts his arms round Phil's neck, kisses him Italian style. 'How else was I gonna get you here? Celebrate while you can, that's my motto.' He turns his attention to Jo. 'Howdedodee, you look good enough to eat tonight. C'mon, let me introduce you to a few of the folks.'

As Ted leads her away, Jo catches Philip's eye: his birthday and he didn't even tell her! She blows a kiss. She's going to have to give him a special present later; one that doesn't come gift-wrapped.

'Have you met Scott?' Ted asks, stopping in front of a gangly bloke in a frilly white shirt and leather pants. Once was enough, Jo thinks, nodding. 'And this is Libby. Libby meet Jo Nowd, all the way from the Emerald Isle.' The lanky brunette mutters 'Ciao' her eyes boring into Jo from under a fringe of false eyelashes, sighing languidly as if worn out by the effort.

'Are you a friend of Phil's?' Jo asks to be polite.

'Sometimes,' she replies, slinking away.

Ted leans over, whispers, 'Very rich, has slept with practically every painter in Florence, in fact anyone who owns a paintbrush. Except Phil.'

'Hey, there's a couple of people dying to meet you. Will, Maris, over here' He lowers his voice. 'Phil's best friends, home today from the Outback. Aussies.'

Two outdoorsy-looking people amble over; what looks like a cat squatting on the woman's shoulder.

'That thing's a monkey. Mind the little mutt, it sometimes bites,' Ted warns.

'Hey you two, this is Jo.' Jo holds out a hand, pulling it back as the animal snaps.

'Sheba likes you,' the woman giggles, petting it. 'I'm Maris, the slob in the Hawaiian shirt answers to Will.' Standing back, she gives Jo a searing look, her face breaking into a smile. 'So you're Jo, Ted's been telling us all about you. Irish, right? And you paint.'

Jo nods, wondering what else he told them. Still she likes Maris' up-front approach although she's not sure about the bloody monkey.

'I'll leave you guys to get acquainted. Food's up in five minutes,' he calls, disappearing into the kitchen.

'Have you tasted Ted's cooking? Boy, I can't wait.' Maris smacks her lips.

'Great! I'm starving!' Jo nods towards the departing American's back. 'I'm beginning to think Italy has this strange effect on men. They all seem to cook. My father doesn't even know where the kitchen is. Thinks it's sissy.'

'Wow, Dark Ages!' Maris strokes the animal's head, eyeing Jo pityingly. Jo stiffens, sorry she mentioned it.

'Isn't Phil wonderful?' Maris continues. 'He's such a great painter.' She makes a face. 'Two in the one house, could be a challenge!'

It might be, Jo thinks, if anyone was doing anything.

'Oh, I don't know,' she says lightly, keeping her thoughts to herself.

'Well, we love him! And Sheba adores him. I think it's a good sign if an animal loves someone.'

Jo glances at Phil, wonders if he and Maris have slept together. Rupert should never have put the idea into her head: she'll drive herself bonkers if she suspects every woman she meets.

'I'll wash,' Maris says, throwing Jo a towel.

Most of the guests have left and Jo can hear Ted, Will and Phil arguing over a football match. Even so, she'd rather be in there lowering grappa, than stuck in the kitchen doing the bloody dishes. Why do women always offer to help!

'What's new with you guys?' Maris clatters bowls round the sink.

Jo shrugs. She's gone off Maris. All through dinner, she kept talking about some sort of "body art" thing she'd been at: people with chocolate daubed all over their skin, prancing about licking each other, talking baby talk. It had something to do with returning to nature and she'd kept raving about it, calling it a "total experience". What a hippy! "You can't call that art!" Jo had finally protested but Maris had just smiled benignly, her brown eyes brimming with emotion. It was impossible to have a proper discussion with her.

'Has Philip started working again?' Maris lowers her voice. 'We were kinda hoping you might be a good influence.'

'What do you mean?'

'We—el, Philip's usually very discreet about his women so Ted was surprised when he introduced you. We decided he must be serious about you. Sorree! What a dumb thing to say, I don't mean it the way it sounds ... I'm always sticking my foot in it.'

Jo is pleased and annoyed at the same time. The truth is Phil hasn't touched a brush since she moved in; not that she can talk. Listening to Maris, it feels as if she's failing some test.

'He's been talking about it,' she lies.

'Cool. Be prepared, he's a demon to live with once he starts. His last girlfriend nearly went demented. You don't mind my mentioning her? Now they've split I meet Mandy for coffee on the sly. She's neat. The thing is,' her eyes widen, 'she knows next to nothing about art or the artistic temperament. At least you do. Philip gets quite moody when he paints. Stops drinking, even stops socialising. Mandy says it was like living with a hermit.'

Jo sifts the information as she gathers up dinner plates, stacks them in a cupboard. No wonder he goes through women if they're prepared to give in to his moods. Well, he'll be waiting if he thinks she will. Let him sulk if he wants to, she'll just do her own thing.

'Thanks for the warning. Think I'll go and see what the guys are up to.'

'Hey, these cups sure are pretty!' Ted holds one up to the light.

'They're Phil's. I think he's friendly with the guy who made them.' She'd thought of saying "ceramicist" but she wasn't sure how to pronounce it; has never said it out loud. 'They were stashed away at the back of a cupboard. Seems a shame not to use them. More coffee?'

'Afraid, I gotta watch it. Phil tells me you paint.'

'Try to.' Jo's eyes stray towards the walk-in cupboard where she's been storing her materials. When Phil had told her earlier he was going to wave off some passing-through Americans, she'd planned to use the time to work: get going on a still-life. Just her luck, Ted would decide to drop by. It's only been a couple of days since the surprise party and she wonders if he knew Phil would be out.

'They say there's only room for one in the family,' he quips. 'My current wife dabbles, water-colours, nothing serious. I guess it burns you up or it doesn't. Been burning me up for years.'

Jo considers saying it burns her up too but not in a way that's helpful. Like a song her mother used to sing: smoke gets in her eyes. Or maybe she's just good at getting distracted.

'How do you like Florence? Great place to live huh?' He makes a little whistling sound. 'What a beaut, no smog, no subways, no elbows in your throat. Some days I take off, go walkies. Start at the Boboli, finish at the Duomo. A little piece of heaven on earth.'

As he talks, Jo thinks she sees a glimmer of tears, remembers what Phil had told her. Is he really going to die? He looks healthy, fit as a fiddle, apart from his eyes. They're pale as if the colour's draining out of them.

'Where's your wife now?'

'Back in Manhattan. She doesn't think anywhere else is civilised. No use telling her how long the Roman Empire's been round, if it's across Brooklyn Bridge forget it.' He guffaws.

'Don't you miss her?'

He scrapes at a patch of dry paint on his thumb. 'Jess is my third wife. I kept trading them in for newer models.'

Jo hides her surprise: three women married this guy?

'I guess something was missing from my life and … well, heck, here I am and it's not missing anymore.' He grins like a cat, the grey stubble on his chin glinting.

Jo wonders if he's telling the truth. A lot of what he says

sounds rehearsed as if he's trying to create an impression.

'So what gives? Is Philip working? Maris told me-'

'Why is everyone so interested in what Philip's doing?' Jo snaps. She's getting fed up with the way they all talk about him: like he's a piece of private property or something they've invested in.

Ted looks into her eyes, a hurt expression creeping into his. 'We care about Phil, I guess. Last coupla years he's produced squat! Pardon my French.'

'Maybe he needs a little room. How would you feel if everyone was waiting for you to pick up a brush?'

Ted laughs. 'Yessirree, you sure are a change from his usual type.'

'What's that?'

'Brainless on good legs. Not that I've seen your legs.' He glances down lasciviously and to make up for snapping, Jo hitches her dress a little.

'Pretty darn good, but you fail on the other count.' He makes a diamond with his hands, looking through it as if he's planning on drawing her. 'Phil's a strange guy. He's one hell of a friend and one hell of an artist. But I like you. You're a nice kid. I don't wanna see you get hurt.'

'I can take care of myself.'

'I guess you've heard he goes through women like a dose of salts?'

'Several times.'

'Heck, when I was putting together that little dinner-party—I'm not offending you, am I? Pays to know the score, I always say.'

Jo laughs off the idea.

'Phil's used to women flapping their skirts. What he needs is someone strong – a woman who can stand up to him. Think you can do that?'

'What do you think?'

'I think maybe you can. Most women-'

'I'm not most women,' Jo interrupts.

'I can see that.' He leans across the table. 'Let's you and me keep this little conversation under our hats. Who am I to interfere with cupid's arrow? A jealous old man, that's all.'

24

Phil hovers in the middle of the kitchen, holding a bag of dirty washing. Recently, even when he's standing still, he's restless.

'I'll do them,' Jo insists, 'I said I would. Then I'm going to get out my easel and get stuck into a bit of work.' There, she's said it; it's out in the open!

Phil doesn't react and Jo tries to quell the colly-wobbles in her stomach: why does it have to be such a big deal!

'The laundromat's a hell of a lot easier.'

'Everything comes out looking grey. I don't mind,' she adds, lying through her teeth. She can't stand washing clothes; knows she's only offering to do it as a way of placating him, paving the way for what she wants to do.

'You amaze me, Miss Nowd.'

'That's the intention.'

'Y'know, I might consider giving you a permanent position.'

'I haven't applied for one,' Jo fires back, dumping some of the stuff from the leather tote into a large basin, shaking in a heap of soap powder. When she shoves her hands in the water, it feels like play-acting: pretending to be a proper woman. A wife. But a wife would know why someone who buys hand-made shoes doesn't have a washing machine. It's funny how inhibited she feels about asking certain questions. His being older and owning the apartment makes her shy about enquiring, seeming to pry.

Sprawled across a chair, Phil chews on a toothpick. 'What other qualifications are you hiding?' he asks lazily. 'Don't tell me you can cook?'

Jo wonders why he's bringing that up now: if he's trying to distract her. The one time she'd offered to cook – out of politeness – he'd refused point blank. Most nights they eat out; when they don't, he likes to spend hours in the kitchen, whole afternoons sometimes, sipping wine, concocting dishes she's never heard of like stuffed cabbage that take forever to prepare.

'Not unless you count a magnificent mushroom omelette. I've told you – that's my forte.'

'I guess I could do something about that.'

'Teach me?' Shut-up, she tells herself but it's too late.

'I might. Hey, make sure you wash out all that soap, I don't want jock rot.'

Jo flicks soap bubbles, giggles as several settle on his hair like snowflakes. Straightaway, he's across the room, his body pressed into her back, a leg between her thighs, a fistful of suds in his hand.

'Please,' she begs, 'don't!'

'That's not what you were shrieking last night.'

She tries to squirm away but he blocks her escape, a soapy hand poised.

'Don't! Honest, I'm sorry.'

'You will be.' He blows the soapsuds and they float away, evaporating one by one.

As his hands caress her breasts, Jo's insides liquefy. Stop,' she protests, bracing herself. 'I've told you, as soon as I hang this lot out I'm going to work. I've been meaning to for ages. In case you've forgotten, it's what I came to Italy to do.'

'All work and no play …' he whispers, nipping the lobe of her ear.

'… makes Jack a dull boy. But Jill a painter!' Sloshing the wet clothes into a basket, Jo dodges past. That's the worst over, she hopes: she couldn't have made it any clearer. Since her conversation with Maris, she's been on the look-out for the right moment. As she pegs up tee shirts and underpants, she can almost feel the pencil in her hand.

Philip has followed her out to the balcony and catching sight of him skulking, she throws a sock, laughs as he dives to catch it, immediately wishing she hadn't. Why is she sending all the wrong signals! She could kick herself. Annoyed, she stomps indoors, Phil on her tail, dangling the wet sock in triumph.

'I meant it. Go away.' Resolutely, she goes to the cupboard, lugs out her equipment. While she adjusts the small portable easel, Phil watches, an ironic expression on his face. He probably regards it as Mickey Mouse, she thinks, as she lays out her meagre supply of pencils and paints. It is Mickey Mouse! If only he'd let her use the bloody studio – she's hinted often enough.

After taping a sheet of acrylic paper to a piece of heavy cardboard, Jo goes through the motions of surveying the room as if trying to make up her mind about what to use as a subject. Inside she's in knots, afraid of making a fool of herself; doubting, all of a sudden, whether she has any ability to draw or paint; even wants to.

Lost in thought, she jumps as Philip's arms encircle her. Snuggling in, he parts her hair, kiss-kisses the nape of her neck.

'I was thinking of going for a beer, wanna come?' he murmurs.

Taking a couple of steps, Jo picks up a pencil, begins sharpening it.

'The offer won't last forever.'

This is it: if she gives in now she's finished. Hearing the kitchen door open, Jo grits her teeth; wills herself to stay put. A moment later Phil returns.

Keeping her back to him, she pretends to measure something, holding out a pencil, screwing up one eye.

The seconds tick.

'Play with being an artist if you want to!' Philip turns on his heel. A moment later, the front door slams.

Fuck! Jo flings down the pencil, restraining herself from rushing after him. So much for her brilliant idea! What made her think she could provoke him into doing something? All she'd wanted was to prove Maris wrong. Now look what's happened!

It wasn't only for Maris, she admits, retrieving her pencil; she needed to give herself a kick-start too. Well, she's not going to let him dictate to her; until now she's gone along with everything. Galvanised, she focuses her attention. Where to start? The whole room would be too difficult; better to go for something smaller, something specific. She hems and haws, eventually settling on an angle that takes in one of the shutters as well as an occasional table – home to a beautiful piece of Murano glass. And if she expands a little to the left the large leaves of a cheese plant will cut into the frame. Once she's decided, Jo allows her mind go blank, her body quieten. Eventually, a sort of brightness flickers at her core, and slowly, what's in front of her eyes transforms into an intricate pattern, a play of light and shadow…

She starts by doing several sketches from different positions – some overlapping – her eye travelling from room to paper, paper to room in one continuous movement; concentrating on getting the rhythm of the composition, nailing the overall effect. Discarded drawings pile up.

It annoys her as soon as she realises she's listening out for Phil, waiting for him to return. Then again, why wouldn't she? It's the first time they've had a fight! On cue, a chorus sets up in her head: look what you've done, you should have waited, you need to learn to play your cards right, you've learned nothing! Phil isn't looking for a doormat, Jo dismisses them, but having started their barrage the voices are not easily silenced.

Unable to concentrate, Jo crosses to the window, her eyes sweeping the square. A Japanese couple are posing for a photograph in front of Santa Croce – smiling shyly as the camera flashes – and she remembers the first afternoon she and Phil had stood arm and arm just where she's standing now. That day, Santa Croce seemed magical; today it looks earthbound, just another building, all the enchantment gone. Or could it be that drunk on lovemaking, she'd conferred the magic herself?

Picking up a couple of the drawings, Jo inspects them, is forced to admit that despite her efforts, they just don't have enough depth. It's not because of perspective either; it's something else. Returning to the window, she studies the way tourists crossing the square set about avoiding each other, negotiate the space between chairs and tables. Can art really be a question of the space between and around objects? They were forever drumming that into them at college: get the negative space right and the rest will look after it itself.

Jo tears out some fresh sheets, begins all over again. When she's finally satisfied with one, she unscrews several tubes of paint, squirts a blob from each onto a plate. Although acrylic dries quickly she applies the pigment cautiously: darker tones to lighter ones-

It's no use! How can she work with one eye on the door, an ear cocked. Phil was right: all she's doing is playing. She should have gone out with him; Christ, they've been together six weeks and she's acting as if they were an old married couple. No wonder he stormed out.

Checking the time, Jo's surprised to discover it's getting on for five. She'll surprise him, make something special, have it ready when he comes in; after all, he's done all the cooking since she moved in. She'll have to watch it, she warns herself jokingly as she picks up a shopping basket. She doesn't want to end up like her mother, slaving for a man. No chance of that, her relationship with Phil is different from her parents'; she's different.

Grabbing a piece of charcoal, she writes a quick note in case he gets back before her. She might not be able to produce anything exotic but she can fry up a couple of *bracuola di manzo* — she'll get the ready-made beef rolls at the butchers — a side serving of courgettes, "*zucchinis*" in Italian, sizzled in olive oil, and a bowl of insalata mista. Wine, candles, her new dress, what more could a man want?

At eight o'clock, Jo dumps the blackened meat into the bin, munches disconsolately through wilting salad. There's no sign of Philip, not even a phone call. Refilling her glass from the bottle of Montepulciano she'd opened, Jo carries it to the window. Sitting there, she'll be able to see him coming. Sipping her wine, she realises how ridiculous it is to be feeling this miserable over someone she's only known a few months. Even more ridiculous to be incapable of doing anything other than wait: as if she's forgotten how to be alone. That's it, she pounces: she isn't alone, she's without Philip. And he's out there, somewhere, without her.

As if wishing could conjure him up, her eyes rake the piazza but all she can see are the same old tourists haunting the square like seabirds blown off-course. One group are clustered beneath a bronze plaque; a guy at the back balancing on one leg to try and get a better view. Jo's heart does a sudden dive. A heron used to stand sentry along the canal where she and Eamonn went for walks; catching sight of it they'd look at one another in awe, fall silent. If they were downwind and quiet enough, they'd sometimes see it spread its clumsy wings, take off, alighting a few yards away, immobile again, focused. As light as the touch of a feather, Jo senses Eamonn's presence, nesting in a corner of her heart. No wonder Phil's gone AWOL, he probably knows she doesn't love him; maybe even suspects he's part of a grand experiment to prove she can have a relationship without falling in love. "*I gave you my heart but you wanted my soul*" – Dylan's words. What does it mean to give your heart and not your soul? She'd given Eamonn her soul without thinking. Do women love differently from men? She might not 'love' Philip the way she loved Eamonn, but she enjoys having sex with him, finds him exciting, interesting, likes being with him, most of the time. So she loves him in a way. Draining the glass, she pours another, gulps it down, willing it to go to her head. Maybe there's more than one kind of love: maybe we love different people differently. Or maybe it's impossible to love a second time the same way.

A rush of good feeling streams through Jo. Cuddling a cushion, she flings herself around the room, spinning until she collapses into one of the leather armchairs. As the room dissolves into a kaleidoscope of colour, she closes her eyes: fly away Eamonn, she's waiting for Philip. When he comes home, she'll apologise; if it's not too late, they can go out for a meal, get mad, mad drunk. Mad drunk, she repeats, putting the bottle to her head. Maybe she's falling in love! Impossible. She fancies Phil, is sexually hooked but that – is – all.

Getting to her feet, Jo stands to attention. Take a bow Miss Nowd: you've landed the best-looking man in Florence. And the best painter – according to no less an expert than Rupert's mother. As she waltzes across to the window another thought occurs: is it possible to go on living with someone and *not* love them?

Jo curtsies to the lights illuminating the square; is surprised to see waiters clearing up. She glances at her watch: 10.35! Fuck!

Where is he! Why hasn't he- Fuck him, he isn't going to arrive back here at all hours and find her waiting like a suburban little wifey. She's not someone he can take for granted. Blowing a parting kiss to the night, Jo giggles. She *is* drunk. Drunk and tired. She'll go to bed. Not drunk and tired, she corrects herself: drunk and happy. Maybe a little sad too, but deep down, deep, deep, down, happy. Really.

It's pitch black when Jo wakes, her head muzzy, her tongue stuck to the roof of her mouth, a thought that scares her forming. Trying not to panic, she gropes for the bedside lamp, switches it on. One o'clock! Her heart stops. Smart-aleck! Too smart for her own good. Thinking of herself and all this time Philip might be in trouble; might have had an accident.

Hurrying to the window, she undoes the shutters, relief flooding through her at the sight of a lone man rolling across the square. She'll say nothing, go back to bed; pretend to be asleep. But the man keeps going, disappearing into the shadows. Jo looks at the clock again, wonders if it's too late to phone someone. Philip keeps an address book in his bureau; she'd flicked through it one day when he was out, curious to see who was in it. Liar: which women were in it! Besides, he'd probably be furious if she rang anyone. He might be the most important person in her life but that doesn't seem to give her any rights.

Cautiously, she peers into the hallway, then on impulse, races down the stairs, out into the street. The piazza's deserted, desolate, Santa Croce looming and sinister. Florence isn't like Dublin: people don't stay out late so where can he be?

Shivering, she runs back upstairs, picks up the phone. She'll ring Ted. No, Maris; he's more likely with Ted. Halfway through dialling, she stops. She can't bear the thought of him knowing she's in a state. She'll make tea. Think.

Sitting at the table, Jo watches the liquid scum over. He's no right to do this, she'll kill him. Straightaway, she imagines the phone ringing, a voice telling her about an accident, an attack. Phil hurt, injured. Dead! She's filled with remorse, regret. It's her fault he's out there. Her and her stupid painting.

A faint tinkle of music drifts into the bedroom. Throwing off the duvet, Jo sits up. Philip!

Tiptoeing to the kitchen, she sees him bent over the table, a cigarette dangling from his lips. Jo's taken aback; she's never seen him smoke before.

'I didn't know you smoked.'

'I don't,' he answers, absorbed in rolling a wodge of modelling clay.

'Where were you?'

'Why?' he asks. With his free hand, he flicks away a ribbon of ash. Jo hadn't meant to sound accusing but she can't believe he's sitting there as if nothing's happened.

'I was worried sick. You were out all night!'

Concentrating, Phil picks up a metal clothes hanger and after untwisting the neck, winds both ends together. Taking his time, he moulds the softened clay round the home-made mount, gouging and smoothing with precise, deliberate movements. More ash drops.

'There's something you need to understand,' he says as a woman's body breaks through the clay. He holds the torso away from him for a moment before placing it on the far side of the table. 'I don't need a mother. Is that clear?' His eyes meet hers and Jo nods. 'And I don't like being questioned if I decide to stay out.'

Jo dams up a rush of words.

'Now c'mere.'

Warily, she walks towards him.

'You've been crying!' Gently, he traces the track of her tears. 'I didn't know you were such a cry-baby.'

'I'm not,' she protests. He's right though: it was silly to get so worried. They're both adults: they can do what they like.

'C'mon get your glad rags on.'

'We're going out?'

'Yeah, I saw the steaks.' He laughs. 'We're going shopping.'

'Prova signorina, prova. Try.' The shopkeeper lifts a sliver of cheese with a spatula, offers it to Jo. 'Buono,' she kisses her fingers to her lips.

Jo grins anxiously. She's not a "cheese" person; the only Italian one she likes is ricotta which Philip doesn't consider cheese.

'It's a local *pecorino*, made from sheep's milk,' Phil informs her. 'Straight from the sheep's udder.' He says something in Italian and the woman nods vigorously. Jo bites into it warily, is surprised to find she likes it.

'*Buono*,' she agrees.

'*Quanto costa*?' he asks as the shopkeeper cuts a large chunk. He makes a face when she answers, mimes changing his mind. Laughing, the shopkeeper slaps it down in front of him, writes a number on a piece of paper.

Phil nudges Jo. 'See, that's better. *E meglio!*' he tells the woman.

The shopkeeper places the cheese next to the prosciutto and salami Phil's already selected; points to a ring of sausages.

'*Cinghiale, mia marito l'hai fatto.Veremente buonnissimo!*'

'*Damme due kilo.*' 'They're wild boar, her husband makes them,' Phil translates as Jo gazes at the red squelchy meat inside the casings. 'They hunt them in the Maremma, it's a tradition around here. Wait until you taste it!' He makes the same kissing gesture as the shopkeeper and the woman throws her hands in the air, a big smile cracking her face. While the Italian's weighing the sausages, Jo gapes at shelf after shelf of exotic, unrecognisable things: some stuffed, others floating in bottles; the counter heaving with barrels of olives, vats of pickled fish, bits of who-knows-what animals dangling from the ceiling. And the smells! Strong, earthy. Sexy. In Ireland food's food. "No matter how rich you are you can only eat three meals a day" was one of her daddy's favourite sayings. Here, eating's a way of life. And buying food's like courting. The more you flatter the more the shopkeeper loves you; and the better the deal you're likely to get!

Smiling and nodding, the woman wraps each of Phil's purchases carefully – even the tiniest portion – using thin shiny paper so they end up looking like gifts.

'*Andiamo*,' Phil winks at Jo after he's paid.

'*Signorina?*' The shopkeeper offers her a bonbon, chucking her cheek, mouthing something to Phil who gives Jo a quick once-over before answering.

The woman cackles; slaps his wrist playfully.

'What did she say?' Jo asks when they're out of earshot.

'She said you had a little more meat on you than the others.'

'What did you say?'

'That you'll probably last longer.'

I will last, Jo vows secretly and before long I'll be the one doing the shopping.

'Only joking,' Phil tells her, misinterpreting her expression. 'You're just as skinny.'

Jo gives him a dig and he laughs, snuggling in. 'Anyway, I'm going to fatten you up.'

'Before you eat me!'

'Don't be putting ideas in my head!'

Outside the shop they stop and kiss; Jo quickly burying the memory of the previous night. She needs to get to know Phil better – that's all – understand how he ticks.

'Let's go get some vegetables.'

Jo trails round the market with him, happily memorising words: *asparagi,* she's eaten at the Robertsons; *melanzane,* a fat purpley vegetable Philip uses in a Greek dish called moussaka; *pepperoni*, red, green and yellow, and *funghi*, her favourite veg. She sings the names in her head: she's going to learn how to use them, turn into a brilliant cook. In her spare time, of course.

Shopping done, they gulp espressos at the counter of a crowded café, share a moist creamy pastry. Fuelling, Phil jokes, clinking her tiny cup, brushing his leg against hers. Jo's throat tightens.

'Let's go home,' he whispers.

25

Picking up a letter, Jo takes it with her to the kitchen.

'For me!' she waves, parking herself on Phil's knee.

He snaps at her neck pretending to bite.

'It's from the *scuola*. They want to know if I can come back next term. More hours if I like.'

Phil's face darkens. 'You're not going.'

'What d'ye mean?'

'I don't want you taking your clothes off for horny students.' Easing her off, he wanders over to the cooker, his shoulders hunched against her.

Jo's not sure how to respond: has a feeling it isn't up for discussion.

'What about money?' she asks tentatively.

'We have enough.'

"We?" She should be delighted; modelling bored her to death. All the same, she'd prefer if they discussed it; there's no need for him to lay down the law as if he's her father. Folding the letter, she stuffs it in a pocket; raises her hands in surrender.

'I'm to be a kept woman, is that it?'

He looks at her and smiles, but behind the smile Jo catches a flash of something, something she can't interpret, then it vanishes.

'Don't get any ideas. I intend making you pay your way,' he jokes. 'Now, go to the fridge.'

'What are you going to show me today chef?'

'Open. Remove two of those bottles. Hand them to me.'

Jo holds up a beer. 'At this hour?'

'Did anyone ever tell you how exceedingly bourgeois you are Miss Nowd? Beer can be enjoyed anytime. Like now for example.'

Opening both bottles, he hands her one. "Bourgeois": Jo hasn't heard the word since the day she met Camilla. She remembers looking it up in a dictionary but all it said was something like "belonging to the middle-class".

'I'm not middle-class,' she protests.

'Maybe not, but you sure as hell have a lot of their attitudes.'

'Because I don't like beer in the morning?'

'Because you're female.'

Baffled, Jo shuts up. What has being a woman got to do with it? She wishes Camilla were here: she'd show him what a woman was.

'*Vive le donne!*' Jo thinks, forcing the beer down; wonders what Camilla's words really mean?

Jo carries the book on Velazquez into the kitchen, props it against the radio on the table. She'd been hoping to try and get a bit more work done on her painting but for days Phil's been prowling the apartment like a caged animal: grunting if she as much as looks at him. If only he'd let her use the studio she'd be out of his way. Maybe she'll cook something nice later, bring it up again, casually. So far, he's refused to rise to the bait.

With a sigh, she opens the page at *Las Meninas* – The Maids of Honour. Velazquez is one of Phil's favourites; he'd spent an entire evening singing his praises, telling Jo if she could understand the Spaniard's achievements, she'd understand a lot about art. Keeping one eye on the painting, she scans the text on the opposite page: "Painted in 1656 … King and Queen of Spain … visible in the mirror … it's a painting of what they're seeing … In the foreground the Infanta Margarita … surrounded by maids and dwarfs".

Jo studies the scrunched-up face of the principle dwarf; is moved by the ache of resignation in the eyes, the stoic set of her mouth. How terrible, she thinks, to end up someone else's plaything.

She carries on reading: "The painter's mature work depends almost exclusively on the effects of his brushwork; reproductions can give only an idea of the original." Below the text a fragment of the painting has been enlarged. Close-up, it's a blur of random strokes, pinky-red and cream, slashed with a deep greeny-black. Apparently formless.

Jo holds it at arm's length, surprised to see it mesh into the delicate fluff of lace circling the Infanta's wrist. Wow! That must be what Phil was getting at. She repeats the experiment, delighting in it, wondering how on earth Velazquez had managed it. It's extraordinary! How could he have known which strokes and colours would produce the effect he needed? She'd love to call Phil, share her discovery... but ...

Moments later, he wanders in; takes a beer from the fridge.

'You haven't had any breakfast,' Jo remarks over her shoulder.

'So?'

So die of liver failure.

Tapping one foot on a cupboard door, Philip slurps noisily from the bottle. Jo closes the book. She'll make an early lunch; the tension's driving her barmy. As soon as she stands up, he pulls out a chair, drags it to the window. Slumping down, he sits with his back to her.

Humming pointedly, Jo opens a tin of tuna, dumps it in a bowl, adding a tin of anchovies to give it more flavour. The cherry tomatoes they'd been polishing off are finished so she chops up a beef tomato, slices an onion, mixes the lot with dollops of mayonnaise. Hardly Cordon Bleu but along with the focaccia she

217

picked up earlier it won't be too bad.

'Lunch if you're hungry,' she announces.

The only response is a twitching of muscles in his back. Controlling an urge to throw the bowl at him, Jo forces food down her throat.

When she's finished, she retreats to the bathroom, shuts herself in. Why is he behaving like this, treating her as if she's an enemy? This is where she lives; he's no right- she jumps at the sound of the front door slamming; hurries to the living-room, keeping well back from the window in case he looks up.

The square's more crowded than usual but eventually she spots him, heading towards the city centre, a stranger with his head down, hands stuffed in his pockets. As he disappears from sight, a weight lifts. 'I can open my mouth, shout if I want!' she yells, going from room to room, banging doors, relishing the pleasure of being alone, of not having to creep around.

Her high spirits don't last. Phil's presence is so palpable, the apartment so his, he might as well be there. What she needs is out.

As the door of Santa Croce shut behind her, Jo quashes an impulse to remain outdoors; out in the sunshine in the company of ordinary, normal, good-humoured people. Anyone who isn't an artist! But once she's inside, the interior acts like a magnet: taking her out of herself, dwarfing her problems, reminding her of what's important. Subdued, she follows signs for Giotto's frescos, her way lit by stain-glass windows. When she gets to the Bardi chapel she sees a woman is already sitting there, a red scarf loosely covering her hair.

Glad of the stranger's presence, Jo slips quietly into a pew a couple of rows behind. The woman's head is raised and following her gaze, Jo sees groups of figures standing around a sick bed. The fresco's faded in parts, with patches missing, but she knows the dying man is St. Francis, the men looking down at him his fellow monks. Moving her eye back and forth between it and some of the other frescos, Jo grows more and more bewildered. What's visionary about monks standing by a bedside or praying in a desert? And just as she'd suspected from reproductions, they're not that well painted: the figures stilted, clumsy even, the colours dull. There's no comparison between what she's looking at and the extraordinary paintings she saw in Sienna: they're not in the same league. How can Giotto be considered one of the world's greatest artists? And how could these badly executed frescos have revolutionised Western Art?

As the woman rises to go, her scarf slips.

Jo's eyes widen in disbelief. 'Camilla!!'

'*Ce essa?*'

'*Jo, mi chiama Jo. Siamo incontrata a Pavia, ricorda?* We met at the demo in Pavia, remember?'

Camilla's face lights up. '*Irlandaisa! Ma cosa fai- scusa* … What are you doing in *Firenze?*' She motions Jo to follow, linking her affectionately as they leave the church.

Once outside, she kisses Jo on both cheeks. '*Che coincidenza! Andiamo*, let's go and have coffee. You have time?'

Jo beams. Now she knows why she waited until today to visit Santa Croce. Her mammy's absolutely right: God works in mysterious ways.

'So you have left the exploiters,' Camilla laughs, undoing her jacket; smiling thanks as a waiter sets down their drinks.

The café's one of the more popular ones in the square and Jo finds herself hoping Phil doesn't blunder in.

'Months ago. By the way, I met someone in Pavia who knew you. A guy called Massimo.'

'*Che Massimo*? I am acquainted with several.'

'He has curly hair. His second name – *cognome* – is Buda.'

"Buda!" Camilla blows air through her lips. 'Is that what he is calling himself now? Before it was Malatesta. Do you know who Buda was?'

Jo shakes her head, afraid to risk saying the founder of Buddhism in case she's wrong.

'He was a famous Italian anarchist. He blew up Wall Street. Massimo is a big fan.'

'He told me he was an old friend of yours.'

'*Mai*! Never! The group he belongs to – *pericoloso* – very big danger, *capito*? Bad! *Molto cativo*! You must stay away. Trust me.'

Shit! Tim was right! She really might have ended up in jail!

'I haven't seen him since- I'm living in Florence now,' she says, deciding not to tell Camilla the whole story. Being naïve isn't something she wants to shout about.

'*E fantastico*! What are you doing here?'

'This and that. I had a job in a pensione. Cleaning. Yuck! What about you? I thought you were…' she allows the sentence peter out. She can't say 'refugee camps' as if they're something she's familiar with them.

'I am in Palestine – at the camps – but I have come back. *Sfortunata*, my mother is sick.'

How mysterious the words sound laced in Camilla's smoky voice: "My mozzer ees sick. I haf com back." And how extraordinary and wonderful she's here, stuck in Florence.

'Is your mother very ill?' Jo asks, realising she hasn't shown any concern.

'She is improving. She will come from the hospital in a few

days and I will go back.'

Jo feigns delight at the news. A silence follows and Camilla sips her coffee, a look of pleasure on her face. When she's finished, she sits back.

'You like Giotto, the frescos?' Jo asks to stall her.

'He is my inspiration. My family comes from the same village in the Mugello he comes- came from. So I grow up with him.' She shrugs. 'I am lucky. Many people do not understand his greatness. To appreciate him it is necessary to understand the history of art. Have you seen the frescos in Assisi?'

Jo shakes her head, regretting mentioning him.

'*Che peccato!* A pity! You must go sometime. They are beautiful! I have a book I bought for when I can't go.' Camilla's face creases in disgust. 'At the camps, so much suffering, disease. We call ourselves civilised! The way those people are forced to live. But they are amazing, such spirit. Like Giotto. He painted with love, with compassion, so I come and see him. To remind myself.' Camilla gets out her purse. 'I must go to *ospedale* now and visit my mother. We will meet again for coffee, yes, before I leave?'

Jo's heart sinks: all her hopes reduced to a cup of coffee. There has to be some way of seeing more of Camilla, some reason for them to meet.

'I'd love to see the book – the one of Giotto's frescos?'

'You would like? You can come to my house. Tomorrow?'

'Sure. Two o'clock?'

'*Va bene*. I like very much to talk more with you.' Camilla produces a piece of paper, uses an eyeliner to draw directions. 'The street is near Stagione Santa Maria Novella. You can't miss it.'

Hurrying back to the apartment, Jo touches the map in her pocket; wonders why she hadn't mentioned Phil, wonders if she'll tell him about Camilla?

The vibe from Philip is 'keep away'. What would Camilla think if she saw Jo putting up with such behaviour! The problem is she's never lived with anyone so she's not sure what to expect – what's considered normal? Anna and Tim were like cats and dogs sometimes and she can remember the horrible atmosphere whenever her father was in a bad mood. The house would be like a ticking bomb, everyone keeping out of sight; nobody wanting to be in the line of fire when the explosion came. Growing up, she'd blamed her mother for not handling her daddy properly, not standing up to him; or not having the house tidy or dinners on time. Whatever it was.

Now she's not so sure. She knows she should challenge Phil, tell him straight up she can't stand another minute of being treated like she doesn't exist; confronted by his back, her courage gives out.

Picking up the volume on Velazquez, Jo carries it listlessly to the bedroom, gets in under the duvet. She'll leave him alone, wait for it to pass. Apart from stories and anecdotes, he's not much of a talker anyway. A lot of men aren't. They don't seem to need to. Her daddy didn't, was always slagging her mammy. "Can't keep her mouth shut," he'd mock, opening and closing his hand like a set of teeth, "Yap, yap, yap. Even when she's nothing to say." Like clockwork, Jo and her brothers would laugh.

"It's not right teaching children to laugh at their mother," her mammy's voice objects.

"Aahh, where's your sense of humour, it's only a bit of fun!" her father would reply.

Well this isn't fun, Jo thinks, turning the pages until she reaches Las Meninas. Holding the book away from her, she squints, trying out varying distances, seeing if she can ascertain the exact moment it ceases to be daubs of paint, becomes the ruff. It must be our eyes that fuse the haphazard strokes, transform them into something recognisable. Still, to have the know-how to get it right is mind-boggling. She's never paid much attention to the application of paint, had assumed the less obvious the better. But Velazquez seems to want people to be conscious of it, to grasp how paint works, how it creates the illusion of something solid, real – yet remains paint.

Jo's suddenly seized with a desire to see the actual painting, examine it up close, touch it although that's probably forbidden. They could go to Madrid, have a little holiday. Carried away with the idea, she's already walking into the Prado when she remembers she and Philip haven't exchanged a word for days. The dwarf catches her eye and she slams the book shut. Sighs. What's got into him? She's certain it isn't anything she said, their last conversation had been about his favourite meal which she'd cooked, following his instructions; had spent flippin' hours blanching cabbage leaves. She'd half-enjoyed it, especially when he'd complimented her, told her she was improving.

Rising, Jo tiptoes to the door, puts an ear to it. All she can hear is one of the radiators gurgling, a faint thrum of music from downstairs. Peering into the hallway, she can feel the gloom that's begun to permeate the apartment. A terrible helplessness overcomes her and returning to the bedroom, she throws herself on the bed. A tear falls, then another.

It's no use, she decides, she can't go on like this. No one could. She'll have to move out. Only a dread of letting Ted and Maris down – of not living up to their ridiculous expectations – is stopping her. Pride. The realisation energises her. *Carpe diem*, she urges herself. Arriving at the kitchen door, Jo's resolve wavers then she's in front of him, gabbling incoherently. To her surprise, he puts his arms around her, holds her, rocking her, telling her not to cry, it isn't her fault. Sitting her on his knee, he explains it's something inside him that builds when he isn't working; something that fucks things up, turns him into a bastard. Overcome with relief, Jo clings to him, hears herself telling him they'll find a way, telling him she loves him.

'I know, I know,' he assures her, kissing her wet cheeks. 'Go back to bed, I'll be in soon.'

Unwillingly, Jo returns to the bedroom. She can hear him moving about, wonders what he's up to. Things will be different from now on, she comforts herself. Now she knows she's prepared to leave if- Jo stops, hears herself telling Philip she loves him. Repeating the words, she realises she's not sure anymore. She loves him and she doesn't love him; she could leave him or she might not be able to.

The door swings open and Phil – a pair of stripey boxers on his head – struts in carrying a tray. 'Midnight feast,' he announces, turning his free hand into a trumpet and blowing. Jo laughs.

'A little wine?' Holding the glass, Philip presses it to her lips. Their eyes meet over the rim and Jo sees love shining there; realises again how gorgeous he is. This beautiful man is hers, she thinks. Hers.

26

Jo takes ages looking at each fresco; afraid of blowing it by saying the wrong thing. 'What did you mean by Giotto inspiring you?' she asks Camilla, playing for time.

'You wish to know? Giotto was a humanist. *Capito?*'

Jo nods, even though she doesn't; with a bit of luck, she'll pick up the gist from whatever else she says.

'In medieval times, artists were in the service of God, the Church. They were not free to do what they liked. They had to paint with certain colours; make Jesus and Mary so many times bigger than ordinary people. People weren't free either. The *contadini*, peasants, are supposed to look at these high, lofty paintings, forget about the real world. Can you imagine: plague, disease, death; everyone at the mercy of whoever owned them. Women dying in childbirth! Endless misery. And this God on high- *Boh!*' Camilla's shoulders rise disdainfully. 'Then Giotto! He opens his eyes and everything is shaken at the roots-'

'Those other paintings probably helped,' Jo interrupts, unable to resist. 'When I look at a painting by someone like Simone Martini it's as if I'm ... looking at something miraculous. Not that I believe in miracles-' She clams up, wishing she hadn't opened her mouth.

'Aahh! You are a fan of Siennese painters? Yes, they are good but not so important. In the end they choose to sacrifice truth for... beauty, harmony. Do you know while they were painting their masterpieces, Sienna suffered more death than any other city in Italy, possibly Europe. Wars too.'

'But art has to stand above wars and death. It's there to remind people there's more to life, it isn't just one long struggle.'

'For many people that is what it is. The paintings you are talking about appeal to the emotions, make us blind to what is happening. They flatter their owners. That is their real function. But it is this,' Camilla taps her head twice, 'we have to use. Women especially.'

Jo hopes she isn't referring to her. 'What's wrong with being emotional?'

'Nothing, as long as it doesn't get in the way.'

Meaning I let it, Jo thinks, a wave of anger washing over her. Who does Camilla think she is lecturing her! Implying she likes Siennese paintings because she's a woman!

'I don't think you're right,' Jo fires back. 'And you have to admit compared to the Siennese, Giotto isn't that good a painter,' she adds, throwing down her trump card.

An exasperated expression crosses Camilla's face. 'Art is not a question of- oh if only you spoke Italian I could explain.' She throws her arms up. 'Art is about seeing, understanding. Of course there are better painters, many, even some of your precious Siennese, but it was Giotto who made the leap. He had the vision. He painted real people with real bodies; gave them space to move about in. He showed us their lives, their hopes, their sorrows. That was his great achievement. *Accidenti*, if women had such a vision! The future, the history of the world, would change.'

'How? I don't know what you mean.'

'We are stuck. It's so normal most women don't realise we have to change. Life has been drained out of us. The more we flaunt ourselves the more disembodied we become. We need to take up space, become what we are meant to be. Do you think women have a right to be human, to be whole ... yes?'

'Of course, but-' Jo flounders. 'Women have themselves to

blame. They should stand up for themselves, do what they want to do. What's stopping them?'

'You think gender, economics, history, doesn't play a role? You think women are free in this society? *Veremente*? Really? Women, most women, are imprisoned the same way the images in those old paintings were. Everything is *proscritto*, we are told how we should look, what we can wear, what we can be. Look at you, you have a body, desires, ambitions – are you free to express them? In whatever way you choose?' Camilla's eyes pierce into Jo's. 'I am sorry. But ... I must be cruel to be kind, yes?'

Jo tries to think: she's always done what she likes, has never tried to be sweet or feminine. Well, maybe ... sometimes ... in the past. But her body's her own now; her relationship with Philip proves it.

'Women aren't sweet, angelic creatures always ready to sacrifice themselves. *Boh*, when I think of the Catholic Church going on and on about one man sacrificing himself! Women are sacrificed day after day, and for what? You don't agree?'

Jo pushes away the unease she's beginning to feel, tries to make her way back to safer ground. 'I still don't think art should be political.'

'Everything's political! The food we eat, the air we breathe. Come to the camps, I will show you if you don't believe!

'Come to the camps?'

'Why not? They always need people. You are too busy? What are you doing?'

'I'm- I'm living with someone. An American painter.'

'Yes ... but what are you doing?'

Jo's suddenly conscious of Camilla's steely eyes, the determined chin; remembers her "*Viva le donne!*" on the march: the energy it had sent shooting through her body.

'I'm a painter,' she admits in a low voice; waits to be bawled out.

'Ah! *Fortunata!*' Camilla exclaims. 'I suspect. What are you painting?'

Jo hesitates.

'*Momento.*' After a quick search the Italian takes a book from a shelf.

'I want to read you something. It's in Italian ...' Camilla flicks through the pages. 'It says, excuse my translation ... "The painter, Giotto ... tore down the veil ... which for centuries hung between man's soul and his body ..." Of course our job is women. The veil exists: we are either virgins or whores. Our bodies belong to God or men. We must reclaim them.' Camilla laughs. 'Now you have a subject for your painting, yes?'

27

'I want you to sit for me.'

Jo looks up from the book on Vermeer she's reading. Since her discovery with Velazquez, she's been working through Phil's art books; Camilla's remarks firmly at the back of her mind.

'I don't believe it!' she laughs.

'What's so funny?'

'Don't take it so seriously, I was only joking.'

Phil squeezes her arm, 'I never joke about painting.'

Jo would love to stretch but she doesn't dare. She's sitting with her back to Phil; at a slight angle so only a part of her face and side is visible, one arm resting on the arm of a chair, the other out of sight. Her neck aches but now he's begun to he's paint, she doesn't want to give him any excuse to stop. It took the best part of a week to arrive at a pose he was happy with – satisfied anyway; she'd had to change positions over and over while he tore up drawings, cursed pencils, cursed her; sometimes abandoning her, goose-pimpled and afraid to move a muscle in case he deigned to start again. Most days, he spends hours staring into space or into his hands; if she speaks, he ignores her. Evenings are worse. She's never met anyone with as much capacity to say nothing. Mandy was right, it's like living with a hermit, one who's taken a vow of silence. Jo wonders if she doesn't prefer Philip when he's not painting. It's not like one of his moods either: he's simply not available; has locked himself away in a world of his own. She'd go out of her mind if she didn't have the art books for company; at least she's using the time to educate herself.

'Call it a day.' His voice is flat.

'Can I have a look?'

'When I say so.'

He's given her the same answer every time she asks. Pulling on a robe, Jo plods to the kitchen, goes straight to the fridge. Sitting on your ass certainly works up an appetite. Making a pocket in some ciabatta, she piles in salami and tomatoes, a handful of chopped olives. She makes a second one, leaving out the olives and adding cheese.

'Sandwich,' she calls on her way to the bedroom. A mumbled 'thanks' reaches her in the hallway. At least this way he's eating; the meals she'd painstakingly cooked the first couple of nights had ended in the bin.

Shoving a couple of pillows behind her head, Jo props the clothbound volume against her knees. Reading through the introduction a sentence jumps out: "There are wrong reasons for disliking a work of art." Jo pauses to mull it over. "Reasons" have never come into it for her – she's always trusted her own instincts: paintings either touched her or they didn't. The dividing line had been the Renaissance until she'd stumbled on Bernini's St Teresa. Velazquez had made a big difference too: set her thinking. It isn't that she didn't know painters like him or Vermeer and Rembrandt were great artists; she just hadn't known enough to comprehend how amazing they were, hadn't realized the genius of what they'd achieved. Even so, they don't make her soul quicken.

If Camilla is right when she'd tapped her head and said "It's this we have to use!" Jo must be wrong. Of course, in the strict sense Camilla had admitted Giotto wasn't as good a painter as Velazquez or some of the Siennese artists but she'd also said to really appreciate him it was necessary to understand the history of art.

Jo opens the chapter on Giotto: maybe after she's read it she'll grasp what Camilla was getting at.

"One could never have imagined that the honeyed perfection of fourth and fifth century Greece could give way to a more primitive style as it did during the whole of the Byzantine period. It was certainly not an age of incompetence. Craftsmanship was at a high level, and the Christian Church took the utmost pains to control its direction and turn it into an effective propaganda machine. If art was to serve Christianity it had to evolve a new language: a mystical language where the world of the senses had no place. To do this, it broke from realism creating a new set of forms so remote from visual experience, so engendered by a state of mind, that it becomes almost purely abstract. Byzantine and medieval art developed from an aesthetic disdaining earthly reality, revelling instead in the brilliance of colour, the sparkle of gold, wanting above all to move the soul to a contemplation of God. Siennese art adapted but never broke free of this aesthetic and can be seen as a last gorgeous flowering. The coming of Giotto who suddenly saw life in the round was the marking point for a new epoch."

Jo sinks into the pillows: so Byzantine art is primitive and Siennese art the flowering of a dying tradition. What she thinks of as her "unique" response was manufactured, manipulated – just as Camilla had said. She throws the book aside. So what, she shrugs, ditching her newly acquired knowledge. She's well aware the paintings she loves don't concern themselves with "earthly reality", that's precisely *why* she loves them; it's what gives them the power to awaken in her what they do. Even if Giotto heralded a new era, she can't make herself like his clunky figures, humdrum colours, *earthly* concerns. And even though she's beginning to see what Clive Mullins and Camilla are getting at – something still doesn't add up.

Her discoveries with Velazquez weren't a "Damascus" moment after all: she hadn't been converted. It was more a "eureka" moment: a sudden understanding of the potential of paint; an appreciation of its ability to create illusion. The truth is she still doesn't like Velazquez's work. "There are wrong reasons for disliking a work of art!" Angrily, Jo turns to the colour plates at the centre, goes straight to one of her favourites. In it, a group of saints, lost in contemplation, gaze out impassively; the ultramarine the artist used out of this world, the painting emanating a stillness beyond measure. Jo orders herself not just to look at it but to try and see it – think about it: "use her head".

By lunchtime the following day, Phil's covered most of the canvas and when he finally lets her see it, Jo gasps. He's been concentrating mainly on her back; the background barely sketched in. From where she's been sitting, it looked as if all he'd done was borrow a tube of her make-up and squirt it on. Up close, she realises it's nothing of the sort: among the mix of colours there are hair-thin threads of blue, green, even a touch of red.

'It's fantastic! Honestly! Amazing!'

'It's getting there,' he concedes. 'Hey, I'm not nearly done. Back on your butt.'

Happily, Jo returns to her pose. Fucking hell, she hadn't realised he was that good – as good as a lot of the painters she's been learning about, Ingres for example. Velazquez can take the credit: if it hadn't been for him, she'd never have been able to appreciate what Phil's doing.

'Stop fidgeting,' he roars.

Slowly, afternoon turns to evening, their breathing and the

swish of the brush the only sounds in the room. Jo ignores pangs of hunger. Food! Smood! Who cares! The important thing is to get the painting finished. What about her own painting? a voice pipes but Jo gives it its marching orders. Phil's working; that's enough for now.

Several evenings later, Phil pulls the canvas into the centre of the studio, asks Jo's opinion. As soon as she begins to speak, he cuts her off. She's like all the others, he tells hers, imagining it's a matter of putting paint on canvas – 'capturing reality'! Any idiot with a little training and patience can do that, he sneers. Reality has to be bent. Paint has its own laws. So many things are involved – harmony, balancing shape, colour, filling the space. He gets her to stand in front of the canvas, begins by pointing out the warmth in the skin tones, wanting her to grasp how too much blue would have tipped it the other way. Has she noticed, he continues, tracing the arc of the chair leg, the way it repeats the curve of her arm? Curved outwards, it would have led the eye in the wrong direction.

His hands grip Jo's shoulders. Framing everything, he tells her, is the artist's vision. What the artist sees, what he wants to impart. That can't be taught. 'Now go to bed.' His face is drained.

At the door, Jo turns. He's sitting in front of the canvas, his head sunk in a pool of light. Wrestling with what?

The following morning Jo pulls on a sweatshirt over her nightie; no point getting dressed to get undressed.

'*Bon Giorno*,' she calls, wandering sleepily into the kitchen.

Philip stops whistling. '*Bon giorno signorina*, you must have smelt the coffee.'

What's with the good humour, Jo wonders. Whistling too! He

hasn't done that for a while. Pouring herself a cup, she eyes the taut muscles in his upper arms, catches a glimpse of boxers as he leans over to get at a tin of turpentine. Desire percolates through her.

'Wanna start soon?'

'Ah-ah,' he shakes his head, looking up a moment from pouring oil on a rag. 'We'll work later. Why don't you go out for a while? I've had you cooped up long enough.'

'Are ye sure?' What she'd like to do is drag him back to bed.

'Sure I'm sure. Scoot. I've got some thinking to do.'

Closing the front door behind her, Jo feels banished. Sitting for Phil each day, not having to think about what to do or how to fill her time is addictive. It feels weird being cut loose. She's grown to like the muggy atmosphere, the repetition, each day a kind of reverie. She'd much prefer to stay home, locked in the intensity.

Deciding to test her reactions, Jo sits in the Bardi chapel contemplating Giotto's frescos, waiting for something: a light to go on, her emotions to catch up with her brain. She might as well not have come. The longing for something other, something mystical is as strong as ever. Whatever it is that smoulders inside her refuses to be extinguished; refuses to exchange knowledge for feeling. Camilla had pitched intellect against emotion, the way the Catholic Church had pitted body against soul. She understands now that Giotto was the catalyst for something new; without him the Renaissance could not have happened and without the Renaissance there would be no modern art. The old had to be sacrificed. But is the art which came in its wake better than what went before? She doesn't think so. Of course, modern art doesn't claim to be trying to reach the soul; most artists probably deny its existence. Even if they don't, the work they produce hasn't reached hers. There are exceptions – Bacon for one although she's no idea why his contorted figures seem to touch her. But surely a way should be found to unite old and new, intellect and heart, body and soul. Isn't it essential to hold on to all these things?

Jo makes her way back to the main chapel. Halfway up the aisle, her feet encounter a circle of colour as light pouring through a rose window above the main altar creates a replica on the floor: fainter but perfect. She steps into it, her shoes dappled with colour; wonders, if for some reason, she couldn't see the window or didn't know it was there, how would she explain the marvel in front of her eyes?

"A sadder and a wiser man,

He rose the morrow morn."

Lines from *The Ancient Mariner* reach her from the past. It was one of her favourite poems at school – those lines especially – although something about them always troubled her.

A thought hovers at the edge of her mind. As she pushes open the heavy door of Santa Croce, it surfaces: shouldn't real wisdom bring joy, not sadness? Unless, she thinks, as the door clangs shut behind her, they are inextricably linked.

'Hi! Wait!' Maris calls, rushing to catch up with Jo. 'I thought you guys must be out of town. I've been ringing all week, don't you answer the phone?'

'Sorry, been busy.' It's on the tip of Jo's tongue to tell her Phil's painting but she's not sure he'd want her to.

'Saw you coming out of Santa Croce. Don't you think it's neat: Galileo buried in the same place as Giotto's frescos.'

Unsure what she's getting at, Jo gives her an encouraging smile.

'I love coincidences. One gave birth to modern art, the other to modern science. Both argued for looking at the real world, huh?' Reaching under her poncho, she produces Sheba. 'You know all about that, don't you Sheba? Did I tell you friends of mine rescued her from an animal experiment laboratory? Didn't they baby?' Tickling the chattering monkey, she makes squeaking noises into the small puckered face.

Watching, Jo thinks of Massimo, remembers the way he'd preyed on her sympathies. Looking at the funny little creature, she wonders how people get involved in saving animals or chose to work in refugee camps. In Dublin everything was simple: you did and thought the same as everyone else or so it seemed. Maybe that was the problem!

'It's why I love Philip's paintings, he looks-' Maris stops, gives Jo a quizzical look. 'Is something the matter? You seem ...'

'Phil's almost finished a painting! I've been sitting for weeks.'

'You're kidding! That is so cool! Can I come up, accidental like, have a quick look?'

'Not now. And I better go, I promised I'd be back. It's brilliant though.'

Maris claps the monkey's paws together. 'What about you? If you're doing all that sitting you can't be getting much work done.'

'I'm giving it a break, for a while.'

'Be careful,' Maris grins. 'You know what they say: "Behind every man!" Women! We'll never learn! *Ciao*, gotta run. Give my love to Phil.'

Jo watches her disappear, a ball of colour bounding along. As she mounts the stairs to the apartment, she tries to dismiss Maris' remarks but they dog her. "Giving it a break!" What a joke!

It's none of her bloody business, she fumes, shoving a key in the door.

'Home,' she shouts, letting herself into the studio.

Her voice boomerangs and seeing Philip motionless in front of the canvas, a chill runs through her.

'I met Maris, she was asking-'

'What did that vulture want?'

'I thought you were friends!'

He glowers. 'Sometimes I don't know whether you're naive or just goddamn stupid.'

'They're your fuckin' friends!'

'Right. Can we get on with things?'

She should tell him to go to hell. She looks at Phil, hoping for a smile of apology but he's staring at the painting, brows knitted, and she realises he's forgotten her.

Jo wakes to find a blanket draped over her; Phil at the table cleaning brushes. The canvas has been moved to a corner.

'Sorry,' she whispers.

He doesn't respond.

Wrapping the blanket round her, she creeps across to have a look. Despite the hours that have passed, he seems to have done very little.

'We can keep going if you like?'

'Tomorrow,' he answers in a throwaway voice.

28

It's eleven o'clock by the time they end up in a bar near the Duomo and Jo insists on sitting at a table. Maris and Will can prop up the bar with Phil if they like; they haven't been on the tear for the last week. To her surprise, Maris gives Jo a grateful look and drawing up a chair, flops down beside her.

'Can't keep up the pace eh Ireland?' Phil slurs. He giggles and Jo winces. Placing his fingers to his temple, he stands to attention: 'America, America ...' he bellows then losing interest, slumps against a stool.

Will guffaws, slaps him on the back. 'Watch out, the Aussies are coming.'

The two men hug sloppily.

'What are you girls having?' Phil shambles across.

'Women,' Will interjects, following him. 'Women.'

'Where?' Philip's eyes dart around the crowded bar.

Jo asks for cioccolata; she's had enough pissy beer to last a lifetime. She could sink a ship with the amount she's drunk. Shadow-boxing one another, Phil and Will shuffle back to the bar.

'Is he drinking?' Maris whispers.

Oh God, Jo thinks, here we go again. She's sick to death of Phil and his friends. What about her? They could at least pretend to show a bit of interest!

'What does it look like,' she answers, too exhausted to be polite. What do they want to hear? That he'd been pouring the stuff down his throat since the painting disappeared – unfinished – into some cubby-hole.

'Phil's so sweet! I hate what he's doing to himself.'

That's what you think, Jo sneers inwardly, instantly feeling guilty. As always, thinking of herself. They're his friends, his so-called friends anyway, why shouldn't they care about him? It's her who needs to try harder. Love him the way she'd loved Eamonn: she'd have done anything for him. But the idea was *not* to love Philip; the idea was never to love anyone with that intensity again. She watches as Phil bumbles towards them: she might as well be in love for all the difference it makes.

'Maris, Maris, want to hear my new recipe for roast lamb?' Phil leans in confidentially. 'It's out of this world. First dress the leg in the usual way, rosemary, garlic, the whole caboodle, then pop into the oven.' He winks. 'Now listen carefully, this is the important bit. Open a bottle of wine. Drink it, fall asleep and-' he makes a slurpy kissing sound, '*buonissimo*! Am I right Jo?'

Jo nods and they all laugh. He'd told the same story earlier and every night for the last three nights.

Maris tugs Phil's sleeve.

'Don't look now but Stefano's on his way over.'

An arrogant looking guy swaggers towards them, a blond sewn to his arm. At last, the famous Stefano! He stops at their table, the bombshell letting out a theatrical yawn. Jo gives her a sympathetic smile but with a disdainful sniff, she looks the other way.

'*Amichi … come stanno?* Friends, how are you? And Philip, my old chum.'

'Isn't it a bit late for you to be up?' Phil counters. 'I thought you needed your beauty sleep.'

'Always the tease, he loves me really. And where did you find this little oil painting?' He holds out a hand to Jo. 'Stefano di Montefiore … delighted to meet you.'

'Josephine Nowd, delighted to meet you.' Jo laughs, blushing at being singled out; secretly pleased in front of the others.

'Not tonight Josephine – ah it is always so.' He puts a hand to his heart, sighs deeply.

'Very original for you.' Phil's face darkens and despite his drunkenness, Jo can see he's furious. As if sensing the tension, Stefano takes a pace back.

'I am giving a little party on Saturday, you are all invited.' He looks from one to the other, his bright teeth smiling, his eyes lingering momentarily on Jo. 'I hope you can make it. Just a few intimate acquaintances.'

'You mean half of Florence will be there,' Phil scoffs.

'Friends, only friends.' With an airy wave he takes his leave, one arm carelessly around the woman, their lips touching briefly as they move away.

'Asshole,' Phil mutters and Jo hopes that doesn't mean they won't be going. Stefano looks interesting and she'd like to go, meet some new people, proper Italians, find out what an Italian party is like. She could do with having some fun; she's been walking on eggshells for weeks.

'He's a painter?'

'His prick does a hell of a lot more than his brush.'

'No need to be coarse Will,' Maris protests, grinning. 'Men, they're so jealous of one another.'

'Jealous of that louse!' Will sneers. 'Did you hear Philippa slept with him and he dumped her straight up? Because he's a prince, he can pull any woman he wants. He's one dick!'

All ears, Jo looks at Will. 'A real prince?'

'His grandfather bought the title,' Phil butts in. 'Christ, Italians will do anything for a whiff of royalty. As for Philippa-'

'Who's Philippa?'

'The tyre heiress. She's worth millions,' Maris explains. 'I guess that means she won't be at the party.' She turns to Jo. 'She trails Phil round like a puppy. It's embarrassing. You think she'd have a little dignity.'

'You can't embarrass money,' Phil laughs and Jo sees his mood has changed. 'Did I tell you about the time she invited me to lunch? Her parents have a little palazzo near San Gimenano-'

'Little!' Will snorts.

'Little, big, freeze your balls off,' Phil chuckles. 'While we were waiting for food to show up, we decided to play a game of tennis and Fizzy – that's Mom – turns up to watch. About ten minutes into the game she shouts: "Change courts darling, time to tan the other arm." It's true! Can you believe it!'

Phil laughs uproariously, repeating the punch line over and over.

'I'm falling asleep,' Jo says, making a face at the others behind his back.

Philip stares glassily in her direction. 'Time to get Cinderella to bed,' he kisses her hair.

As they walk home, he puts an arm round her, snuggles her into the folds of his coat.

'I can't breathe,' Jo murmurs but he doesn't hear.

The following morning, a postcard arrives from Camilla. "*Come va il dipinto?* How's the painting going?" scrawled in red ink on the back. If Jo was in Dublin, she'd send a card back saying – "Slowly!" But she isn't at home and it's not a joke. Jo sighs. She'll start again one of these days; they just need to get over this hump. "They?" Phil, she means. The painting of her has vanished, is never mentioned; the studio off-limits. She and Phil are out most of the time, or in bed, or recovering from hangovers; the unwritten rule seems to be if he's not painting, no one else can. Meaning her.

Hearing a knock on the door, she opens it expecting to find

one or other of the usual suspects.

'Rupert!' she shrieks as a pair of arms encircle her, hoist her into the air. 'What are you doing here? Put me down!'

'Aren't you going to invite me in?' he asks, landing her back on her feet.

'Of course. Come in. *Benvenuto*, welcome. Phil's out,' she tells him, glad to have him to herself. Relieved.

'So, how are you? How's it going?'

She sees him glance around for clues.

'What does it look like? Gone to seed. Too much pasta and wine. You on the other hand look wonderful.' He does: bronzed and thinner, his hair bleached even blonder. A flicker of regret passes through her. Is it too late? Too late for what! Things are okay between her and Phil. What's got into her, for goodness sake!

'Would you like a coffee?'

'What have you been up to?' he asks, following her into the kitchen.

Jo searches for something interesting to tell him. 'Living, I guess.'

'How's Phil? Is he getting any work done?'

'Not you too! What is it with Phil's fuckin' friends! Do you work?'

'Hey, that's more like you!'

Jo squeezes her eyes tight. What's happening to her? What is she doing with her life? Turning away, she rummages in the cupboard as if searching for something.

'How was Greece?' she asks over her shoulder.

'You'd have loved it. Coffee's on the table by the way.'

"*You'd have loved it.*" There was a choice: going to Greece with Rupert or moving in with Phil. A third way? There always has to

242

be a third way …

'What is it Jo? Are things alright?'

'Of course they are. Amn't I living the life of Riley! I don't have to work. I can get up when I like – eat, drink and be merry. It's a far cry from *PensioneVanda*.'

'You don't seem very happy.'

'You expect happiness on top of all that! No wonder you're screwed up.'

Rupert laughs. 'I've got this super idea, why don't we go out and have a slap-up lunch? I know just the place.'

'Not a good idea?' he asks, seeing her expression.

The front door opens and Jo starts guiltily as Phil comes in. 'Hi, look who's here. He just dropped in,' she tags on quickly.

Rupert looks at her questioningly but Jo avoids his eye.

'Good to see you Phil,' Rupert throws his arms out and they embrace awkwardly.

'When did you blow into town?' Phil asks.

Hearing the sharpness in his voice, Jo feels ashamed. She should never have told him Rupert was in love with her; at the time it had made her feel important.

'Landed a couple of hours ago.'

Jo can see Phil doing the calculations in his head: why does he have to be so jealous?

'Staying long?'

'Hey man, I wasn't expecting the third degree! As it happens, I'm heading back to England. The parents have convinced me duty calls. I've decided to give it a shot.'

'You're not going to work in a bank!' Jo explodes.

'Afraid so. Sorry to shatter your illusions.' He turns to Phil. 'Jo and I used to have these big ideas. She was going to be a great artist-'

Seeing Phil raise an eyebrow, Jo wilts, hopes Rupert doesn't stay long. Pointedly, she clears the milk from the table, excuses herself as they begin reminiscing about someone she's never heard of.

"Great artist," she taunts herself, hovering by the bedroom door. What a joke! Phil's right: she's only ever played at being one. It was something she did to make her feel like she was somebody. Sure, she enjoys it when she finally settles but that doesn't mean she has any talent. Look at Phil, even when he isn't working he's an artist. What is she? Nothing, she thinks, seething at the phoney laughter coming from the kitchen.

As soon as her anger cools, Jo wanders back. 'Staying for lunch?' she asks breezily, knowing Rupert will refuse; that she wants him to, wishes he'd never called.

'I'd love to darling but I have to hit the road. Hey, I'm leaving my address, parents' actually, but if you end up in dear old Blighty give me a bell. Both of you,' he adds, although Jo knows it's meant for her.

When he stands up to leave, she holds out her hand. She'd have preferred to hug him but with Phil looking on she doesn't dare. The phone rings and Phil excuses himself, disappears to answer it. Jo occupies herself clearing dishes.

'Jo?'

She makes a bargain. If he touches her ... once ... that's all he has to do ... that's all it would take.

'Jo?'

She senses him reach out, hesitate.

'Got wheels?' Phil asks coming back in. 'I've got a package to pick up.'

'Borrowed a jeep earlier. C'mon, I'll drop you. Goodbye Jo.'

'Bye Rupert.'

Blinking back tears, she watches at they get into the car, waits until it drives away. That could be her, she thinks, wallowing in the fantasy for a moment. Who's she fooling, she snaps herself out of it: it was never more than a fairy tale.

29

'What do you think?' Jo parades in front of Phil, smoothing down the red silk. The dress is figured to about halfway down her thigh then flares out, the material cut on the bias. She's never worn anything quite so slinky, hopes her bum doesn't stick out too much. 'It's not too tight, is it?'

'I like you better without clothes.'

Jo scowls.

'Ok, ok, it's great, you'd look good in a plastic bag.'

'Thanks for the compliment. You don't look too bad yourself,' she jokes, admiring the green paisley shirt and pale linen pants he's wearing.

'C'mon, the party will be over before we get there and I want to stop for a drink.'

As they make their way into a bar, Jo wonders if Phil's buying a little Dutch courage. Prince Stefano de Montefiore is probably out of his league – definitely out of hers – but despite words like "dilettante" and "plagiarism" being bandied around, going to the party has never been in the slightest doubt. Whenever they were with Maris and Will, the talk was all about who was going and who wasn't; who was in or out of Stefano's golden circle. Jo catches a glimpse of herself in one of the mirrors: I could be a princess, she thinks. Smiling at her reflection, she sips her drink, looks around: the bar's not a patch on an Irish pub – it's the one thing Italians get wrong. Suddenly, she misses home; wishes Eamonn could see her looking so lovely. Feel jealous.

'Hey, it's the guys,' Phil taps her arm as Maris and Will troop in, Ted making up the rear, one arm solicitously around a woman Jo's never seen before. After the hellos and the introductions there's silence. Maris and Ted exchange glances.

'I thought we were going to a party. Feels more like a funeral. What's up?' Phil asks.

'We've discovered what the celebrations are in aid of,' Maris tells him.

'Stefano's lost the last of his milk teeth,' Phil laughs.

'Corvetto's giving him an exhibition – a solo.' Maris fiddles with an earring, her face oozing sympathy.

Jo's heart sinks. Corvettos is *the* gallery in Florence; not the biggest or poshest but the most 'in'.

Phil doesn't react although Jo can see a ripple of shock pulse through his body, the tell-tale muscle in his cheek begin to twitch. She wants to hold him, re-assure him.

'What's the exhibition called: "Painting by Numbers"?' The remark's forced but they all laugh.

'I'll drink to that,' Ted proposes.

As they walk to the party, Maris links arms with Jo.

'You know Phil's big success was at Corvetto's.'

'Shit!' Jo swears, covering her mouth instantly. Phil hates her cursing.

'Marco- that's Signor Corvetto, took a chance on him, he usually goes for big names but he liked his stuff. The thing about Stefano is he sells. Lots of people dig his paintings, they go with their interiors. A blue room, we'll have a blue nude by Stefano. A pink bathroom, why not a voluptuous pink one. And because he studied with Anigoni – attended his classes anyway – people reckon it has to be "art".'

Jo steals a glance at Phil. If only she could get him to finish the painting. Once he got over that hurdle, the rest would be a cinch. She'll do it: she'll put everything she has into it. This time next year, it will be Phil having an exhibition at Corvetto's and they'll be throwing a party.

When Jo eventually catches sight of Stefano, people are swanning round him like kids round an ice-cream van. He returns her glance and she holds it a moment, is about to move away when he raises his glass, his eyes travelling slowly over her body. Jo turns away, confused by a tremor shooting through her. What a power tripper, she thinks, topping up her drink from a passing waiter; he probably expects women to throw themselves at him. She can hardly blame them: not only is he royalty but he's attractive, even if his smile is part sneer. She'll give him this, he knows how to throw a party. There's so much to eat and drink it makes the Robertson's do look like afternoon tea. She ought to go and get a bite, she's drinking too much. You can't drink too much champagne, Jo giggles, dropping into an armchair. On the other hand, you can have too much shouting in half-baked Italian, and abba-bloody-stanza of gorgeous Italian women in fabulous evening dresses, breasts popping, making her silky number look positively nunnish. What is it that makes Italian women look like real women, one version anyway? And where's Phil? He'd abandoned her almost as soon as they got there, making a beeline for someone Jo didn't recognise. Maybe she should go and look for him or maybe she'll go and sample some of the gorgeous food. Soak up the alcohol. Make room for more!

As she gets to her feet, a man brushes past almost knocking the glass from her hand. '*Scusa, scusa,*' he laughs and Jo laughs back lazily. Eating can wait, she decides, stopping to watch a couple jiving; riveted as the man hurls his partner across the floor; the woman whirling back into his arms without losing a step. Time to find Phil: she needs to dance, use up some of her energy.

Excusing her way through tangles of perfumed bodies, Jo goes from room to room, glancing around casually; the last thing she wants is Phil thinking she's keeping tabs. At last, she spots the paisley shirt, is dumbfounded to see him with his arms wrapped around a tall, dark-haired woman, her face buried in his neck. Phil's eyes are closed as they slow-dance to breathy come-to-bed music. Jo stares, half-dreading, half-wanting Phil to open his eyes. Changing her mind, she tears herself away; is at the door when a hand grips her shoulder.

'They make a lovely couple don't you think?' Stefan smiles spitefully.

Shaking herself loose, Jo keeps going, waiting until they're in the hallway before answering. 'They're dancing, so what!'

'You're not jealous? A man and woman dancing like that. If it was my woman I'd-' He makes a slitting gesture across his throat.

'Don't give me the macho stuff. Women and men can dance anyway they like. It's no big deal.'

'I don't think you believe that.'

'How do you know? Excuse me, I have to go to the loo.'

Jo makes a getaway, ducking into the first room she comes to, losing herself in a sea of writhing bodies. She feels mortified. Hurt. Stefano must have seen it on her face, no matter what she said. And from what she's heard, it will be all over Florence tomorrow. What does she care! Fuck him! Fuck Phil! Who's the woman anyway? Fear and panic suck at her stomach and she positions herself where she can be seen, willing Philip to come looking for her. If he comes, she'll say nothing. Jo gives him five minutes, then another five as the music around her gets louder, drowning out her thoughts, fuelling her anger.

Who needs a man, she decides, launching herself into the middle of the dancers, a big smile etched on her face. An aristocratic-looking guy stretches out a welcoming arm. See, Jo thinks, shimmying towards him, she doesn't need Phil to enjoy herself. Movement spirals inside her and she curls round it, hair flying, dress swirling. Exhilarated by the red frenzy she's turning into, she tunes to an inner rhythm, feels a pulse race through her, sing in her veins. One by one, women stop dancing, their partners seduced into Jo's orbit, competing for her attention. She dances towards each one in turn, until, with an inviting swivel of hips, she twists out of reach. Eyes penetrate her as she spins in and out of each man's gaze; aware she mustn't stop, mustn't break the spell. Desire surfaces, flickers from eye to eye; her willpower keeping her in motion, keeping them at her fingertips. She clicks and twirls, faster and faster, heart pumping, her body carving space.

Amid the blur, she recognises someone, his eyebrows raised in curiosity. Stefano! Let him look, see if she gives a fuck. Closing her eyes, she goes with the beat, a hand touching her here, there, someone laughing as she stumbles; a guy with frizzy hair steadying her, grazing her cheek as he tries to grab a kiss. Life, she gloats, this is life, and she's living! She's never felt better. Nothing can stop her. Nothing. Opening her eyes, she's surprised to see Stefano among the dancers. As he struts in her direction, the other men fall away. Jo tosses her head, angles her hips and with little stamping movements gyrates towards him. Their bodies glance off each other, lips almost touching as she unwinds, one hand trailing to brush his cheek.

'*Amore*,' he whispers.

Guests form a wall around them; Jo spots Maris among them. She waves without missing a beat, slithers across the floor. Stefano goes with her, keeping eye contact, coiling closer and closer until the gap between them disappears. The music stops. Gently, as if kissing a baby, he puts his mouth to her ear.

'Let's go upstairs and fuck.'

Jo bursts out laughing.

'You must be joking!'

'No,' he protests, his expression disbelieving.

'I'm not interested. More music,' she shouts.

'You dance like this but you don't want to fuck? Is that what Irish girls do? Tease?'

Several of Stefano's friends edge closer.

'Grow up for God's sake! Because someone enjoys dancing doesn't mean they want to fuck you. Most girls probably don't know how to say no.'

She feels giddy; giddy and deflated like a burst balloon. She needs to keep going.

'If a man and woman put their bodies together like this...' Stefano thrusts his pelvis against her, 'they get excited and making love is natural. Unless you stop it,' he jeers.

'Stop what?' Phil asks, pushing between them.

Jo blinks: she'd completely forgotten about Phil.

'You must excuse me, my friend. I was explaining the facts of life to Josephine. She doesn't appear to know them.'

Jo gasps. Prince or no prince he's not getting away with that!

'That's where you're wrong! It might be news to you but not everyone finds you irresistible.'

'You don't think so, no? Believe me, I can make any woman want to make love.'

Phil's eyes bore into Jo.

'Oh yeah! Well, try me.' Inwardly, she congratulates herself. Bet he wasn't expecting that!

Stefano glances from Phil to Jo; a hush descends on the room as he reaches out, strokes her neck. Some sixth sense urges her to walk away but it's too late. In what seems like slow motion the Italian's hand inches down her dress. Wetting his lips, Stefano circles one of her nipples with his finger. A spark of desire quivers inside Jo but she damps it down, keeps her gaze steady. 'I told you, nothing.'

A door slams shut, reels on its hinges.

'I think your boyfriend just left,' Stefano smirks. 'Perhaps he didn't understand what you were trying to prove,' he tosses over his shoulder, as he walks away.

Jo stares at the door. Phil … she was only … only what? Her head swims. The room sways. What was she trying to do? It doesn't seem clear.

'Are you out of your mind?' Maris grabs her arm.

Jo looks wildly about her.

'Christ Jo, what were you playing at? How would you like …'

'Did he say anything?'

Maris looks at her helplessly.

'Maybe I should go after him. Explain.'

'I'm not sure that's a good idea. Who knows where he'll go.'

Seeing the look on Jo's face she relents, 'You're pissed aren't you? Hang on, we'll take you home. Hopefully, he'll have calmed down.'

Jo's face crumbles.

'Don't worry, you can crash at our place if you have to.'

'Is he in?'

'The light's on.'

'Want us to stay?'

Maris and Will huddle together, regarding Jo sheepishly. She shakes her head. If Phil's going to explode, she'd rather be on her own.

As soon as they've gone, Jo realises she hadn't brought a key; is obliged to knock. When there's no response she knocks a second time.

'Piss off tramp,' a voice lashes her through the door.

Jo flinches; steels herself. 'Phil,' she whispers as loudly as she dares. 'Please open the door. It's not- I can explain. Please.'

This time there's only silence.

Maybe she should go to Maris'; it's only ten-minute's walk. Then what? Come back tomorrow? She rattles the handle. If he opens the door, she'll apologise, tell him she'll pack her bags in the morning. It's over between them and she's glad.

'Phil... please Phil!'

'Fuck off.'

'Just let me in.'

What right has he to lock her out! It's her home. He invited her to live there; stopped her earning money, made her dependent on him. Well, if nothing else belongs to her, her body does and she can do what she likes with it. If she wants to let someone touch it, that's up to her! What about the way he was glued to that fucking woman!

Hearing people on the stairs, Jo nips onto the fire escape. If she could just get in, get through the night. Then ... adios! If he's not able to handle someone with a mind of her own, he can go back to his brainless dolly-birds! After all she's done, all those hours sitting, putting her own work on hold so he could get on with his. Putting him first just as she'd done with Eamonn. What a fool! A fool who's desperate for a piss and freezing to death in a flimsy dress! If he doesn't open the door soon, she'll wet herself.

Jo tiptoes back into the corridor. Please, please, she prays, if he lets her in she'll never get herself into a situation like this again. About to lift the knocker, Jo realises the door's been opened. She eyes it nervously. What's she frightened of? She's not sure: his anger; fear he might attack her? She doesn't think he would but … saliva gathers in the mouth. Swallowing it, she inches into the apartment. She can see him, sprawled in a chair, a bottle of grappa at his feet. Stepping further in, she looks quickly at his face: is met with darkness. She stands absolutely still, trying to make herself invisible; their breathing trembling on a tightrope. It's essential she gets to the bathroom but that involves walking past him. Say something, anything, she begs in her mind. Jo squeezes herself tight, rocks. She's going to faint. Her face reddens; her whole body seems to light up as a dribble of pee trickles down her leg.

'Look at the fuckin' state of you.'

It's as though she's become invisible, or he just can't see her; has an image of something other, something disgusting in his mind.

Jo blunders across the room. As she crashes into the bathroom, her grip loosens: pee flooding down, soaking her dress, her legs. It forms a pool at her feet and she sinks down into it. Howls.

As Jo bundles the red dress into a bin, the memory of showing it off to Phil a few hours earlier stops her but only for a moment. She never wants to see the dress again. Letting out a sigh, she looks down at the freshly washed floor. While she was on her knees, she'd heard Phil stagger to bed, shout something incoherent in her direction. Sorrow weighs her down. A grovelling, shameful sorrow she's never experienced before. She tries to reconcile the Jo who blazed with the cowering mess in the mirror: can't. That Jo was an aberration. This is reality. Leaning in, she examines her streaked face, forces a smile. There has to be a funny side. When it's all over and done with, she'll tell this story, re-tell it: make it funny. But it isn't over and she wishes she knew if Phil was asleep or lying in the dark cursing her. More than likely, he's passed out. She envies him if he is. Dragging a duvet from the hot-press, she dumps it on the couch – the surface hard and unyielding when she lies down. She's being punished, punished for everything. Punished for being a woman, she decides, as a grey sleep overtakes her.

Sensing Phil standing over her, Jo tries not to move a muscle. She couldn't bear a scene; her body, even her mind, feels bruised as if someone's been battering her.

Of course, she's only putting off the inevitable. At some point, she'll have to get up, face him, face the day, leave; see if Maris will put her up or find a hostel. It probably isn't fair to ask her and Will to take sides.

Phil walks away and she hears him leave the room, return moments later. Once again he stands over her, his shadow blocking the light. A hand touches the quilt, tucks it around her. Seconds tick by. Eventually, he goes out and she hears the front door open and close, quietly. Relief surges through her. He's forgiven her! He must have! She can stay. Jo sits up: feels a rush of love for every object in the room. Getting out of bed, she picks up a small Etruscan head, presses it to her heart. She hadn't realised how much she's grown to love the place, how attached she's become. Not that anything's hers – all she brought were clothes and books, her art stuff. Draping the duvet around her shoulders, she scurries to the window. In the frail morning light, the church of Santa Croce is tranquil, unperturbed. Even after such a short time, part of her own history is entwined with the ancient building. That first time when she and Phil stood looking at it; bumping into Camilla in the Bardi Chapel the day she went to see the frescos. What, she wonders, would Giotto paint if he were alive? All of a sudden, Jo feels drained. Worn out. Glad she doesn't have to leave. He could have thrown her out, she deserves it. How could she expect him to understand what she was trying to do? She hardly understands herself. She supposes she'll have to be careful for a while; humour him until he gets over it. Thinking up ways she can make it up to him, Jo pads down the hallway. First, she'll have a bath; wash away every vestige of the previous night.

Two red buds break the surface. Hazily, Jo observes them; traces the contours of her body through the blueing water down to her narrow feet. Out of exhaustion, a thought forms, permeates her whole being, electrifies her: it's beautiful! Eamonn was right: her body is absolutely beautiful. How has she never realised this before? She rises, mesmerised by the glistening droplets pearling her warm, rosy skin. Energy floods through her. This miracle is hers. Hopping out of the bath, she wraps herself in a towel, skips out of the room and along the hallway, into the living room. Water drips everywhere, soggy feet marks leaving a wanton trail. Who cares? She's a goddess! Standing in the middle of the room, she stretches out her arms, allows the towel fall away: stands naked. Mine, she thinks, mine. 'Not yours,' she shouts. 'Not anybody's!' The revelation tumbles through her like a landslide. Bastard, bastard! She'll kill Phil, scratch out his eyes, tear him limb from limb. She'll wreck the place, rip up his paintings, smash his fucking stupid sculptures. Phil's face rises up in front of her ... displaced by Stefano's ... Tim's ... morphing slowly into Eamonn's. 'Fuck all of you,' she roars, 'I'm me!'

30

She'll never get used to living close to the sun, Jo admits, on the look-out for somewhere shady. Her arms ache from carrying the holdall and portfolio; sweat running down her back on account of the bloody jacket she's wearing. She hadn't the heart to abandon it; besides her mother would kill her if she left it behind. For some time, she's been walking in circles, euphoria draining away. As the hours eke themselves out, she feels less and less like a goddess, more and more like an ordinary mortal with swollen feet. Earlier, things had seemed so clear. Her mind jumps. If there are wrong reasons for disliking a painting, could there be wrong reasons for disliking a man? Or liking one. Whatever the answer, she's back where she started, penniless with nowhere to sleep. Maybe she should swallow her pride, go and beg money off Maris or Ted. Go back to Phil and apologise. Go to *Pensione Vanda* and apologise. Hope one of them will take pity on her.

Passing an *Alimentari* she remembers she hasn't eaten and as she pushes through a curtain of plastic strips, the aroma of food in the deli makes her feel faint. What a pity Rupert isn't here, she thinks, as she orders *un panino con ricotta e mortadella:* a roll with ricotta and something processed that resembles meat, two of the cheapest fillings possible. Taking her last and only 5,000 lira note from her purse, she gives it to the shopkeeper. When he hands her the roll and her change, she counts it, even picking up the handful of almost worthless coins he tosses on the counter; Italians leave them behind. Shoving them in the pocket of her Donegal tweed, her hand touches a small round box.

'*Io non parlo molto Italiano ma questa … e un caduta,*' Jo explains to the jeweller. 'A present. *Bisogna di soldi.*' She makes the sign for money, rubbing her fingers together. '*E possibile?*' She smiles into his face, waving her arms around.

'*Possibile,*' he tells her, suspiciously.

'*E buono,*' he pronounces after sticking something that looks like an eye bath in one of his eyes, peering closely at the ring.

When he's finished, he scrutinises Jo from head to toe.

'*C'e indirrizzo signorina?*'

Jo hesitates, wondering which address to give; finally taking a scrap of paper from her handbag.

'*Si. C'e indirrizzo in Ingleterra. Va bene?* English address, ok?'

'*Dammi?*' he holds out a hand.

Jo hands over the piece of paper with Rupert's address on it; the last thing she grabbed as she left the apartment.

He copies it, glancing up at her a couple of times.

'*Devo andare...*' Jo begins. What's the word for "away" she wonders? '*Via,*' she tries, adding '*lontana,*' for good measure.

'*Capito, signorina, capito. Amore eh?*' His shoulders rise to meet his ears and shaking his head sadly, he launches into Italian.

Jo grasps the essence of the story he's weaving: one of jilted love, passions of the heart, a ring exchanged but now being sold. Why not let him think it's true: it might tempt him to give her extra money.

Painstakingly, he counts large lira notes from a wad he'd retrieved from a safe, patting Jo's hand with each banknote, muttering about '*amore*'. Jo's eyes widen. Rupert wasn't joking about the ring's value; she could go anywhere with this kind of money! Paris. London. She could go and see Camilla! For a moment, an image of herself standing next to Camilla in some godforsaken place entices. Impossible! Camilla's her other half: everything she's not; never will be. Camilla's a 'doer'; not a watcher, a looker-on. Then stay here, the voice in her head suggests, go to the *scuola*: it's what you wanted to do.

'*Aspetta signorina.*'

The jeweller disappears into a room and through a tiny window she can see him type something. Go to the *scuola*? Become a student again? Could she? She's always told herself she'd dropped out of art college on account of Eamonn but that wasn't the only reason. Thinking of herself as an artist had scared the living daylights out of her: it had been easier to give up. When Phil says he's an artist he means it; whenever she said it she always felt as if she was an impostor.

Despite all that's happened, at the thought of Phil, Jo feels as if someone's taking a tin opener to her heart. She's not sure if it's possible to stay in Florence; maybe it would be better if she went somewhere far away. Isn't that what she'd done last time? Run away. If she isn't careful, she tries to joke, she'll run out of cities.

The man returns, places a typed receipt on the counter, points to where he wants her to put her name.

Jo Nowd, she signs: her gaze remaining on the signature. *Her signature.*

She came to Italy to paint, to become an artist; the least she can do is give it another shot. Take art seriously. Take herself seriously the way Camilla does.

'*Tanti auguri,*' he calls as she leaves.

Jo drops the good wishes into her pocket. The morning she was leaving Rome, she'd wished herself the same. She hadn't known then what was in store: could never have guessed she'd end up working in a *pensione*, meet a guy like Rupert, live in a cool apartment near Santa Croce with someone like Phil – have a love affair. If she hasn't become a woman of the world, she's made a stab at it: laid the groundwork. She's young: who knows what might happen!

Standing outside the jewellers, she hesitates. In the sky, the sun has come to a full stop. Could that be a sign? We can create the future, she tells herself as she descends the steps, turns resolutely into a street parallel to the Arno. She thinks again about Camilla, the way in which Giotto inspires her, acts as a reminder of what's good, what's possible in the world. Maybe Camilla can be that for her.

Ahead, the Ionic columns of the school are visible. When she arrives at the building, she lingers in the courtyard, contemplating the verdigrised body of the mermaid rising out of the fountain, water cascading endlessly over her wave-like tresses. Half-woman, half-fish: both in and out of her element – the way Jo feels a lot of the time. In the fairy story, the little Mermaid has to give up her voice to become human. Leaning across, Jo touches the scaly tail for luck. Maybe we all have to sacrifice something to get what we want. Pushing open the door of the Nuova Scuola dell' Arte, Jo feels lighter, as if thing have shifted, rearranged themselves, found their rightful place. For the moment. Even if her heart's a little unsure, her feet seem to know exactly where they are going.

Acknowledgements

I would like to thank Ger Burke and Tony O'Dwyer at Wordsonthestreet for publishing this novel and for all their support. I'd also like to thank my partner in crime Pete Mullineaux and my daughter Cassie for their unlimited patience, support and creative input; Celeste Augé for reading the novel at an earlier stage and for our 'writing chats'; Mary Morrissy for reading the novel and making several crucial suggestions; and a special thanks to Nuala O'Connor and Mary Morrissy for their lovely words. Thanks too to all my friends and fellow writers who've been encouraging in ways they'll never know. And to my sister Ita who has accompanied me most of my life, especially these last few months when in the midst of a pandemic we walked our phone conversations up and down the garden. A special thanks too to Jess Walsh for her wonderful author photo.

About the author

Having left school aged seventeen, Dubliner Moya Roddy went to art college as a night student. She continued to paint during a two-year stay in Italy before moving to London where she trained as a television director. *Que Sera Sera* which she wrote and directed won a Sony Award in 1984 and in 1985 the British Film Institute commissioned her to write her first feature film. Several of her screenplays have been optioned in the United States and she's worked for Channel 4, BBC, Scottish Television and RTÉ. On her return to Ireland she published a novel *The Long Way Home* (Attic Press) which was described in *The Irish Times* as 'simply brilliant'. Her collection of short stories *Other People* (Wordsonthestreet) was nominated for the Frank O'Connor International Short Story Award and a radio play *Dance Ballerina Dance* was short-listed for the P J O'Connor Award and produced by RTÉ. With her partner Pete Mullineaux she's co-written two plays for GYT and a radio play *Butterfly Wings* for RTÉ. She did a Portfolio Course in art at GTI (2005) and was awarded an MA in Writing (Hons First Class) from NUIG in 2008. Her poetry was short-listed for the Hennessy Award and her debut collection *Out of the Ordinary* was short-listed for the Strong Shine Award in 2018. She also facilitates meditation at Brigit's Garden.